PRAISE FOR OVER MY DEAD BODY

"*Over My Dead Body* is a page turner with a historically driven storyline... Kelly Fitzgerald Fowler is immensely gifted in leading the reader through generations of Jewish tradition in her characters' family history. The ending will leave you stunned and wanting more!"

~J.T. Tubbiolo, author of *The Charleston Conspiracy*

I enjoyed the use of humor - both in characters and in puns such as *"Over My Dead Body"* I enjoyed Harper's love of food, especially waffles. I think the choice of the dramatic confrontations in Heaven between God the Father and Our Lord Jesus and Lucifer, Father of Lies is unique in my experience and a very creative concept.

~Clarence Fedler, actor, executive producer, co-writer of *John Laurens' War*, the movie

Wow! I've never read anything like this. Kelly Fitzgerald Fowler opened my eyes to the fact that there is a great cosmic fight going on to claim our souls between powers we cannot see with our human eyes.

~Terry Ward Tucker, author of six books & co-author of the screenplay, *Only God Can, the movie*

By the time you finish the first chapter, you will find this is the one book you're unable to put down until finished. Be prepared to be intrigued as the story meanders thru the history of one family that begins in the first century.

~George Wagner, retired NY publisher at CTRC

Over My Dead Body is very cleverly written. Kelly weaves Biblical truths and insights throughout historical fiction.

~Linda Howard, co-author of *Wholly Woman*

OVER MY
DEAD BODY

OVER MY
DEAD BODY

A SUPERNATURAL NOVEL

KELLY FITZGERALD FOWLER

Published by Relevant Pages Press,
Charleston, South Carolina.

Cover design by Moondog Animation Studio,
Cyril Jedor and Suzanne Parada
Interior layout by Suzanne Parada
Edited by Janet Schwind, Dana Frazeur and George Wagner
Family Tree layout by Brooke O'Friel

ISBN: 978-1-947303-33-1
Library of Congress Control Number: 2017958089

Printed in the United States of America.

For every family member and friend who
encouraged me to never give up.

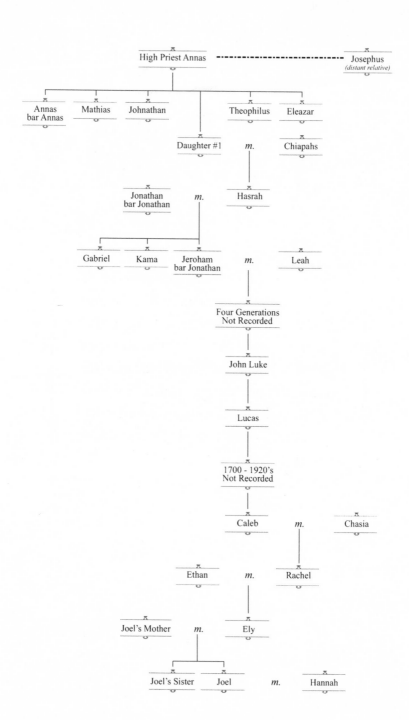

Again I ask: Did they stumble so as to fall beyond recovery? Not at all! Rather, because of their transgression, salvation has come to the Gentiles to make Israel envious. But if their transgression means riches for the world, and their loss means riches for the Gentiles, how much greater riches will their fullness bring!

1

GRIEF

~New York, Present Day~

The shovel in his hand felt heavy as stone as he stuck it into the mound of dirt next to the grave. In the casket below, Joel Cohen could not get the picture of his father's dead body out of his mind. Silence drove through his thoughts, but not on the hectic Brooklyn streets nearby. The hustle and bustle of honking cars and city life were whirring around Joel. People were running, walking their dogs, pushing strollers and going on about their lives. Time was at a standstill for Joel as the weight of gravity on his body planted him in the middle of the cemetery.

Joel was the oldest between him and his sister and the first one in the family to drop dirt on the casket. With tear-filled brown eyes and an ache in his heart, he felt the physical pain of loss. He allowed his floppy ringlets of dark brown hair to fall over his face to mask his leaking eyes, but it didn't matter. If there were ever a time for a real man to have permission to cry, surely it was at his own father's funeral. At that moment Joel didn't care about being a real man.

When the dirt fell and scattered to the sides of the casket, it made Joel think of the downfall of many father and son relationships. His life with his father, Ely, was no different. Joel had always been peaceful and laid back, with an understated drive for success, just a small business owner trying to make enough selling "dead peoples collectibles" as Ely would say. Ely, on the other hand, had grown irritable and bitter. He was a hard-hitting business broker and he expected Joel to be just like him. But Joel was nothing like his father other than his looks. They had a "classic Hebrew warrior" build, as his mom would say. Stocky but not a giant—an acceptable height as far as Joel was concerned. He took good care of himself like his mother had taught him, other than letting his hair get a bit long. His father was shorter than him, but Joel ignored the comparison. His mother had said over and over, "It's not fair to compare" and Joel never did. Ely never spoke it outright and perhaps never came to realize that Little Man syndrome may have been part of his annoyance. Joel only thought this because he had surprised his family with a growth spurt.

Sure, there were good times, but also many difficult times. As an adult, Joel understood his father to have a reason for being bitter. Maybe Ely was in pain and nobody knew. Something had recently changed though. The last few weeks of Ely's life suddenly flourished with joyfulness. Perhaps his father had softened with old age, but even with his newfound joy, he was always preoccupied with something. Ely spent much of his life in a state of concern. Joel had always remembered him that way, but his mother reminded him often of a time when Ely was excited, full of life, and not so irritable.

Something happened to Ely when his own father Ethan, had died. Joel was only ten years old when his grandfather—his zayde—passed away, so he had a faint memory of a time when his father was happy. He remembered his dad calling him "little one" as a young boy. Joel loved it when Ely called him that. After Joel turned ten, he hardly ever called him that again. Perhaps Ely thought Joel was too grown up for the term, but it was the way his father said it that made him feel loved. Joel hadn't thought about it for years. Perhaps grief pulls memories from a valuable place in your mind to ease the pain.

Today he was burying his dad, and Joel felt the pressure in his heart. The loss of his father would bring changes to his life. Yet something deeper haunted him—it burned in his gut—something beyond his present circumstances. Joel would have plenty of time to contemplate it all, as Shiva, the Jewish way of grieving, would start today. Sitting Shiva meant seven full days with family and friends at his childhood home to mourn the loss of his father.

Joel's thoughts quickly moved to his wife, Hannah, who was unable to attend the burial. She was strong, witty, and beautiful. Her strength inspired Joel and she had reminded him of Audrey Hepburn in the movie *Sabrina* when they first met, with her small build and cheeky attitude. Joel's mother had made him watch all the Audrey Hepburn movies, so he had always been attracted to Audrey's look and classy attitude. Hannah proved stronger than Audrey, which was an even better fit for Joel.

The two of them were married almost a year, still newlyweds and supposed to be having the time of their lives. What effect would his father's death have on their lives? Both were in their mid-thirties and fully in love with each other. With kids far off right now, Joel and Hannah were two professionals living in the greatest place on earth, the Big Apple.

Joel owned a successful antique shop, and Hannah loved her work in security with the Israeli Consulate office. The two had met online through a Jewish dating service and had what Hannah called a "fairytale courtship." They connected from day one. Hannah was attracted to Joel's short curly brown locks and deep brown eyes. He was barely taller than she was, and she loved being eye to eye with him. Joel was attracted to her thick dark brown hair and eyes, along with her adorable smile and no-nonsense approach to life. Neither of them had ever questioned the direction of their relationship. They just fit perfectly, and

Joel was grateful. They had even experienced a new level of joy since their wedding day.

His sister took the shovel out of his hands, put her arm around him, and laid her head on his broad shoulder. Her hair fell around him, and he hugged her tight. Looking beyond the gravesite towards the street he saw two men he did not recognize. He wondered how many people he did not know were watching him grieve? The men looked suspicious to him, both wearing sunglasses on a cloudy day. Maybe they were his father's friends and were crying too? The tight hug from his sister, who would not let go, jostled him out of his thoughts and back to his father. How could he be thinking about his wife when his father had just died? And why would he question his father having friends?

This feeling he was experiencing was guilt—a doorway for demons to enter and build lies. Joel had no idea how demons operated or that guilt could do such things to him.

Then, more tension grew behind his eyes and pressure pushed on all sides of his heart. Joel recognized grief. He had grieved for the loss of his real daddy long ago as a young boy.

2

THE THRONE ROOM AND COURT OF HEAVEN

~Outside of Time~

The room was overflowing with layer upon layer of a glowing, translucent amethyst essence. Bright light illuminated overhead from the beaming face of the Ancient of Days, the one who existed before time. His flowing hair was light itself. If there were a ceiling overhead, it was lost in his radiance.

Standing before the Ancient of Days-the Father, the Judge-was Jesus. The sparkling amethyst substance was his robe swirling around Him. He listened as Lucifer spat out the list of accusations against the souls of every man, woman, and child, yet the face of Jesus never lost its peaceful countenance. Finally, Lucifer took a breath, pleased with the case he was building against all of humanity.

The voice of the Father boomed through the courtroom. "Over my dead body!"

As He spoke, Jesus looked into the eyes of Lucifer to measure his reaction to the eternal evidence as it echoed through the chamber. It wasn't often the Father would use an idiom to get his point across. However, Lucifer was not listening well, so the Father tried a different approach, which was laced with a hint. Jesus was sure Lucifer would pick up on the clue to his downfall; however, the adversary let out a nervous snicker and continued pleading his case.

"Eve disobeyed, Adam disobeyed," he hissed as he pointed at them both. "So, I'm entitled to the keys to earth forever."

"You tricked her," the Judge replied as he lifted a gavel. "Atonement is complete; the evidence has been thrown out and is no longer admissible in court. Death died the day the tomb was empty." The gavel struck the arm of the throne with a clap of thunder.

Lucifer gasped as he looked over at Jesus standing in the flesh in the courtroom. He peered behind Jesus, where thousands upon thousands of souls stood in witness to the ruling. Lucifer decided to pretend he didn't understand what had just happened. He checked off the top two names on his list.

"Okay, true, Almighty, I lied to her, but she wanted to believe. But never mind, I will move on."

He continued with his next victim as he started down his long list of names and accusations. The next person standing in line was Cain, followed by a multitude of those who had perished on Earth before the mighty flood.

Jesus moved to his seat on the right side of the Ancient of Days, his robe streaming through the room with precision and flowing grace.

Jesus sighed with a patient breath, "This is going to take a while. When Lucifer has completed his false accusations, I will address the crowd."

3

THE KEY OF DAVID

~Outside of Time~

Elsewhere, inside one of many workshops in heaven, the threefold Godhead—the Father, Jesus, and the Holy Spirit—discussed keys to the kingdom. Jesus took a piece of uncut metal and placed it into a mold. A bright shaft of the glory of the Holy Spirit exuded from the mold, and a key in the form of a medallion was forged into the shape of two combined letters from an angelic alphabet that represented the alpha and the omega. Once completed, Jesus threaded it onto a metal chain and held it up for all to see.

"The key to the House of David," Jesus stated.

"Throughout history, the key will be a symbol and reminder for those who, like David, understand their authority to crush evil on earth and in the unseen world through intimacy with the Almighty," the Holy Spirit said, to explain the divine qualities of the key to those present.

A throne angel, one who is normally posted only before the throne of the Almighty, named Harper was one
of the few on assignment to be allowed to watch the
court proceedings, as well as to witness the Father, Son,
and Holy Spirit forge the key. Beside the angel stood two
other witnesses, Joel Cohen, a human man, and Joseph,
the earthly father of Jesus. Joel listened and experienced
the wonders of heaven as he moved with the angel from
place to place. Once back in the throne room, Joel noticed
someone in line behind Cain who looked familiar to him.
Harper the angel whispered in Joel's ear the identity of the
one Joel recognized.

4

THE CARPENTERS

~Nazareth, Around 15 A.D.~

Jesus and his earthly father, Joseph, worked together to make and sell rare wood storage boxes, tables, and benches in their village of Nazareth.

Annas, the high priest and head of the Temple in Jerusalem, had noticed one of their wood boxes on their previous visit to the Temple and asked Joseph to make one for him. His request honored Joseph, who knew Annas recognized them from a couple of years earlier when Jesus had shown up at the Temple at age thirteen to discuss the written words of Moses and the prophets with the many priests and teachers. Mary had been frantic when she turned around while in the market and realized Jesus had wandered off without telling her.

The box they chose to bring to Annas was a design Jesus had carved and fitted together without nails. The shape was rectangular, and the lid flipped open like all the other small storage boxes they had made. However, the acacia wood grain on this box was more intricate than Joseph had ever seen. He was not surprised at Jesus' skill, or his ability to solve any problem. He had figured out, over time, raising the Messiah would come with many surprises. He knew Jesus was God living his life on earth fully a man. Jesus would have to learn many things just like every other child, but Jesus had allowed himself to be gifted in certain areas just like every other person. Joseph was able to teach Jesus everything he knew about carpentry, but Jesus eventually surpassed Joseph's skills. The box they made for Annas had moving mechanisms and hidden compartments. Jesus had hollowed out parts of the wood. Joseph thought it was a brilliant way to make the box lighter for transporting. He could see no visible way to access the hollow places. It was unlike any other box he had seen or could have made on his own. He was humbled to work with his son on the box for the high priest.

Once the box was completed, Jesus affixed onto the lid a fascinating, intricate adornment crafted from metal. Then, as if the Ancient of Days knew Joseph would have many questions, He allowed Joseph to witness a vision of the workshop in heaven. As Joseph's mind was transported, he saw Jesus create a separate metal piece—a medallion—which when nested into the adornment on the box as it was designed to do, acted as a key. Jesus called it the key of David. Joseph's vision continued as he was then flown like a soaring eagle through the history of the key, witnessing the key being passed down from David and others, and saw it was now in the possession of the high priest, Annas. In the vision Joseph saw that once the key was placed on the wooden box's metal adornment, glory light from heaven shined out and the pieces shifted open like a puzzle, revealing the hidden compartments. He then realized there were supernatural reasons for the light and the secret hiding places. The box displayed spectacular craftsmanship and Joseph had no need to ask about the strange properties of the box or the medallion; he was in awe of being a witness in heaven to the spectacular history and design. There were moments with Jesus when Joseph would remain speechless—this was one of those moments.

The symbol on the medallion reminded Joseph of yet another phenomenal moment like this one. Jesus as a young boy had created his own alphabet. He insisted He be able to share his alphabet with those who studied in the library in Alexandria, Egypt. Joseph took him to the library upon his insistence, where the boy Jesus brought along his symbolic scroll. The scholars brushed Jesus off as a child, but when He opened the scroll to reveal his alphabet, they suddenly became interested and accepted his manuscript. Shortly after, an angel of the Lord appeared to Joseph in a dream, calling them back to the land of Israel. They left Egypt and never returned.

5

THE DEMON NAMED MARQ

*M*y father Zagan was the head of Lucifer's light brigade while still in the Heaven of heavens. His position was pure luck for me as it triggered Lucifer to favor me. My assignment exhilarated me. I was loyal to Lucifer. I mean, I did what it took to skirt by, which broke protocol, but I got away with it anyway. Lucifer was kicked out of the third heaven when his pride got the best of him. My father was part of the regiment that was spewed out of Heaven, along with the rest of the fallen angels.

After spending time on earth, my father seduced a daughter of Adam; I was the result. The shocking flood sent by God destroyed my flesh from my mother's side of the family. That is how we got into our current state of affairs of no flesh. We were called Giants, Titans or Nephilim who never really understood what was going to happen to us when Noah was building that despicable vessel. It took him so long to produce that barge.

We were ruthless in our barrage of taunts toward him, but Noah kept on task for years. We should have taken notice. We thought we were a supreme race and could never be harmed. Not the case. So now I exist on earth in spirit form, a demon.

It's not comfortable for demons here. Finding a host is a constant struggle of moving from object to object and generation to generation. But for now, I make do by attaching to pretty much anything that may have a malevolent use. I can attach to any object and attitude that aligns with evil. I move often within the vicinity of my assignment, unless an object has great significance for evil that could lead me to total success in my mission. Oh, how I miss my flesh.

The only redeeming part of my existence is my assignment to a noteworthy family. I find my work detestable, which is good for demons, but what choice do I have? I have followed the family through the years, since Annas was a little boy. My assignment is the high priest, Annas, and his Jewish dynasty.

My first opportunity to attach to Annas was after his father Seth berated him. Keep in mind—wounds created from father issues are driven deep into human souls. It was easy for me to take up residency on the wound because I acted quickly; it had been exposed just long enough for me to latch on. Then Annas buried it as deep as a well. His father expressed disappointment with Annas when he was just an eleven-year-old boy, so Annas worked most of his life attempting to overcome the pain of his father's disappointment. Seth expected great success from his sons, and Annas was no exception. Fathers berating their sons expose little boys to many opportunities for the likes of me.

Annas had caused trouble in the women's court at the Temple by pulling his mother's head covering off while she was praying. One of his friends dared him, and he fell for it. It's the small decisions people make, even at young ages, that open doors. The look of disdain in his father's eyes was more than Annas could bear. He knew better, but he was just a boy, and little boys are utterly mean and clumsy with their decision-making. The pain lodged deep down in the circular walls of his heart.

All I needed was to get into the part of his mind where he pondered the lie. I was able to capture the lie and repeat it over and over with high precision: "I will never be good enough." Annas retold it like this in his mind repeatedly: "No matter how hard I try, I will never please my father." Those types of lies and pain are all we demons need to do real damage to a child.

Today, I have my sights set on Joel Cohen, a direct descendant of Annas. Joel is different from his father Ely. Not such an easy target since his mother has taught him about grudges and kept him balanced and obedient. I have noticed through time, mothers who spend their energy training their sons to obey create a strong layer that is hard for demons to penetrate. I have been able to watch Joel from childhood, and his mother's bloodline has strong family support along with the pathetic emotion of love. My mother was nothing like Joel's mother, quite the opposite. It is sickening how much his mother taught him about kindness. You can call me jealous, but I'm not. I just happen to hate kindness.

Joel's father Ely was extremely easy to attach to for many of us, just like Annas had been. I became a bit uncomfortable when Ely came close to understanding forgiveness, which is the currency of heaven, but he also had pride. He carried a nasty root of bitterness buried deep inside, and I had squatter's rights. He didn't know how to dig out the roots soon enough to reach his full destiny, which gave us legal rights to stay attached to him.

There were a few of us demons there, holding on for dear life. Bitterness, anger, malice and regret plagued Ely. But toward the end of his life, he managed to harness the vindictive power of forgiveness. When forgiveness moves in, most of us are kicked out. He stumbled upon forgiveness with only three weeks left to spare. We ruined the assignment, as we didn't know our time was so short. We figured he would live much longer, especially after he forgave. Oh, there were plenty of assignments on his head—brain cancer, heart problems—anything to keep him from sharing the details of what was in the box. But usually, after forgiveness sets in, most demons must leave. For some reason, we still had access to his heart. Ely didn't understand his authority, so I took advantage and stayed. Heart sickness got him on a Spring day, which was an unexpected surprise to the family. A bonus point for me since I rode it out and was able to find a chink in the armor.

Never mind all that. Joel has plenty of pain for me to take advantage of at the moment. Currently, I am residing on a bitter relative's journal entry in the box that had anger and unbelief. I am just waiting for the best time to leap on Joel.

It's not relaxing at all when you attach to non-living objects or words. When you find living flesh to connect to, you at least have a bit of a breather. Joel has heartache and grief, but no bitterness to attach to quite yet. He doesn't have a hardened heart like his father. I easily deceived Ely. I just have to bide my time until the right opportunity comes along to get my grip on Joel. Perhaps I could get access to Hannah, his wife; I would have rights to her as well through the marriage covenant. When the two become one, it creates a flesh gateway.

6

SHIVA

~*New York, Present Day*~

Seven days later, Shiva ended. Friends and family had come and gone. The mourning period was a sweet time with his family. They remembered all the places Ely had been and the things he had done. Ely's friends reminisced about them all hanging out together. Some memories Joel recognized, but some happened before he was born. Joel was sad, but somehow found peace with the unexpected passing of his father. Now he had to help his mother make some sense of what happened and what was next for her.

"Joel, we have to talk about the box," his mom said.

Joel was surprised by the topic coming up so soon. The box had been a subject of discussion off and on throughout his life. Nobody except Ely had ever touched it. It sat in his father's office behind the desk for as long as he could remember. He asked his dad about it often as a boy but would only get a few little hints about its contents. Joel knew it was off limits. His father had made it apparent to him.

Ely told Joel that one day he would know what was in the box. As a child, Joel imagined the day his father would share the contents of the box with him. That day never came.

Joel often obsessed about the box as a young man, thinking about its story. After all, it was an antique and Joel was an antique dealer who relished in the excitement that an object could have a history. He adored historical items. His shop was successful because Joel attached adventure to every item in the shop. When he bought a piece at an auction or from a seller, he tracked down the history and shared the details with his clients. The buyer was not just buying a piece of art or a knickknack - they were buying into the experience of that item.

Even after Joel moved out of his childhood home, the box was on his mind. He had waited with great patience for his dad to finally share it with him, but it was too late. Now his mother had given it to him. She told him his father had left a sweet note along with his will to pass it on to him. Joel was heartbroken when he realized his father had never intended them to open the box together. Where had their relationship gone wrong?

Joel was put off and offended by the attitude his father had given his mother over the years. His mother always said offense was bait used by demons to lure people into depravity. That always stuck with Joel as semi-comical folklore but good advice, so he worked hard not to be offended.

However, all this time the box had been sitting right there, untouched. Joel was irritated by the secrecy surrounding the box. It ate at him.

"I'm going to put an end to this mystery right now!" Joel said. "This is ridiculous." Anger surged to his face. "I can't believe Father never told you what was in the box. Let's just open it together."

"Your father said in the letter he left me it was for your eyes only, and I'm not going to betray his dying wish," his mother consoled.

Joel calmed a bit as he looked into her soft, puffy, red-lined eyes. He could see she loved him.

"Mom, you've got to be kidding me; this is crazy. Come and open it with me," Joel begged, interlocking his hands as if in prayer. He had again assumed his boyhood role of pleading with her to get his way. Somehow when he was with her, he became her little boy again. It made him long for simpler times. "I want you by my side when I open it. I know you want to know what's inside. Please look," he petitioned her, as he tried to assume a more adult approach.

She cut him off, cross now, and stubborn in her quiet way. "Your father said if you want to tell me you can, but he specifically asked me not to look unless you understood what it was and what the consequences would be."

"The consequences?" Joel didn't like the sound of that. "What happened to Dad after he opened the box? You said it changed him." Joel's tone had changed to one of fear, and his mother noticed. She had said many times before that fear squelches the ability of people to reach their destiny. She knew him so well.

In her quiet voice, she said, "Son, don't be fearful. Whatever's in the box, you're the person chosen to handle the contents. Your father changed, but this is a different time, and you are in a different place." It was evident she wasn't going to look with him. He was disappointed.

Joel looked at the office door and saw a fleeting outline of something, a white shape. He just realized he had seen this before throughout his life, always near his father's office - a silhouette of what looked like a man with a sphere next to him. In a quick glimpse, he questioned what he saw as he squinted his eyes. It disappeared as if it had walked through the door. *Some strange light reflection,* Joel thought, but then he felt a cool breeze and peace overwhelmed him for a split second, and then vanished, as if sent to strengthen him.

Joel decided he had no choice. He would face this without his mother or father. His whole mind entered the reality of all the possibilities as he turned the knob of the office door.

7

ACACIA WOOD FROM EGYPT

The simple yet captivating box was behind the desk. The only thing Joel knew about the box was that it was made of acacia wood. That's because his father had explained to him the story of how Jacob, after moving to Egypt, had planted the acacia trees in Goshen, Egypt. Joel recalled the voice of his father: "Jacob told his son Joseph, who then told his own children, 'When you leave Egypt, take the acacia wood with you.' Later, when the Ark of the Covenant was built, the acacia wood from Egypt was used." His father knew the box itself was valuable and told the same story many times. Joel realized the old heirloom was one of the reasons he had gone into the antique business in the first place. Joel appreciated history. Ely had created great curiosity for him as a child, and Joel thought about the contents often. He grew especially interested when Ely told the story of Jacob and Joseph and the acacia trees.

"Father, when they left Egypt how did they drag these trees with them through the Red Sea?" Joel remembered asking one time after he had watched the *Prince of Egypt* animated film. He looked at the box in wonder and awe as if he was part of some massive fairy tale. That was one of the few pleasant memories he had with his father on the subject. "How did they drag those trees, again? Is our box from one of Jacob's trees?" Joel would ask over and over.

"I don't know, little one," his father answered, growing tired of the questions over time, wishing he had never told Joel to begin with.

"How did our family end up with a box like that?" Joel kept asking, unaware of his father's irritation.

"Joel, it has been passed to us from generation to generation," he snapped. "Don't ever touch it or open it unless I say it is okay," his father finally said.

That was the end of the conversation. Ely would not say when or how they would open it, or what was in the box. Joel had a healthy curiosity about the contents but gave up asking, afraid he would cause his father more annoyance.

Now, here he was. He sat in front of the box that had held so much intrigue for him as a child. The acacia wood was magnificent and the way the box was constructed, it had the appearance of being woven together like the sides could shift. The box was lighter than Joel expected. It looked more like a small chest, with an embossed metal symbol on the lid—not Hebrew, but familiar to Joel.

Joel had learned the Hebrew alphabet as a young man, so he could read the Torah at his Bar Mitzvah, but the symbol was different than anything in the Hebrew alphabet. He wondered about the symbol. It could have been a logo of some sort, representing the wood carver, the antique dealer in him believed.

Heaviness started to build in Joel's mind, and he felt an invisible weight on his head and shoulders. He plopped into the office chair. The peace he felt earlier had departed.

Then, an unusual thought entered his mind. Joel was considering a prayer before opening the heirloom box. He had never considered prayer, much less saying one himself outside of synagogue. *You don't talk to God. You let the rabbi pray to God,* he thought.

Today was a different day. He was grief stricken, and through the pain, his mind had been drifting to places he had never imagined.

Joel was heartbroken when he thought about his relationship with his father. Did his dad love him? At some point in his life, Joel believed they would be good friends. *Wanting to pray must be part of grieving,* Joel thought. His head started to feel like a medicine ball in his hands, as tears formed in his eyes. Joel decided to hold back the tears, but roll with the thought. *God, if you are real, help me know what to do,* Joel prayed in his head. *Short and to the point,* he thought. Again, a strange thought, since he never prayed outside of guided prayers at synagogue.

Joel was already wondering what was happening to him. He admitted in his mind: he would have never considered this sort of thing just seven days ago.

As he opened the box, Joel felt a hand on his shoulder. He swirled around in the office chair, afraid of what he might see. He saw nothing but felt a definite presence. He looked around the room. Every hair on his body prickled and he could feel something was different in the air. Joel lifted the lid of the box. He was stricken by the thought of God being real and in this very room.

Joel looked down as he flung the lid opened. The inside was a carved-out rectangle with thick sides and there appeared to be other moving parts inside the box that did not make total sense. Inside was a rolled-up scroll on top of a small, old journal. Both items were placed on top of a typed manuscript in a clear-cover notebook. The thick scroll was rolled up and tied with a piece of leather, and had obviously been placed inside a clear plastic bag for protection. The scroll itself appeared to be papyrus. On top of it all was a letter in an envelope with Joel's name carefully hand-printed on the front.

Joel's mind reeled as he thought of what all this might be. He picked up the bundle and noticed Hebrew writing on the scroll.

"Is it an old copy of the Torah?" he asked aloud.

These things belong in a museum, he thought. *Okay, maybe it is valuable, perhaps ancient, but what's the mystery?* He needed a Hebrew dictionary. He had not read Hebrew since he was thirteen.

He held the envelope with his name on it and opened the flap. As he pulled out its contents, he realized it was a handwritten letter to him from his father.

8

THE ANGEL NAMED HARPER

I am a throne angel. I am not omnipotent. Only the Almighty has that type of power. He created throne angels to be able to see several places at one time. I have many eyes. The Almighty gave me the ability to focus consistently on Him, and currently, my remaining eyes are focused on my assignment, Joel.

I am not a scary angel like Michael. That angel is frightening, even to us. I'm a sphere with golden wings. I don't look like a huge muscle builder with long silky black hair like Michael. I am honored to be a uniquely created being with supernatural qualities and abilities.

My name is Harper, which means harp player. You may think it's not a very original name for an angel. I know most humans believe angels sit on clouds and play the harp. The funny thing about my name is I don't play the harp at all. My throne angel friends think my name is hilarious. I enjoy their laughter. It is an honor to be named by the

Almighty. I asked the Almighty why he named me that yet He did not put the desire in me to play the harp. He told me that my voice sounded like a harp to Him. I love that.

I'm not the only angel assigned to Joel. There are several of us assigned to him and to every human. The Almighty tells me what to do, and I carry out those assignments.

My weapon of warfare is to worship and watch. My worship of the Almighty is keeping most of my focus on Him and the rest on whatever task He gives me. Humans could learn a lot about worshiping from me. Being obedient is a potent form of worship.

Throne angels are intense in their warfare, and I take my position seriously. I also love my assignment to watch Joel and his family. It has brought me great delight to enjoy the looking glass humans call "time."

The Almighty created time on the day he made night and day. I had the honor of watching him create the earth as well as the sun and the moon. Being one of the first created beings is an honor.

Here's an interesting truth. Most humans probably don't even realize light was created before He even put the stars in the sky or the moon out there to enjoy. I was fortunate to be a witness. The Almighty created us just in time to watch and see the rest of creation unfold. We angels rejoiced every day as each discovery came forth of what the Almighty revealed in creation. We were dazzled, to say the least.

Once, I had the honor to be one of the throne angels who ushered the Almighty toward the earth on a great moving throne, when the Almighty fed a scroll to the prophet Ezekiel from his own hand. Ezekiel told me later it tasted like honey, with the texture and taste of what you would call filo dough. Ezekiel saw the angels and described us as a wheel, but we are spheres. He took the correction well when we met in person.

Here I am talking about time and food again. Time is an odd concept. We angels don't have to reside within time, but we find it fascinating to watch.

Food, on the other hand, we love. For example, what you call a blueberry waffle today tastes very much like manna. The funny thing is, manna literally means, "What is it?" I tried to get the Almighty to tell Moses it was a waffle, but of course, He wouldn't. The Almighty usually plays along with my jokes. Did you know He has a sense of humor? After all, His joy in you is your strength. If you don't think so, then just take a look at a seahorse. He made them with the head of a horse and tiny baby fins and the male species has the babies. So, I asked the Almighty if I could appear to Moses while he and the Israelites were wandering in the desert to tell him that manna tastes like waffles. Again, the answer was no. Now that Moses is here in Heaven, we joke together about waffles. He always gets a good chuckle out of the conversation. Then he says, "What is it?" and tries not to *laugh at the fact he had never even tasted a waffle. They created waffles in the Middle Ages at the place you would now call Belgium long after Moses left the earth.*

Laughter is good, but we need to get back to Joel; he is reading the letter from his father. The Almighty is quite interested in what's happening with Joel right now, as Joel just struck up a conversation with Him, which has not happened since he was thirteen.

9

A LETTER FROM ELY

My Son,

If you are reading this letter, it means I must be gone. I know our relationship has had its awkward moments. Please forgive me for being such a bitter old man. I hope you will realize over time the burden I carried for far too long to keep your mother, sister, and you safe.

The reason I am writing you this letter is that I want to make sure you understand the contents of this box is of great value. Our family has preserved the details and scrolls for over 2000 years. The document you are now in possession of is a detailed account of what your ancestors have done with the box up until now.

The box itself must hold a supernatural power for preservation because I can't explain how the contents have lasted for so long.

Remember the story I used to tell you about the acacia wood? It must contain a type of preservative. There are also supernatural powers at work surrounding the box at all times. I know it may sound crazy to you now, but I believe angels guard the box. You may even feel their presence now. If so, don't be afraid. Remember what mom always said about fear, that it will destroy your destiny.

~~~

Joel stopped reading and froze. He was taken aback by his father's acknowledgment of angels. Then he even mentioned the story of the acacia wood and fear. Was it a coincidence Joel had just thought about those very topics a few minutes earlier? His heart raced while his ears and head became hot. The next thing he knew, his whole body collapsed as if melting and he slid from the chair to the floor.

Out of nowhere, Joel was surrounded by a sensation of weightlessness. A rush of warm glowing light flowed over him with a flood of peace. He could see waves in his mind's eye as they poured over him as if he were in a calm ocean. Each wave hit with a deep color, bringing with it a more profound sense of peace. The waves were not any shade of color he had ever seen. He couldn't explain to himself what had happened. Fear and doubt tried to overcome him but was forced away by the powerful waves of peace.

He felt a sensation of floating and bliss, yet knew he was lying on the floor. *What are these waves?* he thought.

Joel wanted to know what was happening to him. He knew he wasn't dying, but he couldn't feel the weight of his body.

Suddenly, Joel's eyes popped open naturally, and he had no idea how long he had been in this peaceful state. His heart was experiencing a melting sensation as if it were made of wax. Joel tried to identify what was going on. All he could think was that he had never felt more alive and refreshed. This was peace, as earth surrendered to Heaven on Joel's behalf.

Angel Harper

Joel doesn't understand he just drifted into what we call "earth as it is in Heaven." Angels are allowed to provide a glimpse of heaven to humans who need strength. It's like a little taste of manna. Joel's guardian angels are holding his spirit so he can take a look. It will refresh him and renew him for his task ahead.

At the moment, several angels are working with Joel - a few angels to strengthen him and myself. He and his family have a significant legacy to fulfill. There have always been many demons surrounding his family because the fallen angels and demons want the box and its contents. The Almighty sends us to make sure everything is legal and fair.

I see one demon has attached to the journal in the box. That demon is on the hunt for bitterness. He is trying to get to Joel, but so far, he doesn't have the right angle because Joel is not like his dad. Joel doesn't have a bitter bone in his body. That demon is just hovering and waiting for a chance to pounce. It's sad how they linger forever. I wish they would give up.

~~~

Unsure how to react, like a man in denial and needing an explanation for what had just happened, Joel gathered himself up from the floor. He had to press on to read his father's letter.

~~~

Your ancestor Annas purchased this box from Joseph, the father of Jesus. Yes, the real Jesus. According to the scroll, Annas purchased it when Jesus was a young man of fifteen. It's believed to be hand-crafted by Joseph and Jesus together.

As you read the details following this, little one, please know I had a decision to make about this valuable information, as our ancestors did before me. I did what I thought was best for my family, and my decision hung heavy on me for years. I felt like a coward, but they—people with great power—threatened our lives, our family. I figured out early on that the contents compromised our family and our culture. I wasn't willing to sacrifice, and so I lived in fear. There are forces both natural and supernatural that will fight to keep you from making this public, simply because of their need for power. I know you are stronger than I ever was, and I know you will make the right decision regarding the contents of the scrolls, but please protect our family. To take it public, you need finances for lawyers. You will be scorned by religious people from every walk of life and sought after by supernatural forces you cannot see.

If you decide to keep the secret and pass it on to your children, know it is well with me. When I got this box from your Bubbe Rachel, I never wanted to burden your mother. I felt like it was something I had to decide on my own.

Bubbe and I never discussed it openly again, once she initially told me about it. I think she was surprised at my negative reaction, which I now regret. I believe there is even more to this than meets the eye, but she stopped telling me details once she realized I wasn't ready. When we moved her into the assisted living space, I found her diary and put it in the box also, as it contains details of what happened to the box during WWII. It made me sad she never passed the key she mentioned in her journal on to me.

An interpretation of the Annas scroll is in the enclosed typed notebook. I had to have it translated and the dates researched from Hebrew to English by Leona, a Hebrew professor back in the eighties, so I could read it. I also figured it would keep the fragile scroll from having to be handled by people. I typed up a translation from Italian to English of Bubbe's diary, so you could get all the up-to-date details, which I was missing until your Bubbe got sick and I read her diary.

Each generation has recorded the details of how and why they decided not to reveal the truth. No matter what they decided, they were all in grave danger so be careful! Please make sure you record your decision and keep it in the box for the next generation, unless you choose to bring it forward.

I'm sorry, son, the burden was too heavy for me as I denied the truths my whole life. Even once I had all the details, I couldn't believe what I was reading. I didn't recognize the real truth until my old age, but still did not have the courage to put the family in danger by bringing it forward. Ultimately, it is up to you and God.

Seek Him with your whole heart, and you will find Him.

In the name of Jesus, the Messiah,
Your father,
Ely

10

THE BIG SECRET

Joel's heart sank as his father fell short of writing that he loved him. He was used to it, and yet it stung, again. And, what was this? Joel couldn't believe his eyes! *What did that say?* His mind ran into overdrive. His father had never mentioned Messiah or the name of Jesus in their house. Once in a while, they would talk about the fools who followed Jesus, but his name was never allowed in their home.

His father hated those people who called themselves Messianic Jews and referred to them as traitors. Even though Joel knew their family didn't exactly follow all the laws themselves, he and most of his friends were Jewish in culture, if not religion. Plus, it was pretty clear following all the laws would be impossible.

As a young boy, Joel saw his friend's father spit on the "Jews for Jesus" who came to their neighborhood and handed out pamphlets to try and convert them to believe

Jesus was the Messiah. Even Ely would get angry with them. His father would say, "Don't look at them; they are liars." Now, his father signed his letter in the name of Jesus the Messiah?

The world was upside down. His father was not only talking about angels but now Jesus, too? Joel didn't know what to do with this information. His mind pictured the great abyss of doubt his father had dealt with throughout his life. Suddenly, he realized more clearly why his dad had been so secretive. The secret in this box was a *big* secret and a dangerous one.

Joel considered what might have happened if Ely had taken the box to one of the rabbis. He was sure the rabbi would have called in deprogrammers. Joel had seen the circus of what happened when a Jewish person decided to believe Jesus was the Messiah.

His friend's father from his Jewish high school decided to try to prove to his Christian wife Jesus was not the Messiah. So, he studied the Torah hoping to show her proof and convert her to Judaism. As he dug into it, he was convinced Gentiles would have a chance to accept the Jewish Messiah.

That one piece of information had stuck with Joel for all these years since high school. It was not something he had ever heard any other Jewish person say. It nagged him occasionally, but the mess that took place in their school after he said it was frightening.

The deprogrammer gathered all the families to explain why Jesus was not the Messiah. But his friend's father had studied so much, and he had details from the Torah, which were contrary to what the expert rabbi was saying. They argued in a meeting in front of parents, students, and teachers, until the rabbi realized his friend's father was too far gone, and they asked him to leave.

Joel was too busy with his studies to pay much attention, but he knew the situation had made everyone crazy for a while. After that, his friend could no longer attend their school. A few other students left the school also, traitors who believed Jesus was the Messiah.

Joel turned his attention to the supernatural thought of angels. Chills hit him, and he realized what he had experienced earlier. *Could he see angels?* His father's letter made it seem like it was no big deal but make no mistake—his father was talking about angels.

Occasionally, throughout his life, Joel had experienced the feeling he was not alone. The angelic activity his father referred to explained plenty. However, *if God wasn't real, how could angels be?* Joel pondered as he realized his belief in God really was just tradition. Joel remembered some details from studying the prophets in school. All the stories were so far-fetched, but he was fascinated with the idea of angels. Joel had even written a report about angels in ninth grade. He remembered the Seraphim angels had six wings. With two they covered their faces, with two they covered their feet, and with two they flew. Joel had even sketched a picture in his notebook of what he thought Seraphim angels might have looked like. During his research it had occurred to Joel the prophet Daniel had several experiences with angels. He specifically remembered how Daniel had fallen on his face in terror until the angel told him not to be afraid and strengthened him. Joel looked around the room as the thought caused his heart to race, but he didn't see anything. But he did have a new awareness of the possibility divine messengers could exist, and not only in ancient Hebrew writings.

Joel turned his attention back to the scroll and the manuscript. He took his dad's advice and decided to read the translated document, rather than open up the ancient, delicate scroll.

11

HEROD AND BETHLEHEM

The manuscript of Annas was put together in a notebook, typed neatly on an old typewriter, with a clear plastic cover. Joel picked it up and began to read.

High Priest Annas Son of Seth, 4th day of Nisan 3830

(April 1, 70 A.D.)

I must tell the beginning from the end and the end from the beginning.

I recall the first time I saw Jesus, son of Joseph of Bethlehem. He was in the Temple with a large group of leaders. Jesus was sitting at their feet, soaking in their knowledge. I approached the group to listen to the questions of the young man. The rabbis were answering his questions with more questions, as was

the custom when teaching. As I drew near,
I realized this young man was answering
their questions with even more questions,
as if he had studied for several life-
times. The priests and rabbis were astonished by the boy's knowledge. I was
jealous of his gift.

I remember I once asked Jesus, "How
will you recognize our Messiah?"

He answered, "The prophet Habakkuk
said, 'The earth will be filled with the
knowledge of the Lord's glory, as the
waters cover the sea.'" Then he gave me
a pleasant smile I never forgot, even to
this day. He was a typical boy in many
ways, but I will always remember the confidence he carried when he answered that
question.

His circling questions continued for
two days before Joseph found him, having
wandered off from his parents. It never
occurred to us his family didn't know
where he was. We had no idea where he
had gone the previous evening—we assumed
back to his home or wherever his family
was staying. When he showed up the next
morning in the men's court, we thought

his family had extended their stay in Jerusalem beyond Passover.

After this, our first encounter, I would see him and his family often when they would travel to the temple. I would even talk with him and his father to see how he was progressing in his studies. I knew he was gifted.

During one of their visits, I noticed a box they used to transport small meals. The hand-carved craftsmanship was perfect. It was hard to believe so much knowledge and skill came from a family of carpenters from Nazareth. Nazareth was a small fishing village, and a Roman garrison occupied Galilee from that location so anything from Nazareth typically repulsed me. But I wanted one of those boxes. I asked Joseph to bring me one the next time they came to Jerusalem. He enthusiastically agreed and made this box, which currently holds my writing. I was surprised by their generosity because I believe they knew I was not fond of Nazareth. Jesus even added intricate ironwork on the top to give it a regal appearance. I learned later they made it from acacia

wood — the same wood used to make the Ark
of the Covenant — and the ironwork was
placed there for a specific purpose. Now
I own this masterpiece. It has become my
prize possession. I expect the family to
treat it with great care. I am especially
fond of the metal design on the top and
the secret locking mechanism.

But much happened long before I even
met Joseph and Jesus. Let me start at the
beginning. I am an old man. Forgive me.

Thinking back on the crossroads that
led to my truth, I recalled being in
the temple, long before I was named high
priest, just a young elder in the Saddu-
cee council. King Herod the Great called
a small group of us before him to discuss
a recent visit by three Magi or priests
who arrived from Persia in the East. The
Magi had asked Herod the Great about a
prophecy of a baby born to be King of the
Jews. They explained how in their belief,
they had studied the stars for years and
realized an ancient prophecy from Daniel regarding the night sky had come to
pass. They had seen a bright star in the
East, and each followed as if an invisible hand led them. They all decided on

their own to leave their kingdoms to seek the prophesied child.

King Herod the Great, being a paranoid tyrant, had summoned us to ask where the Messiah was to be born. We told him the prophet Micah had written the answer 750 years earlier, recording what God had spoken to him, saying "But you, Bethlehem, though you are small among the clans of Judah, out of you will come for Me one who will be ruler over Israel." The Messiah would be born in Bethlehem.

It was only a matter of time before Herod the Great had every male child in Bethlehem under the age of four killed. His paranoid fear of losing his throne caused him to order the butchery.

When we heard of the atrocity, we wept and mourned for our brothers and sisters in Bethlehem. We had contributed to the killing of all those children; their blood was on our hands. Not again! We wailed as we remembered our baby boys being thrown into the Nile in Egypt during the time of our slavery. I questioned the existence of God, Messiah, and any truth I had ever believed.

Tears still flow even now from the memory of this incident.

Demon Marq

I remember Herod the Great. There was a legion of insanity demons assigned to that man. Manipulating him was easy, as it was evident from the look on his face and his actions that he welcomed them. It was pure evil in motion as they manipulated his every word. I was with Annas when this exchange took place. Annas was still a young man when Herod the Great murdered all those innocents. I used this situation often, to remind and convince Annas to do whatever it took to hold onto his power in a worthy quest to never let something like this happen again. Convincing humans to do the wrong thing using their own self-righteousness is an easy task if they have pride and regret. I can still see the demons of regret that followed him around after that incident.

12

PROPHECY-ANNAS SCROLL

High Priest Annas, Son of Seth, 16th Day of Nisan 3830 (April 12, 70 A.D.)

This is how I came to understand more about Jesus.

As the high priest, chosen by Rome, my power grew stronger and stronger. Everyone looked up to me, and I relished this role in the seat of leadership. I understood the best way to preserve Israel was to keep the peace. Whenever a new person claiming to be the Messiah showed up, I would discount it every time.

So many women would come to me and ask if their baby boy could be the anointed one. Everyone was looking for a king to

save us from the Romans. We were looking
for a political savior, not a spiritual
savior. I had sacrificed plenty of innocent animals for my sins. I pretended,
along with everyone else, that atonement
for our sin was assured through animal sacrifice. But if it was working,
it didn't feel like it. Too much blood
everywhere, all the time. Preparing myself with constant washing and following
every little law, then killing, was ex-
hausting and never-ending. I convinced
myself it was just a performance for the
people and for Rome, necessary to keep
my job. I convinced myself eventually
that Adam and Eve, Noah, even Moses were
just tradition, not believable.

I worked hard to assure people the
time for the Messiah was not now, but
many believed differently. I regularly
dismantled their philosophies as wish-
ful thinking. We had not seen or heard
from God for well over four hundred
years. I had convinced myself God was
made up. Since I was not legally chosen
to be high priest, I didn't have the same
convictions of those before me. Rome was
in charge.

Occasionally, the thought that Jesus might be the Messiah crept into my mind after studying swirling prophetic details, but then I would remember Jesus was from Nazareth, not Bethlehem. Of course, I considered in my study of the topic how some prophets said the Messiah would come from Nazareth. I also knew he was about the age of the murdered children in Bethlehem. However, there was no way he would have survived the slaughter. The Romans were ruthless and meticulous in carrying out orders.

Long after his crucifixion, when it was too late, I learned he and his family had also lived in Egypt for a time. Most of my life after the crucifixion I had discounted the possibility of Jesus being the Messiah. However, it became apparent he had fulfilled another major prophecy from the prophet Hosea who said, "Out of Egypt I called my son." The Messiah would come out of Egypt, Bethlehem, and Nazareth. For me, it was just another one of God's riddles and I was weary of finding prophecy after prophecy Jesus had fulfilled.

When digging further, I realized Joseph of Bethlehem, the father of Jesus, would have been there signing up for the census around the same time I stood before Herod the Great.

I learned later, after I had persecuted Jesus and his disciples, Joseph was told in a dream to leave Bethlehem. They fled to Egypt just before the slaughter. This truth was gut-wrenching. I realized then how I contributed to the death of so many people. Recording this makes me physically ill. I do so only because I want my family to know the truth, no matter how disturbing. This is my confession. I need a rest for now.

~~~

Joel put the manuscript down and rubbed his eyes for a moment. He needed a break. He got up from the couch and left his father's office. His mother was sitting in the kitchen at the table holding a cup of tea. She knew from the look on his face her son was not going to share any information with her—a Jewish mother's intuition. She wanted to know what was in the box and could probably convince Joel to tell her now, but on this rare occasion, she was resolute to obey her husband's wishes. Joel forced a smile at her and opened the refrigerator to piles of food, brought to them from various friends. Joel grabbed a tray of pre-made sandwiches and a plate. Still, there were no words between him and his mother.

Joel sat down across from his mother. He smiled at her, and she smiled back. She noticed it looked as if he had been crying a bit, but she didn't mention it to him. She wanted to talk, but nothing came out.

"So, what's up today?" Joel asked as he shoved an entire half sandwich into his mouth.

She chuckled at his adorable boyish manner and said, "I have to go to the bank to figure out some things from our accounts." She paused. "I also need to stop by the lawyer's office."

"Do you need me to take you?" he asked, with food still in his mouth.

"No, honey, your sister is already on her way." She paused again, looking at his wet eyes. "You need to get back to Hannah; I know you miss her. I am sure she is missing you, too," she said, as she drew in a heavy sigh.

As he chewed, Joel nodded a bit in agreement with her. The whining boy who went into the room to look at the box had stepped back into his role as a grown man. He was dealing with the loss of his father as an adult now. His mother knew he would have to grow up in that office and sure enough, he did.

She stood up from her tea to head off to her bedroom

for a shower. She kissed Joel on the forehead as she left the room. Joel shut his eyes as she kissed him and knew he wouldn't tell her what was in the box and she wouldn't ask.

Joel's mind went back to the letter. He needed to process what he was reading. *I need to do some internet research on who this Annas is,* Joel thought. He had heard about Jesus but didn't know much. His Christian friends had never crossed the line to talk to him about Jesus.

Joel gobbled down the remains of his sandwich, so he could get back to the office and finish reading.

Angel Harper

I knew Annas had unbelief and of course he didn't like the slaughter of innocent animals, but when he was a young priest, he would consume plenty of the meat. He may have grown weary in his old age by the time he wrote this down. Other humans have told me, as you age you eat less. I am just preoccupied with earthly food, so I ask lots of questions when I get a chance. Anyway, after following Annas around most of his life, I can tell you he loved his choice meats. What do you think they did with all the animals they sacrificed? They had barbeques to feed the priests. The Israelites had five different types of offerings for various reasons. All of them included food the priests were allowed to eat, except the one called the "Burnt Offering," which had to be totally burnt up. But the rest of the offerings, the priests could eat to their hearts' content. Don't get me wrong; it was their job to go into the Holy of Holies, which was the location in the temple set apart for God's unique dwelling place. Not an easy task to stand before the presence of God—I am just saying Annas liked a full belly.

13

JOHN THE BAPTIST

Joel picked up the manuscript where he left off before he got hungry.

~~~

High Priest Annas, Son of Seth, 24th Day of Nisan 3830 (April 20, 70 A.D.)

I am sorrowful to read what I have already written. But I must go on, as I have no idea how much time I have left to tell my story.

Since the Romans do as they wish, they appointed me high priest. I assured them I would be supportive of their tax needs and demands from the people. This elated the Roman legate Quirinius - who chose me for the position - and also ultimately pleased Augustus, the emperor of Rome at the time.

I remained high priest for nine years. Then Ishmael took the post for a short time. However, within no time I got my son Eleazar appointed high priest. After Eleazar, I managed to get my son-in-law Caiaphas appointed. I still had all the power and felt like the puppet master.

Around that same time, John the Baptizer was creating a disturbance, claiming people could be cleansed symbolically of sin by being dipped in the Jordan River. John was stealing from us by teaching people how to bypass our lengthy, expensive rituals at the temple. We found it offensive and wanted it stopped. For that reason, at first, mostly peasants followed John. Who could blame them? So few of them could pay for the animal sacrifices required to cover their sins. It was clear to them only rich men could get into heaven.

It wasn't difficult for me to get John arrested after he spoke out against Herod Antipas for marrying his brother's wife. Plus, Antipas was nervous about a possible revolt and had to answer to the prefect of Judea, Pontius Pilate, so he arrested and beheaded John. Anyone rising to power threatened the Herods.

As I mentioned, men would present themselves in Jerusalem and claim to be the Messiah. John was different; he would only talk about the Kingdom of Heaven and the coming Messiah.

I was not there, but at one point John identified Jesus as Messiah in public. I wish I had listened to John. There were so many stories from those who were present, so it was hard to clarify what happened that day. Many came to the temple proclaiming they had heard the actual voice of God. Others reported thunder. Who were we to believe? Nobody had heard the voice of God for four hundred years.

~~~

Joel put the manuscript down on the desk.

I have got to do some research. He slid over to his father's computer to do a quick review of Annas' history.

He found out Annas did have a son named Eleazar who was also high priest. One article he read said, "Annas was an unscrupulous schemer who violated many canons of Jewish justice to get Jesus the death penalty."

The prospect saddened Joel. *If it were true, this one family member had single-handedly caused grief for over two thousand years. No wonder his father didn't want to tell anyone,* Joel thought to himself. It was evident Annas had made some catastrophic decisions.

Demon Marq

That was a glorious day, when Antipas took the head of John the Baptist. Imagine how surprised and discouraged John was while in prison. That was Lucifer's doing. I joined in too and had a chance to convince him Jesus did not care about what happened to him. I know it was a lie, but that is what we do. We tell a lie and hope we are not discovered—it's not our problem if you believe the lie. Just imagine John sending word to Jesus asking him if he was really who he said he was. It was a wicked moment in time. I was sure Jesus would be embarrassed that his own blood relative suddenly did not believe. That's not exactly what happened, but I am not going to talk about it. I played a small part in the victory by discouraging John even if only for a moment.

14

MESSIAH KILLED

High Priest Annas, Son of Seth, 28th Day of Nisan 3830 (April 24th, 70 A.D.)

The Messiah showed up, and we killed him. Many wondered if he really was the Messiah, when we later walked through the events of that day. I was no longer the puppet master; now I was a puppet on a string. The real puppet master was pride. I wanted to tear down any resistance at the temple that threatened the power I loved so much. I wanted to protect my family from the Romans who at any time could decide to wipe out our whole race.

The night the temple guards went to the garden and arrested Jesus and brought him to me, I had them drop him in the cell below my home. I had to act fast. I called the council of the Sanhedrin, and we conducted a trial, which was illegal to hold during the Passover feast. I ignored the laws for my comfort.

Many people did not realize the pressure we faced to keep the peace in the temple during the feasts. Pontius Pilate threatened us with elimination weekly. He was a ruthless leader with no mercy. We acted the way we did to protect our families, our people, and our way of life.

Of course, this was just an excuse for the fear I faced. My greatest fear is not leaving a legacy. If my family does not survive, then my name and my life are for nothing, and nobody will remember me in history.

My ultimate pride was thinking my legacy was the only thing that mattered. Stay away from pride, my sons. Run from it! It will trick you and lie to you; it will invade your soul and murder you from the inside. It took me until the age of ninety - and supernatural intervention - to convince me of the truth.

I am ashamed of my actions. I have cried many nights, tortured by the realization of my sinful pride. I pleaded and begged my Messiah for forgiveness. In his grace, he granted it as he reminded me gently of his last dying prayer on the cross, "Forgive them, for they know not what they do."

His prayer stunned me when I heard him say it. Who would pray such a prayer for his murderers? At some point during the crucifixion, I thought to myself, "If God is real and Jesus is his son, he would step in and stop this." God did nothing from what I could see, and it added to my unbelief. I had no idea Jesus knew what would happen and God would allow it.

Many smart rabbis had identified Jesus as Messiah many of them my friends. They were fools to me. Now I know I was the fool.

When the body of Jesus came up missing, I wanted full punishment for the soldiers who were supposed to be guarding the tomb. Pontius Pilate would not comply. The soldiers on guard at the tomb said they saw Jesus in the flesh

three days after they had seen him die.
We tried to bribe the soldiers to give
false reports, but they took our money and still spoke what I thought were
lies, but turned out to be the truth.

All this was over his dead body. I
interviewed the soldier who offered the
punishing thrust of his spear into the
body of Jesus. The soldier, Longinus,
gave me the head from his spear and even
the nails he used, as he pointed to the
blood of Jesus still present on the tips.
Longinus convinced himself Jesus was the
Son of God and was sure Jesus had died
before he ever pierced his side with the
spear. It was brave of him to say so,
with my intimidation tactics. I didn't
have time for his nonsense about the
darkened sky and the earthquake. Just
a coincidence, I thought. People were
going mad over this, especially me, and
now the body was missing. Where was the
body? We couldn't find it because he was
not dead. He had risen.

I learned the truth much later when
Jesus himself appeared to me in the
flesh. I was walking on the bridge from

my home to the Temple Mount. I saw a
man walking toward me in a white robe
and his tallit swaying in the breeze. I
thought perhaps one of my sons had given
this rabbi access to the bridge to our
home. I looked closer and recognized his
face, his stride, and his demeanor. It
was Jesus. As crazy as it sounds, all I
could think was, "Only the high priests
and their families have access to the
bridge."

It was a ridiculous thought at the
time, but power corrupts.

I thought I was hallucinating, but
when he came closer, he stretched out
his arms and gave me a hug. I felt nothing but total peace. It had been over 50
years since I had witnessed his death
myself and yet he didn't look one day
older than the day he died.

I happened to have the medallion key to
the House of David tied under my shoulder sash that day, something I would occasionally secretly do to remind myself
of the power I once wielded. After the
hug, he said to me, "I have come back for
the key," pointing to it. My heart leapt

out of my chest as I noticed he still had
nail marks on his hands. How could it be?
He was alive.

Then he said, "Thank you for securing
those items in the box for me from Longinus."

I knew what he was talking about, but I
was unable to speak. He untied the medallion and chain from my garment, enclosed
it in his robe, turned around and walked
back across the bridge toward the temple.
Just a few days before this encounter I
had discovered the metal emblem on the
top of the box bore the exact emblem of
the key of David. I had never made the
connection before as I kept the key a secret since I was not supposed to own it.
When I put the two together to see if they
matched, the box opened, revealing hidden crevices. I decided to hide my secret
valuables in the secure places in the box.
It was as if Jesus had waited all those
years for me to figure it out before he
came back and took the key I had stolen.
I was fine with him taking the key; I was
not supposed to have it anyway. It was
supposed to be passed down to the kings

of Israel, but I stole it from Herod the Great on my next visit to his palace after he murdered the babies. He left it lying out and had no business with the sacred key of David after what he had done, and he didn't even miss it. The fool probably didn't even know what it represented.

I had heard Jesus appeared to Saul of Tarsus. I remember being frantic when I found out, swearing it had to be a lie. There was no real proof other than Saul's word and his drastic change of heart toward "The Way." Saul had been on our side and persecuted all followers of Jesus with great severity. At one time, our mission was the same: wipe out anyone who would try to change the Law of Moses. Little did I realize then, but the Law was pointing to Jesus as Messiah.

I didn't want to see the truth, so it was hidden from me until this moment when Jesus came in the flesh and revelation fell from heaven. We received word from Caesarea that Saul was now going by the name Paul and he had come to believe Jesus was the Messiah. Many others converted after Paul. I had an experience like Paul. Except Paul was made temporarily blind and I was given only kindness.

Pain gripped my heart and I wept following the realization. The fact his followers were willing to die for him is part of what threw me into grief. If they would rather die than deny, that is substantial evidence for truth—but back then I had no tolerance for fairy tales. Now, Messiah Jesus had given me an undeserved gift of grace at a time I least expected it.

The night after Jesus appeared to me, I had what I thought was a dream of a fallen angel named Zagan who demanded I give him the box and the key of David.

I stood up in the dream with boldness and told him to get out. He said to me, "Your time is short; your family will be murdered and then I will take the box." I laughed at him in the dream and mentioned my age and proceeded to tell him Jesus took the key. As soon as I said the name of Jesus, he vanished. This dream or vision confirmed for me we had to get out of Jerusalem. I am today writing this from a cave outside the city.

We heard from a couple of others hiding in these caves about the total destruction of the temple by Titus, which made me realize the fulfillment of the prophetic words Jesus had spoken: "Not one stone would be left standing." I cry out daily to God for truth.

The followers of Jesus had warned us to leave the city long ago. I am still perplexed as to why Jesus spared me this long. The followers of Jesus left long before Titus showed up. My guess is God told them to leave long before the worst of it; they didn't stay and fight for the temple. We needed their manpower, so most of the leaders in the temple were offended and made it clear their group would no longer be welcomed back to the temple after God defeated the Romans.

My family and I had to make decisions about what would be pulled out of the temple as things started escalating with the Romans. We had a plan to get at least some of the most valuable items out.

Many valuables from the very first Temple had been removed and hidden before the Babylonians invaded. The most elite of those items, the Ark of the Covenant, has not been seen since. As high priest, I know where the ark is, but I cannot bring myself to record such a thing here, as I have no idea who may read this document, and we never felt led to put it back in the latest temple. We just operated as if it was there. I must pass the location on by word of mouth to one of my children for the future of Israel.

Angel Harper

The host of heaven watched as Jesus our King offered himself as a sacrifice. We did not understand what was happening since it occurred before the foundation of the earth. The archangels were told to stand down. Satan, the king of pride, couldn't put his finger on why Jesus seemed to be an easy target and gave himself up in the garden. But Satan ignored truth all the time, so it was clear even if he knew the truth, he would lie to himself about it. The worst lies are the ones you tell yourself.

15

ANNAS ESCAPES

High Priest Annas, Son of Seth, 30th Day of Nisan 3830-(April 26th, 70 A.D.)

This is how I escaped from Jerusalem with all I could carry of the Temple treasures, which I know the Romans desperately wanted to take from us. My namesake Annas, the youngest of my five sons, insisted we smuggle out as many items as possible. He worked along with Phineas, the current high priest, so we could hide the items. I escaped two weeks before Titus surrounded the city of Jerusalem.

My son happened to have overheard as he was rounding a corner in the marketplace a couple of "The Way" followers talking about dreams and visions of the city being surrounded by Roman soldiers. My dream of the fallen angel and this incident convinced him the dreams were accurate, so he acted swiftly and made a plan for as many remaining family members as possible to get out of the city and fast. But I am brokenhearted he and his wife stayed.

Within three days the plan was in place, and they loaded supplies into my cart. We expected some of the Roman soldiers to stop us, but it was as if we were invisible to our enemy. We packed and rolled out of town by the light of a golden purple sunrise.

The Roman soldiers were barely awake as the shift change was taking place and they were laughing and joking as they greeted one another for their day's work. I had not dressed in priestly garments, which would have drawn attention to my activities as most of them would have recognized me if I had been wearing my own clothes. Most people have not seen me for some time. My granddaughter Haserah and her husband Jonathan have been

taking care of me since my daughter, her
mother, died. Her father Caiaphas died
a horrid death in one of the revolts. I
have trouble keeping track of the sadness now.

We saw soldiers on the road out of
town, but this group of Romans was deep
in political debate about Rome's latest
decisions. News traveled slowly to Jerusalem from the empire. Most of the soldiers were disappointed in their assignments. Jerusalem represented significant
anxiety for the empire since the revolts
by the Zealots broke out four years earlier over Florus trying to steal from the
temple treasury. The Zealots were trouble, and the soldiers complained about
it. All the better for us on that day as
we left the city undetected.

We recorded and hid a complete list
of items taken from the temple. Yahweh
will reveal it in due time. I pray this
document stays in the hands of my descendants, if indeed we survive. I am
not comfortable enough to disclose the
truth, as followers of Jesus hate me. I
don't have the energy or courage to step

into their world and declare to them Jesus is Messiah as Paul did. I do have the courage to record here what has been revealed to me so future generations can have a clear understanding.

One of the largest sources of pain for me is my family believing I was crazy when I told them about seeing Jesus in the flesh. Every time I began to discuss it with them, my sons would get angry and blame insanity and old age.

Here I was involved in false trials of Jesus and his followers and brother. It seems what I used to be proud of is a curse to me now. I'm a hypocrite just as Jesus said. Oh, how I wish I had recognized him when he was walking on the earth!

So here we sit in a cave at the end of my life. Many from my extended family have to have died in the desecration. We can't get into Jerusalem to confirm all the horrific things we have heard about or who has died. I pray one of my living sons, grandsons, or great grandsons will believe what I have recorded here and have the courage to reveal this truth to our people. If not, perhaps my granddaughter and her husband will keep it safe and have the courage to pass it on to the next generations, until truth is finally revealed.

My heart is broken over my lack of courage; I'm not in any position to come forward with this information now anyway. For all I know this attack on my people could mean the end for us. I pray whoever reads this will have the strength to reveal the truth to our people. I must rest now, as my mind grows weary from recording such great sorrow. I will continue at a later date if the Lord allows me to live longer.

16

HEBREW PROFESSOR LEONA

Joel's mind zapped back to his current day reality, needing to digest some of the information in the manuscript before he continued. This document was explosive, and there was plenty more to read.

He dug around in the box looking for a list or a key but didn't find anything. He ran his fingers along the adornment on the lid. The thought of a list of Temple treasures existing blew Joel's mind, but there was no sign of it in the box. His mind was jumping from topic to topic.

The value of this document must be colossal, Joel thought, dumbfounded over what to do with all the information.

Joel flipped through the pages in the rest of the typed notebook. He was astonished at dates that spanned two thousand years. He couldn't believe what he was reading. His ancestors had written tidbits of their lives down for him to see. He stopped and skimmed short excerpts of their reactions to the details in the box. His mother had always said a life worth living is a life worth recording.

It was sad for Joel to learn about some of his relatives who felt tortured over the decision of what to do with the box. Others were not sorry or perplexed by how to handle the information. One translated comment read, "This information is made up, but I will give it to my son since the box is so old." Joel noticed an underlined portion that read, "Likely a fairy tale, just like Adam and Eve and Noah's Ark." Next to it was a handwritten comment that said: "Finally, a family member with some sense! ~Leona"

That must have been the woman his dad mentioned in his letter, who had translated the document, Joel thought.

Demon Marq

Leona was perfect for our purposes. She was an inquisitive professor of Hebrew, full of pride. All of her faith was in academics. A perfect pawn. I hoped Leona would keep Ely from taking the manuscript public and she did. If only she had done what I expected her to do, my full plan might have worked. Then I could have turned my focus toward Joel years ago instead of Ely.

It was my idea to encourage Ely to call Leona. She was a beautiful woman with long black swirly locks of hair, the type of woman Ely could have used to take his mind off the manuscript, which was making him irritable.

Unfortunately, my plan for Ely cheating on his wife with Leona failed once she realized what she was translating.

Leona, although an excellent translator, was also an avid atheist who was very active in a secret society called SAD. You would think as a demon I would welcome her unbelief and bitterness. However, my plan was to cause Ely to leave his family and ruin Joel's life in the process. There was no way she would have anything to do with my plan once she started translating the documents.

SAD stood for Secular Ark Deniers. To be in the group, you had to be a true believer in secularism. Plus, Leona was particularly interested in activism. The SAD group was all about fighting research that might point toward the Bible having any possibility of being proven right. Leona had dedicated her life to learning Hebrew, so she could read the Bible and prove it wrong. She wanted to be a professor, so she could mold young people's minds and recruit them for her cause. I should have been happy, and I was, once I realized Leona had reported Ely's scroll to the SAD group in the State of Israel.

Almost immediately the Israeli SAD group went to work on finding a way to get the box away from Ely. Over time they came to realize Ely was not going to do anything with the box, so they decided to wait and see what would happen with the next person who inherited it. I think their thoughts centered around keeping the box away from the public for as long as possible until they could concoct a plan to get it out of Ely's hands. They were doing Lucifer's bidding without realizing it; he is talented at that maneuver.

~~~

Joel was irritated Leona had added her commentary. *What business was it of hers?* Joel thought in passing, then decided to press on to see what happened to Annas.

17

JONATHAN BAR JONATHAN

Jonathan Bar Jonathan, 24th day of Tishrei 3831-(October 15, 70 A.D.)

I married Haserah, the daughter of Caiaphas. Haserah has asked me to record what happened to her grandfather, high priest Annas. We have lived in this cave for 45 days now and have managed to survive on what little food supplies we brought with us, along with some hunting I have done of small animals that had wandered near the cave. We are planning on leaving this cave very soon as we are plotting to get out of Judea. We're not sure how this will take place, but we are hoping for freedom as we learned from others out hunting for food that many Israelites have been taken into slav-

ery if caught. Sadly, Annas died in his
sleep the same day he last wrote. Haserah wanted me to record about him here
after I read to her what her grandfather
had written. We were aware of Annas becoming a follower of Jesus. Annas spoke
of Jesus often. Our lives are hard. We
are currently on the run from Romans.

Jonathan Bar Jonathan 20th day of Kis-
lev 3831-(December 10, 70 A.D.)

It has been several weeks since we were
in the cave and Haserah has asked me to
record our journey and some details about
what we heard happened in Jerusalem.

We have learned from others who escaped
after they were taken in chains exactly
what Titus did to Jerusalem: The Romans
surrounded the city walls and murdered
everyone. Only those Israelites who escaped or had left the city are still
alive. We had to move to a new location
as we heard and saw some soldiers making
their way along the hills, looking for
those in hiding.

We moved quickly in the dark over the
hills and are now quite far from Jerusalem. We are camped on an embankment and

plan to make our way to the nearest town
or village. We haven't seen many people,
making us feel as if we are the last people on earth.

One of our only possessions is this
box. We labeled what we still had with
us from the Temple and left it where it
sat. We had to leave so much behind not
only due to weight, but Haserah insisted we not be concerned about leaving the
treasure behind based on some dream she
had about angels. She was adamant about
bringing the box, as in the dream she was
told it must be passed on to our children. It's hard to know what to do next,
but so far, we have been able to eat well
since I am a worthy hunter. There have
been some fig and almond trees along our
journey as well.

I am not sure how long we will live
roaming around. We are pretending we are
celebrating the never-ending Feast of
Booths with its temporary housing that
may become permanent, a bit of humor in
a trying time. Each place we have moved
to, we have set up a covering and thanked
the Lord our God for another day. The
Lord provides for us.

Haserah wanted me to record that we found out the day the Temple in Jerusalem was destroyed in the month of Av on the 9th day (70 A.D.), was the same day and month the Babylonians burned it the first time (586 B.C.). Jesus was crucified 40 years earlier to the exact week. Her grandfather had explained this to her while he was alive.

We learned of other horrific reports I am not willing to write down from those who have been lucky enough to escape. We ran into some who escaped before they had sealed the city, who were talking about heading toward Masada, but Haserah and I are not willing to travel in larger groups. The Romans are everywhere, and we need to be able to move fast.

We decided to go west toward the sea and came upon a tiny fishing village along the coast, called Daya. We planned to find a way out of Judea by boat. I secured a job with a local fishing boat maker and will be working for him to earn money to purchase a vessel.

Other newcomers are hiding in the village. The villagers know why there are

new faces. The few of us who survived
shared our stories of escape. This particular community, for one reason or another, had a few people who had not gone
to Jerusalem for the High Holy Holidays.
Now their loved ones have not returned,
so there is much mourning and many homes
sit empty. After learning of the atrocity in Jerusalem, we knew there had to
be empty houses in villages all over the
area.

At first, we watched the village from
afar. After a while, we noticed which
houses were empty. Then by cover of night
we came into town and moved from empty
house to empty house and slept by day.
Then one day, a man came into a house
while we were sleeping. We looked at him
expecting him to be angry and upset,
but he explained that this village is
empty of most of its original settlers.
The only original people here are either old or sick and were unable to make
the trip to Jerusalem, so they survived.
One blind woman in the village had her
youngest daughter stay back to take care
of her. She is the youngest of the original settlers. The rest of the homes are

empty or have survivors who made their way to the village from caves. We were received and welcomed into the community and had our choice of several homes to occupy.

We have become part of a new community and have no idea what is happening with the Romans, but we know they could show up any day. There is nothing to keep them from coming in and killing all of us. It is a peaceful, humble village. The Romans are probably looking for larger towns to obtain more valuables. When we noticed the hidden community from our outlook, we thought perhaps the Romans had not seen it yet. What I do know is we are here and okay, for now, fishing and building boats. There is always a risk, but at this point, we have decided we need to make a real plan.

24th Day of Tevet, 3832-(January A.D. 72)

We are two years later and have set-tled in Daya. I am still working with the boat maker and Haserah is pregnant. We have grown comfortable here with our lives and have not been bothered by the Romans to date.

Since the temple is no longer there, we cannot offer sacrifices. Its loss has left many of us here in much sorrow. Not being able to sacrifice during our feasts is not easy as it means we cannot atone for our sins.

Haserah has mentioned much to me about Jesus being Messiah and what her grandfather had taught her, but my childhood tradition is what I wish to practice. I do not mind recording for Haserah what she requests of me, but I remain unconvinced Jesus was Messiah. I want to raise my child in the ways of Torah. Many in the village who were survivors from Jerusalem are longing for a new Temple, but it is not possible with the current occupation of our beloved city.

Haserah and I will have a child in three months' time. We will stay here as long as the Lord our God allows us to, and hopefully raise a family here. We have had Romans come through the village. Our strategy has been to feed them poorly-prepared bony fish, so they move along quickly. They realize we are poor. The Romans are looking for riches, so we are safe and can build a life here if we choose. We still long for the day we can rebuild our precious Temple.

9th of Av, 3832 (July 10, 72 A.D.)

Today my son Jeroham was born. He is a healthy baby boy. Haserah is excellent, and we are honored to have a new son. His name is Jeroham Bar Jonathan. We have decided to stay in the village forever. All is quiet here. I have made several boats and still have not left. We will grow a family here and stay and build a life as Yahweh allows.

12th of Sh'vat, 3837-(January 22, 77 A.D.)

We have had two more sons since Jeroham was born. They are named Gabriel, born 13th of Sh'vat 5734 (February 5, 74 A.D.), and Kama born 29th of Sivan 3956 (June 12, 76 A.D.) Haserah wanted me to record it for her future family. She has asked me to record we are following Torah and do not follow the sect of Jews who are called "The Way." My tradition is important to me, and we cannot change it now. We don't know how to do such a thing. We are preserving the box out of respect for Annas. Those family members after us who find his journal will be able to decide for themselves how they would like to proceed with their lives.

I believe the followers of Jesus Messiah are practicing mysticism. They are carrying cloth pieces of the disciple Paul's clothes to our village. The material has healed the blind woman, but I am still suspicious. Paul died in Rome, but fabric from his clothing is healing? It's mystifying.

After the healing, there appears to be a growing number of those who follow The Way in our village. I cannot explain the healing, I confess.

Deep in my heart, I feel Haserah believes Jesus is Messiah. I can't make her change her heart, but she is following my lead, and I am doing what my father before me did. I hear her praying to Jesus. She doesn't think I can hear her, but she is doing it as I walk into the house. I hear her use his name and it makes me furious for a moment. Then I look at her and all anger melts away, as I love her so much.

Since she cannot read, she will not see what I have written, but I wanted my sons to know that I love her and how she affects me when I see her. Sons, you will do good to find a wife like your mother. She is delightful, compassionate, unselfish, generous, trustworthy, hard-working, protective, industrious, and loving. I trust her, and she is my helper. Yes, sons, you will do good to find a wife like her.

Tevet, 3845 (85 A.D.)

Jeroham is 13 years old. Today my son became a man.

18

HANNAH

~*Present Day*~

Joel set the document down, and his mind wandered to his own wife, Hannah. He missed her and her essence, and her vibrant, long brown hair with catches of auburn light from time spent in the sun. Hannah was petite, but strong as a horse. The little muscles on her tiny frame astonished Joel. She had been able to drop in throughout the week but was back-to-back booked working security at the U.N. for the Consulate office. She was a perfect wife for him, much like Jonathan Bar Jonathan's wife. Joel wondered what type of mother she would be to their future children. She was such a capable and beautiful woman—he knew he had married up. Hannah had class. His family had fully approved of her—even his dad, which was a nice bonus.

Joel began to wonder what Hannah was going to think of all this. He didn't even know what to think, but her reaction was going to be important to him.

Although they followed many of their traditions together, they were never overly serious about their faith. Both came from Jewish families but held their faith loosely. The more Joel thought, it was like they had no faith at all. Joel wondered what Hannah would say when he told her about having Christ believers in his family history.

Joel was pretty sure Hannah would be on his side—Joel was Jewish, plain and simple. But how could he not consider Jesus now that he had learned his father had converted, and with all this evidence from Annas? Then there was the angelic activity to take into account, both good and fallen—although there were angels in the Jewish faith. Joel started to wonder if he believed in Judaism. Was he more of a secular humanist? Was secular humanism a religion?

The questions swirled as he went down the tunnel of "what ifs" in his mind. Too many people had fought over religion for too many years. Joel knew Hannah would still be supportive, no matter what happened, because that was just the type of person she was. He was looking forward to seeing her reaction.

Joel started to realize more and more the problem his family had faced throughout history. The problem his dad had been confronted with. He decided to suspend this line of thinking until he had finished reading the entire document.

19

JEROHAM BAR JONATHAN

Jeroham bar Jonathan Sh'vat, 3855-(95 A.D.)

I am Jeroham Bar Jonathan and am 23 years old. Of my brothers, I am the only one who can write, so my father has given me the task of recording what has happened to our family.

When I was 13 years old in the month of Tevet and the year 3845 (85 A.D.), a group of Roman soldiers came to our village. They stayed for about two weeks, and everyone was fearful. The leader was a Hebrew, a scholar, and Roman. His name was Flavius Josephus. He watched what we were doing in our synagogue and became very close to my father. After discussing

our family lines, we learned we were related. Josephus asked if I could go with
him to Rome as an apprentice scribe and
a friend to his sons. My mother pleaded
for me not to go, but our family agreed
to the arrangement. Father was thrilled
to find a relative. He was hesitant, but
since Josephus was Roman also, he believed he would keep me safe.

I have returned to my village for a
short visit before I go back to Rome. I
will take this box to Rome for safekeep-
ing, as I am with Josephus working in
the house of the Emperor Vespasian. My
father has explained to me what is in the
box and I am not sure it is a good idea
to take it to Rome. However, he has insisted I hide it in a safe place. Father
is unsure if Yeshua was Messiah. For me,
this thought would mean death in Rome,
so I cannot visit it.

When I arrived in Rome at age 13, there
were many Jewish slaves. I rode into the
city with a known Roman citizen and Jewish noble, so nobody bothered me. I could
smell burning flesh from outside of the
city. Josephus told me not to look at any

of the bodies. Some were Hebrews who believed in The Way, according to Josephus.
They called them "Christians" or "Christ
followers." Josephus thought the Christians had fallen into a trap and been
confused by the disciples of Yeshua.

I overheard a soldier say they used
much of the valuables gleaned from the
Temple Treasures from Judea to make the
Amphitheatrum Flavium. I was horrified
at what I saw happening to my people,
but I have been living with Josephus, so
people treated me with respect. I asked
Josephus why he was not persecuted. He
told me it was a matter of survival, with
no further explanation.

Josephus treated me like a son, and
I finished my teen years with his three
children, two of whom were also scribes.
I lived with the servants at the house
who belonged to Vespasian. I have returned here to get married, and then I
shall return to Rome as I still have work
to complete there. Josephus has given me
permission to stay in the village. However, my life and my friends are in Rome.
I saved my earnings to purchase a house

and some land eventually. I invited my
family to move with me to Rome once I
have my own home.

Again, I am not sure it is a good
idea to take the box with me to Rome. If
anyone finds it, I could be killed. But
my father believes Josephus will protect
me, so I will obey my father. I hope to
find a good hiding place for it.

My bride is a sweet village girl named
Leah who I have grown up with since we
were babies. I have been dreaming of re-
turning to get her for five years, but
my work did not allow me. Now I shall get
married and have children of my own. I
pray my extended family will join me in
Rome. My wife is very upset about having
to go to Rome, but I know she loves me
and has waited a long time for me to return for her. She will grow to love the
hustle and bustle of the city. She is
quite beautiful and will be admired to
be with a man who is a scribe of such a
respected Roman citizen as Josephus who
is from a priestly and royal household.

Elul, 3864 -(September 104 A.D.)

Leah was most beautiful on our wedding

day, and the weeklong celebration was
fantastic. I am writing this to state
I have found a woman like my mother as
I saw my father wrote such kind things
about my mother.

My first week of our journey back to
Rome was somber. My bride was unhappy to
leave her family but happy to be with
me. It took us a month to get back to
Rome. We took our time, but it was longer than my journey to Daya as the winds
were not in our favor. Once we arrived,
we went to the house of Vespasian, and I
introduced Leah to Josephus. It took her
at least a year to adjust to Roman life.
She was sad for a long time. Everything
was different, so I was easy on her. She
was horrified to see people treated the
way the Romans treated the Jewish slaves
and even more terribly, the Christians.
Leah had led a sheltered life in a small
village.

Four years later Josephus died, leaving me in need of my own home. He had
left me an inheritance and that, along
with my savings, helped me obtain some
excellent land and build a home in Castra

Taurinorum (Turin, Italy). I had heard that area was affordable, so shortly after the funeral of Josephus, we set out for Taurinorum. I convinced some friends to help us move our things to the north. It was an adventure I will never forget as we encountered plenty of challenges with our horses, but we took our time. Some days we traveled all day and others we went only to the next village and would stay for a day or two to rest. Once we made our way to Taurinorum, I was proud to build a home for my bride and children.

I have since moved my family here from Daya. I created a place on our farm to hide the box. It will pass down from generation to generation within our family, along with the farm. I don't know why I have recorded all the details of my move except perhaps a future grandson will want to know my history.

My advice regarding the box is to hide it forever. I am compelled to pass it on to my children for the sake of our family history. It is an interesting part of history, but from what I have heard from my friends in Rome over the years, surely most of the Christians are gone. If Jesus is Messiah, his story will be carried to the whole world, and nothing will stop it. But from what I have witnessed, the Christians are nearly obsolete in Rome. Once Nero blamed the burning of Rome on the Christians, it took most of the focus off the Jewish people. The Romans went after the Christians in a way I have never witnessed. I am sure it was similar to what my father experienced in the death of the Jews in Jerusalem. The Romans used them as human torches, and many are still dying today in the Gladiator Games.

The one thought that haunts me about the followers of Jesus is how many of them would not deny their faith. Often the emperor would make an offer to spare their lives if they would deny Jesus as Messiah. Not one of them I witnessed took the offer. What devotion they have! So strong, it would allow them the strength to die rather than deny Jesus is Messiah. The emperor used them for entertainment. If I brought this box forward now, they would throw me to the lions. Rome was out of control. I could not wait to get out of that place.

So, I built a barn and set up a location to store the box below the floorboards. I will make sure my children and their children keep it safe for a long time to come, as I pray this land will be in my family for many years.

20

FLAVIUS JOSEPHUS

Joel was delighted to read an account of an ancestor who was related to the real historical figure Flavius Josephus. Joel had studied him in one of his Jewish history classes. Almost everyone knew him as the author of *The Jewish Wars*. Josephus recorded the early history of many of the Judean revolts against foreign rulers. *This document really does belong in a museum,* he thought again.

Angel Harper

I am a close confidant to one of Flavius Josephus's guardian angels. Josephus was a rough assignment much like Annas. The two of us hung out together in Rome while I was on assignment with Jeroham Bar Jonathan and the box.

Josephus, a great leader and commander in one of the Jewish/Roman battles in Galilee, kept the Romans from taking over in the area for 47 days. Josephus was clever and did many unusual things to keep the Romans from taking the city. My friend told me, in the end, Josephus was surrounded by Romans and led a group of 40 warriors into a cave trying to escape. Shortly after, Roman soldiers surrounded them. Plus, they had no food, an even worse problem.

According to my friend, Josephus talked the group of fighters into killing themselves in a suicide lottery rather than be taken over by the Romans. What a mission. The demons of death and murder were warring against angels on assignment over the entire group. They were outnumbered in this spiritual battle and the assignment was to convince Josephus he had a hope and future. As the horrible suicide pact played out, they all agreed to murder each other.

They cast lots, which left Josephus and one other as the last two in the group. Josephus changed his mind at the last minute, and the two of them surrendered to the Romans.

Josephus was taken prisoner and held until he convinced a next possible Roman leader he had a gift of prophecy. It took Josephus a couple of years, but eventually, Vespasian recognized Josephus for predicting he would be emperor. When Vespasian became emperor, Josephus won over the household of Vespasian, who released him from slavery.

Vespasian also used him as a mediator for the Jewish people in Jerusalem. Josephus was with Titus when he arrived in Jerusalem and tried to convince the leaders to give up the city to the Romans, but they just shot him with an arrow. They considered him a traitor because he survived the suicide pact.

All I know is Josephus ended up in the village of Daya and recruited Jeroham Bar Jonathan. When the box headed to Rome, I was not happy. I had to go also, and Rome was a horrific place in those days.

21

JOHN LUKE

John Luke Hebrew calendar year 4060 -(300 A.D.), Turin, Italy

I am the great, great, great, great-grandson of Jeroham Bar Jonathan. For 200 years, my family has owned this property. I recently tore down the barn Jeroham wrote about, and found this hidden box in the ruins. The barn was in shambles, but the box is in excellent shape. You can imagine my surprise when I found this with Hebrew writing. I recognized enough of the writing to know it is not something to share with others, so I will record here that I will make sure my ancestors get this box and I will leave its contents a secret.

Lucas, son of John Luke Hebrew calendar year 4010 -(350 A.D.)

My father John Luke gave me the secret location of this box. He said it is a family secret and I should see it and record some of our family's history within. But I am ashamed of what is in the box. There is no way Jesus was Messiah. The entire Roman Empire has gone mad since Constantine named Christianity his religion.

The story of the resurrection is simply not true. I am not planning on passing this information on to anyone or giving it to my children. I am Jewish. My children are Jewish. I plan to hide this box, and if God wants it found it shall be found by whom He wills. It seems the whole world is converting to Christianity. Annas was wrong. I will not even document my family record in this or give it any value. My only reason for recording this is to show that someone in this family had the wisdom to recognize a lie. The box itself is of some value, and I will provide select details about some of my ancestors. I will leave it up to God to decide if anyone should find the box again.

22

TURIN FAMILY FARM AND THE MENACE OF VENICE

Demon Marq

I preferred hanging out on the farm and following the Annas family bloodline around as much as possible through the years. There was no action with the box and the information from Annas was not shared for hundreds of years. Nobody even knew it existed for most of the time on the farm, so I was on a bit of a sabbatical from terrorizing the family. I lurked around the barn and attached myself to animals and different types of flesh in an attempt to haunt the barn, but I knew once the box was removed, I would have to go with it and all my haunting efforts would be lost.

John Luke and Lucas were farmers who moved into banking once they had plenty of wealth. Farmers can be a challenge for demons because they are too busy to get into trouble, but bankers are not a problem. They are greedy.

Life at the farm became extravagant for a long time, and the family of Annas kept building wealth for several years. Each new generation became more enamored with wealth than their traditions, which made my job easy. I was sure there was no way the corruption would ever end. But it did end - and quite abruptly- in the early 1800s when Napoleon was in charge of parts of Italy and declared all debts owed to Jewish bankers null and void. Napoleon wanted the Italian Jewish bankers to assimilate and become real French citizens.

Leaders in the town of Turin grew weary of the bankers profiting from people's misfortune. One day the family at the farm was uprooted and moved into a ghetto. The family lived in the ghetto for many years until one of them found a way to make a claim on their land, and the whole family made their way back to the farm in the 1920s.

Then, something unexpected happened. Little Caleb, Joel's great-grandfather, found the box. I guess it was time for me to move on because as soon as Caleb touched the box, I received direct orders to follow it without fail. Caleb took the box back to Venice with him. At first, I thought it was going to be a pain to be away from the farm. But then I realized I could haunt Venice. I would be able to be the Menace of Venice, a name I gave myself. I reveled in the mischief I was able cause in that town.

Venice is such an evil location on the earth, with stinky water and an abundance of corruption. Then the suffering that came about in the Jewish ghetto in the early 1940s was diabolical. Hitler made a deal with the devil; he was on Lucifer's side from the beginning. The fallen angels and us demons who were on assignment are still famous. Hitler tricked Italy into being his ally and then marched in and took over. We were winning. That was the heyday for me, the Menace of Venice!

The day Caleb left Venice was the worst day of my existence. I wanted to live there forever. But, duty called, and I had to stay with that box and it had moved onward to a church full of monks. Not the easiest assignment for a demon.

23

DIARY OF RACHEL

As Joel read on, he realized the transcript font had changed and the story fast-forwarded, to 1943. Joel was astonished to realize there was a 1600-year gap in the historical record. The next part of the manuscript was a translation from Italian to English. His father had translated it, typed it up, and added it to the notebook. The writer of this portion was a teenage girl named Rachel—his Bubbe.

~~~

~During World War II~

Rachel
June 4, 1943

Dearest Diary,

I should write something interesting in my diary. I have nothing else to occupy my time now that I am stuck in this dome shaped room. The room has a hidden door that appears to only open from the inside. Father said it is quite clever. I am sure nobody would catch us unless someone told the Nazis we were hiding here. I never in a million years thought we would have to hide out, but here we are hiding like rats. There are some other people hiding with us who must have family friends who are members of this church. My parents knew them as customers from Venice, where my father is a tailor. My parents work together repairing and making clothes. My father is famous in Venice for his work making unique clothing.

The past few months have been unimaginable with the Nazi's invading many parts of Europe. I had no idea how sub zero it had gotten until my father came and picked me up at my after-school job at the bakery and we jumped into the back of a truck where he insisted we hide under straw with the others. We drove for hours.

When we arrived in Assisi, a beautiful city on a hill, we hiked straight up to the St. Francis of Assisi Church along with other Jewish neighbors.

Our government was working with Hitler and did nothing to protect the Italian Jewish people. A man in fancy robes named Bishop Nicolini told Father he would work on our paperwork with the local printer to re-create documents to allow us to leave Italy. The bishop has put Father Rufino Niccacci in charge of taking care of us.

The latest news is Adolf Hitler, the chancellor of

Germany, is demanding the Italians deport the Jews from Italy to work camps. We have heard of hideous things happening in Germany to the Jewish people and never thought Hitler would come here and make demands. Mussolini had told Hitler no some time ago, but now the Nazis have rolled into Italy and are demanding compliance.

It's almost impossible for Jewish people to get out of Italy now. We were shocked to find this out yesterday before we went into hiding. We heard a rumor the Nazis are going door to door throughout Italy looking for Jews, even here in Assisi where there have never been Jewish residents in the past. I imagine many are hiding in attics and basements and, others, holes in the ground. I have always heard it said we are people chosen by God. Why in the world would so many people hate us? Why can't God make them love us? I don't feel chosen or special. I am just a sad sack in an awkward body with fuzzy brown hair, boring clothes and nothing to write about. I wonder how long we will have to stay here?

24

A DOZEN IN THE ROOM

Rachel
June 5, 1943

Dearest Diary,

There are twelve of us right now, two more since yesterday. We still sit here waiting for paperwork. That is a dozen in this small room. The fear is increasing, as we don't have much to eat, and lack of easy access to water and toilets is making it uncomfortable. My mother has to hold up a sheet so I can relieve myself in a bowl. It's humiliating.

I guess everyone here is in a state of shock trying to escape the clutches of Hitler. I have been trying not to cry because there are a couple of little girls here who would be scared if they saw a big girl cry. Their names are Samira, who is 10, and Miriam, who is 8. I think their mom, Ozara, is trying to convince them we are playing some

sort of game, but you can see on their faces they're not
amused by it, plus the other adults are talking about what
is going on with the Nazis. You can tell some of them are
not used to children because they're talking about all the
political stuff without a thought to how it might affect the
children. It's angering their mother.

Samira is so dilly. Her hair is so smooth and beautiful, I am a little bit jealous. She talks about art and
brought her sketchbook with her and has spent much of
her time drawing pictures. Her sister Miriam is timid and
has shoulder length hair and brown eyes, like her mom. I
recognize them from their many visits to the bakery with
their mother. They would come in with smiles on their
faces—smiles that are long gone. They would buy a loaf
of rye and a loaf of Italian, and their mother would allow
them sweet bread for the walk home.

People have brought different things with them, which
is interesting. I happened to have grabbed this empty
diary before I left my room. I had plans to write about a
drooly boy I like at school on my evening break at work.
Never mind now. When my father showed up to get me it
changed everything. My mother brought her sewing box
with her, and my father brought the family's strange box. I
don't know what's in it, but he carries it around with great
care and concern.

The box has been in our home since I can remember,
and father tells me that one day it will be mine and I can

learn the family secret. I have begged him to let me know, but he has said repeatedly that I would know soon enough. I can tell he wants to tell me. Since it's so rare-looking and the only thing he brought, many in the room have been asking him about it. He is extremely protective of it and has finally found a place near his head at night to keep it safe from others' curious eyes. He even uses it as a pillow. I am sure he is not sleeping well with that hard box under his head.

Mother is busy helping others repair their clothing, which is inducing the group to like our family, making up for Father's secrecy. Depending on how long we are here, I will have to write more about all the others hiding with us.

25

FATHER NICCACCI AND SPENCE THE MONK

Rachel
June 6, 1943

Dearest Diary,

Father Niccacci brought us several jugs of water, a few for bathing and a few for drinking. We were all thrilled as we were starting to smell salty.

He had two other monks with him to help carry. These two were young and from two different foreign countries who don't speak the language. One was swoony with short sandy blond hair and a smile that would light anyone up. I think his name was Spence. I did not expect to see young monks here. Even after he left, everyone was talking about his smile - I guess we're not used to seeing people smile.

The other monk looked like he was from the Far East with dark skin and dark hair. He was not as friendly but was robust enough to carry large containers of water for our use. Father Niccacci told us to use it sparingly as it's difficult to get the water up to us. I was so grateful for more drinking water. Being thirsty is horrible and smelling bad was even worse. Spence also came back later with prepared food, which he assured us had been prepared in their newly set up kosher kitchen, which had followed strict rules. Father had told Father Niccacci earlier in the week when he asked about the rules of preparing food for us. I am guessing Spence had just arrived in Assisi because he was asking Father Niccacci plenty of questions. We were tired of vegetable soup and bread. Spence brought us some noodles, so we decided we liked his smile and his cooking.

Rachel
June 7, 1943

I just woke from a dream about Spence last night. He was swimming around in a large bowl of soup. He decided to dive to the bottom of the soup bowl, but he never came back up. I watched, waiting for him to surface again, but I realized it was taking him too long to return. When I decided to dive in to save him, the soup turned to blood, confusing me. I continued my quest to pull him out of the soup bowl and when I grabbed him by his robe and pulled him to the surface, his robe went from brown to red to white. He climbed out and said to me, "Now I am clean, and you can be too."

I awoke to loud voices. The Bernstein couple was arguing about whether they were going to stay here longer. Mrs. Bernstein was going on about being caught and that she could not stay here another day as the anxiety was too much for her. She started hyperventilating and Mr. Bernstein was trying to calm her down. It woke everyone up. Mrs. Bernstein's crying was bothersome, and Mother tried to soothe her. There were still many at the church who were probably unaware of the secret hiding place. We were sure she could be heard through the walls.

Thank God it is Monday morning and not Sunday during service. We could hear their service yesterday as the choir sang. There was peacefulness in the room. I felt goose bumps. It made me think twice about these Catholics and how they were treating me, us. It seemed the rest of the world rejected us, but these monks in Italy had taken us in. I began to like them yesterday.

26

MR. AND MRS. BERNSTEIN LEFT

Rachel
June 8, 1943

Dearest Diary,

Father Niccacci brought Mr. and Mrs. Bernstein monk's robes and escorted them out early this morning. It made me want to cry and scream out loud, so I could also get out of here. Mother said we were close to being caught and she knew I would never want to be someone who created such a scene. Father Niccacci is working on papers for all of us, but it could take some time. I learned today at least 200 people who had stayed in this room already got papers. I wonder how many of them made it to safety?

Father Niccacci told us today we had to make some hard decisions about what we would bring along with us when we leave. Knowing that most had nothing when they arrived, it was very clear he was speaking to my father about his box. Father looked concerned and had a long discussion with Mother about the box. The decision weighed heavy on his mind until he decided he would have to leave it with Father Niccacci. He talked with me about my diary. Samira had to leave behind her sketchbook as well. I guess if you are disguised as a monk, it makes no sense to have anything with you. Besides, my diary was relatively new and only had a few bad days recorded in it. Father assured me that somehow we would come back and get our belongings. It made me not want to write anymore, but then I have nothing else to do with my time and who knows, this might be an interesting read to me when I am older.

27

HEAD LICE

Rachel
June 9, 1943

Dearest Diary,

Last night my head was itching like crazy. Mother had to keep telling me to stop moving all night, but I could not help it. This morning we discovered I had lice. I am horrified. It is an epidemic and is rumored to cause typhoid fever. Mother went to work immediately pulling eggs from my hair with her fingernails. Chaos broke out in the group. Nobody else found any yet, I feel like even Samira and Miriam have been staying away from me. I have been crying non-stop all day. Mother finally stopped pulling them from my hair and slathered some oil on my scalp from Father Niccacci. I feel humiliated! Oh, diary, how much longer do I have to look at all these people who don't want to have anything to do with me? What if I get sick and die in this place? No chance to know a husband or children? Mother says to think on happy thoughts, but this has caused me to focus on the worst. I am starting to cry again.

Angel Harper

How did she get that infestation of head lice? Those things don't like dirty hair. It had to be the handiwork of that demon Marq. A weapon they have used since the fall, a cheap parlor trick in my opinion. I don't know how they do it, but maybe the little bugs are so light the demon does not need flesh to carry it and plant it on its victim.

As if this family doesn't have plenty to deal with already, having to run from the Third Reich. They already left their entire lives behind.

Head lice are particularly evil in my opinion. It just puts all the pressure on the momma, and she carries enough burdens as it is. Thank goodness I was able to influence the good Father Niccacci to find some oil to drown the little stinkers before they all made Rachel shave her head. Take that demon. I am sure that's what he wanted. The shaved head is a tool for humiliation. Hair is one of human beings' best features and a symbol of glory.

Did you know the Nazis are shaving the heads of all the Jewish people when they go to the death camps? They are saying it is because of head lice, that's not true. They are turning it into yarn and felt for use in lining army boots. Some companies in Germany are even buying the hair to create cushions for car seats.

Sometimes I wish there were no free will. The Almighty disagrees with me. When people make the righteous choice it's glorious and all of heaven erupts in applause. But some people choose evil, and it is tough to witness. Angels see all the warfare the humans are faced with, so making a good choice gives us something to celebrate.

~~~

Rachel
June 11, 1943

Dearest Diary,

Yesterday I spent most of my time lying around feeling sorry for myself. But today is a new day. Mother says there is no evidence of lice. The oil drowned them, and the eggs are gone as far as she can tell. I can tell Mother is exhausted having to look through my thick head of hair.

Last night Father talked to me about the box and told me my diary would go into the box for hiding. If the Germans caught us and read it with all these details, the entire staff of the church could die, and others hiding in this room could be captured. I understand. I just wish I had thought of that before I put all these details in here. Father has promised we will come back and get it.

Father started revealing to me the truth about the box, and I am utterly speechless about what he has told me. He had to tell me in whispers. The others became suspicious, so he stopped telling me the story halfway through. I wonder when he will get a chance to tell me more? I am looking forward to hearing more about our ancestor Annas. He told me about where he found the box also. If Italy were not infested with Nazis, I would want to go see the old family farm. Maybe one day I will have a chance.

He is working on removing a floorboard in the room to see if his box will fit. He does not want to give it to Father Niccacci. It's not that he doesn't trust him, but he intends to preserve the contents for a later time and purpose. He believes it would cause more problems for us, the Jewish people, if someone found the box.

The world is a crazy place. Everything I ever knew or understood in my life can turn upside down in an instant. It is quite scary and I don't understand. It has to do with Jewish history, which is not my favorite subject. If only I had paid more attention in class.

28

GOODBYE DEAREST DIARY

Rachel
June 12, 1943

Dearest Diary,

Today seven of the ten remaining people left our room. We spread out once everyone left. It's made me realize how hard it is to share small spaces with several people. Father started searching right away for a place to hide the box. He and Mother spent most of the day trying to figure it out. The main problem is Father Niccacci knows we have the box and we cannot take it with us. He might try to find it, but that's a risk we are going to have to take. Father finally found a location under a loose floorboard. The room below us is a chapel, so the curve of the ceiling in that room allowed a deeper space near the corner to store the box. Father worked all day looking for options and figured it out by tapping on the floor. It was almost as if the space we found was custom-made for the box. Father was so excited he wept when he realized the box fit perfectly in the spot.

He has given me this evening to write what I want before he puts this diary in the box with the rest of the writings and Mother's sewing box. He said there is a possibility I will never see this again and that if by chance we don't survive our escape, someone else would find this diary along with the rest of the items in the box. I begged him to let me write about what was in his box. He said no. He did ask for a few pages of my diary, so he could write something of his own to put in the box. All I can say is I hope we will be able to come back and get our things, so we can keep it in our family. God, if you are real, let me come back and get this stuff for my family. Goodbye, Dearest Diary!

Your friend,
Rachel

29

CALEB HIDES THE BOX

June 12, 1943

Dear Rachel's Diary,

This is Caleb, Rachel's father.

To whomever may find this box. I am recording this in my daughter's diary, as I do not have any place else to write it. I am sad I have put this off until this moment, as I had planned for a very long time to record something for the family. Time, business, and mere survival has pulled me away from doing so. I am but a simple tailor who lived on the outskirts of the Jewish ghetto in Venice. I grew up from the age of nine in the ghetto and worked my way out with God's hand on my family.

The value of what is in this box is priceless to me. I dug up this box on the farm of my youth in Turin. It was in the ruins of a stone barn on the land of my childhood home where I would go play with my brothers and sisters.

Preservation of the barn was futile. Many trees and weeds had grown around it, and it made a perfect place for hide and seek.

One day I was there alone and digging in the dirt. While digging, I came across this hard surface and decided it was buried treasure. Over time, in secret, I recovered the box without any other siblings seeing it.

My mother asked me about it once and I told her it was just an old empty box I had found. She did not ask any further questions. I knew, even at a young age, the box was something special. I couldn't understand the writing on the scroll at the time, but through the years have researched it. After reading the enclosed recordings, I found out someone buried it over 1600 years ago. What a great surprise. How it survived that long is nothing short of amazing. The history of the family farm was passed down through oral tradition. My ancestor did not find this particular piece of information beneficial to the family. My ancestors did own the farm for over 1600 years, but poverty fell on my parents, and we had to leave the farm because we were unable to pay the local taxes. It caused great pain to my parents to be the generation to lose the farm. My parents never knew about the written journal of Annas preserved here. They passed away before I ever gained a full understanding of the contents. The last person who recorded anything in the box wrote that it was up to God to send someone to find it. I was that someone and have decided to hold it to be passed down in my family if it survives this crazy war.

I am not Christian. I am a Jew. I have no idea if I would consider Christianity. The Catholic Church is currently saving my family, and I have a new appreciation for them, but it is clear their help is not for my conversion but due to their high moral character.

We are hiding in the dome room of St. Francis of Assisi Church as Rachel told you (I am sorry, Rachel, for reading your diary. I love you and adore you.)

Maybe one of the reasons we are safe is because of this box? I have noticed some strange things in my life that have led me to believe there is a phenomenon surrounding the box. I am not interested in recording anything about it now, but I will agree some miraculous things have happened while having the box in my possession. Being saved by the Roman Catholic Church is one of them.

I pray it lands in the hands of my descendants only, but if by chance a monk from Assisi finds it, I pray he will preserve it until someone from my family can recover it. Myself, my wife Chasia or my daughter Rachel may return to retrieve the box of our belongings at a later date. The Nazis are closing in, and we must make our way out of Italy any time now. I pray after this war ends, I have survived and can return to pick it up.

I also want to make it known how grateful I am to the monks. They have taken care of my family and I am forever indebted to them for their kindness. It is evident the preservation of my people will happen no matter what. The monks who have prepared kosher food for us as well as carried water to us for our needs have most certainly demonstrated the greatest form of service to God. I know it will be greatly rewarded. I have hidden this box only because it's too awkward to smuggle out under a monk's robe. Father Niccacci has asked me to give it to him to hold, but I don't want to cause trouble for him either, so I have chosen to hide it in a place surely God prepared in advance as there is no other place in this whole room the box would have fit. The future is out of my hands. One more note, if you have this in your possession and you experience extreme spiritual circumstances, it is due to the angel who protects the box. If you are not chosen by God to have this box, I pray mercy for you.

With love,
Caleb

~~~

Joel set down the script of the ancient document, rubbed his eyes, and breathed out a heavy sigh. He wanted to call Hannah and share it all with her immediately, but she was on assignment at the moment. Caleb was his great-grandfather. He couldn't wait to show her the incredible history recorded by his family. Since Joel felt the presence already, he couldn't decide if he was scared or excited when he saw Caleb mention supernatural activity.

Not sure how to react to what he was reading, he glanced at the next section. Joel looked at the date and realized it was the exact time Israel became a state. Discussions with various people about Israel becoming a state started rushing back to him. The topic was explosive within the Jewish community. He tried very hard to stay clear of discussing the issue because of the various strong opinions on the subject.

The Jewish people getting some of the land back in 1948 that was given to Abraham in covenant by God was a huge deal. Some did not like the way Israel just took the land from the Palestinians. It was a hot button topic, and Joel could not go into detail about how he felt about it to most of his friends—mostly because he knew it was a topic in which no one would win.

Sure, plenty of Jewish people after World War II moved to Israel and made homes for themselves. They wanted to live in harmony with the Palestinian population, which had settled there through history. However, there was nothing but bloodshed and heartache over the years in Israel. The Palestinians did not want to share. The land was under British control at that time. It was a big mess. Anything would be better than what happened to the Jewish people during the Holocaust though. Gaining their state seemed like a way to say they did not all die in vain. But that didn't make sense either. Six million is a big number and dirt is so insignificant.

Then, growing up in New York, the opinion of the American Jewish community was a different animal. They were divided, and it seems there would never be an answer to which every Jewish person would agree. It was just a better plan in Joel's mind to stay clear of the topic because he didn't believe there was a right answer.

Now Joel was staring down at his ancestor's journal and her firsthand account of what happened. He couldn't wait to dig in further, but he missed his Hannah. He would see her soon enough. Joel picked up the journal again to press on.

30

ISRAEL BECOMES A STATE

~After WWII~

Rachel

May 14, 1948

Dearest Diary,

I have returned to you in one piece. But I am broken-hearted, because you are still here. I was stunned to see what my father had written in my diary, but also happy to see his handwriting. I was hoping my father had recovered the box already and that would be a good indication to continue watching for him at the museum in Turkey where we planned to meet if we ever got separated. Since I have the box, it has stolen some of my hope that my father is still alive. I have the grim task of telling Mother.

Today is the first day that Israel is a state. I am sure someone is celebrating. I am here in Assisi alone, in the room where we lived. The box was in the same place my father hid it in 1943. After spending the last few years studying Torah, it is evident a prophecy from Isaiah has been fulfilled today, which states,

"Who has ever heard of such a thing? Who has ever seen such things? Can a country be born in a day or a nation be brought forth in a moment?"

A new day begins for the Jewish people. Who would have considered a day like this would exist after such horror? A day like today is one every Jew has dreamt of since the fall of the Temple to the Romans in 70 A.D. My mind is wild with scenarios of what will happen next, especially after what has happened to me since then and seeing everything in the box. I can't bring myself to put what I have discovered into words at the moment.

However, much has happened since 1943 and I intend to explain as much of it as possible here in my journal for historical record.

The evening we placed the box under the floorboards, we left the room around midnight. Father Niccacci made us legal baptismal certificates that showed we were Catholic, residents of Assisi, and were baptized at St. Francis of Assisi Catholic Church. The story we were to tell someone if stopped was that we were on our way to visit our family in the south of Italy. We looked Italian, so we could say such things, and we memorized details on our way to the meeting point. Father Niccacci gave us a train ticket to

Bologna, with other instructions of how to make our way to Turkey. It was the scariest day of my life when we left. We were dressed as a monk and nuns, and walked down to the base of the town. There, a car was waiting to transport us to the train station in Perugia. The train was not scheduled to leave until 8 a.m. and we arrived by 4 a.m.

The train station wasn't open. They had moved us in the middle of the night, while the whole town was sleeping. We sat at the station in sheer terror of being discovered. When daylight arrived, I was sleeping on a bench, but Father was wide awake with Mother right by his side. The train appeared; we boarded and rode successfully to Bologna. The tickets and the disguises worked well. People were kind to us on that train. They thought we were people of the cloth. I enjoyed it but had a nagging suspicion our luck would run out eventually.

A Nazi soldier stopped us as we were disembarking. He asked us for our papers and looked them over quite extensively. It took everything in me to stay put and not run. I lowered my head as if in prayer, as I had seen the nuns do before while walking on the streets of Venice. My mother did the same thing as the soldier spoke to my father, who was quick to smile and give him our papers. The soldier looked at my mother then back at me and my father. I tried to keep my head bowed and prayed for real because I thought he was noticing how much I looked like my father, the priest. Our noses were very similar.

We figured out right away that he was suspicious. My father convinced the soldier to go off to another location to talk. Father told us he would rejoin us in one moment to catch our next train. That was the last time I saw my father. He saved our lives by leading the man away from us. He and Mother had a plan, if they ever had to separate the other would promise to take me as far away as possible. Mother took me to the toilet and explained to me Father knew where we were headed and would have to catch up with us later. She said if he was not outside the bathroom when we were finished we would have to run. They had split money and details, so they would know where to meet. Our meeting place was the Hagia Sophia in Istanbul, Turkey.

My parents shared a passion for architecture. Many times, as we stood in St. Mark's Square they would debate with each other over which building was more spectacular, the Hagia Sophia in Istanbul or St. Mark's in Venice. My mother loved St. Mark's architectural details and mosaics. My father argued the Hagia Sophia was even more spectacular. They discussed how Sophia meant wisdom and that Hagia Sophia meant the wisdom of God. Father had learned about the cathedral in the papers in 1935 when Mustafa Kamel Ataturk became the first president of Turkey, and had turned the ancient church into a museum. He told Mother we needed to see it one day. When we left the house to head for Assisi, Father had said we should look at it as an adventure, a holiday to look at architecture, instead of feeling like we were running. Little did he know he would not see his beloved Hagia Sophia.

As we came out of the restroom, the Nazi soldier was gone. My father was gone, and we realized we would have to run just in case the Nazi came back or sent other soldiers for us. Panic set in, but Mother grabbed my hand and took off from the train station and started shedding her nun's habit and instructed me to do the same. We ran and ran until we could run no more. We finally settled down in a short alley to gain our composure. Mother and I wept there for who knows how long.

Mother started plotting right away how we could possibly get to Turkey to take her mind off what might have happened to Father. It sounded like an impossible task, but we needed to find transportation across Italy and the Middle East to Izmir, then north to Istanbul. I was amazed at my mother and her calmness. She had a peace about her I would never have dreamed of obtaining. Her calm manner helped me not panic.

Demon Marq

Israel becoming a state is a bitter topic. However, they did not get the entire promise land back even to this day.

I played a major role in Caleb getting caught. It didn't take much to convince my Nazi "friend," a fallen angel in disguise, to take a second look at the family as they arrived at the train station. I gave him a hint to observe their likeness. He clearly saw the face of the father in the daughter and knew what was happening. The habit framing the girl's face made it easy to see her father's eyes.

I thought if I took out the family all together, the evidence in the box would be hidden in Assisi forever, and nobody would notice we had lost the key to Jesus, a topic of discussion my father, Zagan, had been hiding from Lucifer for eons. That's the only reason my father agreed to let me follow the family and leave the box unattended in Assisi. My father was keeping the box away from Lucifer until we found the key and I was ordered by him to get the family caught so we could keep an eye on them just in case the key resurfaced. I was proud of myself for alerting my friend to grab Caleb so we could keep a close eye out for the key. Then I immediately went back to Assisi to keep an eye on the box.

It didn't occur to me Hitler would be looking for the box, too. Hitler was looking for artifacts for Lucifer also, but my father was keeping this one a secret since the key went missing.

Somewhere, somehow, word got passed to Hitler that a box full of artifacts may have been in Assisi. I would like to know how that information was obtained. My best guess is my Nazi friend beat some information out of Caleb. They figured out the family had traveled from

Assisi. *Being omnipresent would be so helpful in times like these.*

Hitler believed religious artifacts would give him special favor with Lucifer. It's a good thing he killed himself. He was even given special access by Lucifer to use stolen supernatural angel technology to look for Noah's Ark. The Nazis were flying it over Mount Ararat. Everyone knows Ararat was an entire range of mountains, not just one mountain. They were never going to find it anyway.

I don't know what the big deal is about discovering Noah's Ark. Supposedly finding it could make the whole world rethink their position on what has become a cute little children's story. Just like when others claimed to locate it, the scientific community would work in our favor to debunk it.

You would think my own fallen angel father would acknowledge my work in getting Caleb caught was diabolical. Since Noah's big flood, the fallen angels hate us demons. We remind them of their failure and we hate them because they let our flesh die in the flood.

I was also surprised to see Rachel survived the war. I should have encouraged the Nazi soldier to get the two ladies out of the bathroom at the train station. It's almost as if he let them go on purpose.

31

RACHEL AND JOSHUA

Rachel
May 14, 1948 [Continued]

Mother and I decided to stay in Bologna for a couple of days to figure out a new way to Turkey. We walked the streets of Bologna and took a few pieces of pasta along the way from restaurants with noodles hanging outside for drying. Not our proudest moment, but perhaps I will be back and can make up for our thievery.

We came upon a few groups of homeless people gathered around fires in trashcans, talking. We walked up to one of the groups, unsure what would happen. All I knew is we needed a friend, a real friend who would protect us from the evil taking place in this world.

Then a memory rushed into my mind, and it was as if someone forced this flash of memory into my head for such a time as this. Father had told me one day I might be in trouble and to not tell anyone this secret, but to ask Messiah to save me. I spoke it out loud at that moment. I said, "Messiah, save us."

A moment later, a man by the fire gestured for us to come over and warm up. He was clean and polite and asked us if we wanted to listen to a story. We agreed, and before we knew it, he was deep into a story we had never heard before.

It was a story of a king who threw a feast for his son. The king invited specifically chosen guests, but they refused to come. The guests who were invited also killed the king's servants who had delivered the invitations. The king got upset and decided to send an army to destroy the city of the people he had invited who killed his servants. The king then came to the feast and noticed some were there without the required clothes for the feast. The king forced those who refused to dress appropriately to leave. Later the king sent his servants to the street to find strangers and invite them to the feast and give them the appropriate clothes for the occasion.

When the man finished the story, I looked him in the eye and asked if it was the end of the story. The man said yes, and I asked him what it meant. He said, "It's a parable. Ask God what the story means." I found that an odd answer, then he added: "Just like when you have a dream, you should ask God what your dreams mean also." Suddenly I was back at the dream I had about Spence the monk and the soup that turned to blood with his robe that changed from brown to red and white. Then the man said, "If you go to the restaurant two blocks down on the right and tell the host that Joshua sent you, he will give you a place to sleep tonight and a ride in the morning to the outskirts of town." Mother and I looked at each other, but when we turned back to look at the man, he was gone. Chills went down my whole body, and I almost fell, except Mother grabbed ahold of me.

I looked at her and asked if she had seen the man, and she had. And she heard what he said about the restaurant. When I asked her what he meant about the story he told about the king, she said she didn't understand the story or why he told it to us.

Mother and I hustled down the street to the corner and went into the restaurant. I was speechless for most of the rest of that night since I knew I had asked minutes before we met Joshua for Messiah to save us and he sent us to the restaurant for help. When we arrived at the restaurant a man named Luigi greeted us and asked us if we wanted a table for two. We said Joshua sent us and he smiled and politely told us to follow him.

We walked through the restaurant to the back room and into an office. The man moved his desk and pulled up a rug beneath the desk, revealing a hatch. He pulled the hatch open to a set of stairs leading to a basement. It was a room with a place to sleep, canned foods, and a means of cleaning up. There was also a rack of beautiful clothes. The man told us we could help ourselves to any food and clothes we needed. He said Joshua left them there for us. Then he handed me a jewelry box and said it was also from Joshua. I opened the box and inside was a pendant necklace made of what looked like glowing pewter cast in a shape I did not recognize. It was stunning, and I tried to tell Luigi I could not accept it, but he insisted. I gave in with tears in my eyes for the kindness of strangers. I have worn the necklace every day since. He said Joshua had asked him to pass it on to me when we arrived.

Mother and I looked at each other in awe of what was happening to us. Joshua knew we would be coming to this place.

As Luigi placed the necklace around my neck, I had a flash in my mind's eye of the story Joshua told us at the fire, about the king giving garments to the people he invited to the banquet. I could instantly feel the presence of peace and pure love. It was surreal, a peace that surpassed my understanding.

Mother and I ate and cleaned up and found some lovely clothes to wear. We wept together over missing Father, but we were so grateful to God for sending us what we could only describe as an angel. I pondered the story he had told of the king and wondered why Mother didn't understand it. We talked for a long time about Joshua, the necklace, and the clothes, as well as the kindness of Luigi and how he had known we needed help. I knew all along God sent him, but I never forgot how I asked Messiah for help that night.

The next morning the hatch opened, and Luigi greeted us with fresh bread and jam for breakfast. We couldn't thank him enough for his extravagant kindness. Did I mention fresh bread and jam? Luigi said he would be willing to give us a ride. Mother asked if we could stay for a couple of days. He was accommodating and said, "That will be fine, you can stay. Just let me know where you would like to go." Mother told him of our situation with my father and how we had to make our way to Turkey. Our host asked us if he could have the honor of setting us up for a train ride to the southeast coast of Italy, where he had a friend who could help us catch a boat to the Middle East. Mother and I began to cry, and the sweet man hugged us. We were lost but found.

After a week of our host spoiling us with some of the best Italian food we had ever tasted, Mother and I pulled ourselves together for the journey. That is when Luigi said we would be taken by car to the next small town on the rail lines called Imola, where we caught a train to Lecce.

The train took about eight hours, and we would have to make our way from the train station to the coast on our own, to Marina di Novaglie. Once there, we were told to contact a boat captain named Guerriero. So, the next morning we caught a ride with Luigi to the train station and had all our paperwork in order. We were dressed quite nicely, as Luigi had given us each a suitcase of expensive, fresh clothes. We saw Nazi soldiers at the train station. However, we dressed smart and looked like we knew where we were going, so they did not even blink an eye at us.

Once on the train, we realized Luigi had purchased first-class tickets for us and we had a compartment to ourselves for the whole ride. The conductor came by for our tickets and treated us with great respect. It gave us a glimpse of what life was like for people not battling evil. This part of the trip went smoothly. Luigi had packed us plenty of food so there was no need to go into the dining car.

Angel Harper

As I am reading along with Rachel recording this, I notice this was during the time I had to stay with the box in Assisi. It's clear Joshua had it all under control, but nobody mentioned the amazing food. I am not a fan of the lunchmeat bologna unless it is fried with an egg and of course a blueberry waffle on the side. Bologna is one of the best cities for food.

Thank the Almighty the demon Marq had to hurry back to Assisi. Otherwise those sweet girls may have never gotten away from the train station. How evil of him to alert the Nazis. He was not supposed to leave Assisi, but demons don't always play by the rules. They never have. They talk big about legal rights yet break the rules. If you can catch them breaking the rules, you can ask the Almighty for justice. Rachel should ask for justice. Once she understands the power of the key of David, I hope she will.

32

CODE NAME CAPTAIN GUERRIERO

Rachel
May 14, 1948 [Continued]

Once we arrived in Lecce, we sat at the train station for a while, to decide how we were going to make our way to Captain Guerriero. While we were reading the map we had picked up, a local woman working in the train station cafe noticed and asked us if we needed a ride. We told her we had to get to Marina di Novaglie. She knew the village well and said it was not too far by car. She said her husband was a taxi driver and would take us there for a fee. We were trying to be conservative with our money but decided to go with her since we didn't have a better plan.

Her husband was a short man with glasses and a mustache. The taxi was fancy, but he gave us a discount since his wife arranged the ride and she was coming along. He told us news of the war in Sicily as he had relatives living there who had escaped the battles and were now staying at his house. He also mentioned military activity near Brindisi, near the Royal Italian Government Headquarters, not far from where we were traveling. He said it was dangerous and suggested we stay the night at a local hotel near the marina.

He and his wife were both helpful and did not suspect us to be Jewish (at least, they didn't ask any questions about us being Jewish.) We realized that even if our fellow Italians thought we were Jewish, they were not looking for a way to turn us into the authorities. We found out later there were thousands of Italian people who helped Jewish people escape. Out of 32,000 Italian Jews, 7,682 died at the hands of the Nazis. However, 8,369 got out of Italy while the rest were in hiding or incognito, much to the credit of the Catholic priests who mobilized their congregations.

We arrived at Marina di Novaglie by sunset and were dropped off at the marina. There were several boats there, as well as members of the Royal Army. They approached us to ask for papers and our business there. Mother gave them our information and told them she was looking for a captain who would have some fresh fish. They waved her on.

We went from boat to boat asking for Captain Guerriero, but nobody recognized his name. But finally one of the men said, "That's me." We figured out it was a code name. He was part of the resistance of people in Italy who were helping Jewish people escape persecution. He welcomed us aboard and offered to clean some fish for us for dinner. Mother talked to the captain about trying to get to Turkey. He made it clear to us it was a bad idea, but we could stay aboard his boat for a few days while he worked out some details for us.

We agreed but were not allowed to come up from below. The conditions on the vessel were better than what I have heard others experienced. We got tired of the constant sway of the boat but had no choice. The fifth morning Captain Guerriero hopped on the boat in a hurry, and started out to sea. He said there was a change in plans and he would personally take us to Turkey. We were thrilled but wondered what caused him to change his mind. We learned from the newspapers after the war ended in May of 1945 that many of his friends were part of the Italian Resistance Movement, a group of Italian citizens who opposed the occupation of German forces in Italy. The Germans had rounded many of them up and taken them to work camps; he caught wind of this that day and decided it was time for him to leave the area for good. We were at the right place at the right time.

Life at sea was daunting for us, but I learned how to sail like a real professional. We discovered Captain Guerriero's real name was Marseille. He had been helping the resistance since the beginning of the war. Marseille was calm, steady, and had a peace about him that made me envious. What was it he knew that I did not? I had to find out.

The trip was long, and we had to fish for food as we sailed. We also had to take turns keeping watch, as there was plenty of activity on the seas. Thank goodness most of the ships were large enough to see from a way off. We were hard to notice since we were on a smaller sailing vessel, but still we had to sail off course at least five times to avoid other ships. There were luxury liners in the seas as well as military and smaller boats. I remember wondering who would be on a luxury cruise at a time like this? Later I learned that many of my fellows Jews were on those ocean liners and military ships, some disguised as soldiers. Many found safety with another helpful captain who defied his orders and took a whole ship full of Jewish people to Egypt.

I learned all about Marseille's life in Italy as a boy. He had grown up there with Catholic parents. His father had considered a life in the priesthood as a teenager, then met his mother and realized being a priest was not a good idea. However, his father had learned so much about the life of Jesus he would tell his son all the great stories of Jesus healing the sick, casting out demons, and raising the dead. I was interested in hearing about Jesus because, first of all, I knew very little about his real life and second, my father had mentioned Jesus might have been the Jewish Messiah. He would never talk about it outside our house with other Jews and told me not to talk about it, but here I was with someone who knew details and was willing to share.

Marseille said Jesus spoke in symbolic language, in parables, and he told us a few. When he got to the story Joshua had mentioned, we jumped out of our skins. Joshua had told us to ask God what the story meant, so I secretly asked under my breath, not expecting an answer. We hadn't realized it was one of Jesus's teachings when we heard it from Joshua. I told Marseille how we met Joshua and what had happened with Luigi. He got the largest grin on his face I had ever seen. He knew who Joshua was and what the parable meant.

Marseille explained to us how he and his father had studied parables in detail in the Torah. That surprised us. He said it wasn't normal for a Catholic family to study Torah, but when you read what Jesus said about the scriptures, it makes you dig for answers, and that is what he and his father had done most of their lives just for fun. He gave us an example: Joshua in the story of tearing down the walls of Jericho was a type of symbolism for Jesus breaking the hold evil has over the world. Joshua in Hebrew means "God is my salvation and bringer of truth," and Jesus is the Son of God and the bringer of truth and salvation. Then he said, "You probably had a face-to-face discussion with Jesus at the fire. Not to mention the name Joshua is Yeshua in Hebrew."

When he told us this we were astonished. Just because he said this did not mean it was true, but I felt heat all over my body, which made me think he was right. Mother had a similar reaction. We couldn't understand why this was happening, but we knew what the captain was saying could very well be true and it explained why Joshua had just disappeared.

The captain told us Jesus is alive. We knew about him dying on a cross, but the story of him rising from the dead had to be a fairy tale, and we did not consider it truth. Marseille talked to us about the Holy Spirit and how when Jesus was on the earth he came as a man, but all his power for healing came through the Holy Spirit. When Jesus ascended into heaven, the Holy Spirit came and filled all his followers, and they proved it by doing miracles too. Just like Jesus proved his power. I could have been on that boat for a year for all I knew because the captain had so much information about Jesus and I could not stop asking questions. I asked him why he was helping us, and he said, "Your own Torah says of God 'He will bless those who bless Israel and curse those who curse Israel.' Plus, it is right to help your fellow human being who is in trouble." Then he said he enjoyed our company.

I asked him more details about the parable Joshua had told us. The captain said he discussed this one many times with his father. Then he explained it like this:

The king in the story is God, and Jesus is the son. The feast was for the Jews who refused to come and who even killed the messengers, the prophets. The king sends an army to destroy the city where the people killed the prophets, which is believed to be the Romans destroying Jerusalem in 70 A.D. The king sending them to invite people off the street is about King Jesus sending the disciples to the Gentiles to teach them about the Kingdom of God. The garments are what people will wear in the Kingdom when they know the truth that Jesus is Messiah.

We had not met anyone who knew so much about the topic. Even our rabbi had not taught us about symbolism. Father mentioned Jesus once in a while, I believe because he was trying to understand the contents of the box. Mother did not want to hear about Jesus from Father as her family had strictly forbidden any of them to consider Messiah as Jesus. She changed her mind after these events took place, but as time went on, after the war, she didn't want to discuss it further. We eventually became part of a friendly Jewish community, and you just didn't tell stories like that or you would be labeled a traitor.

There was one terrifying day at sea where I thought we were in the gravest danger. We came upon a British war ship at night, and they commanded us to make ourselves known. The captain put his hands up, and a soldier speaking Italian with a British accent asked him what he was doing on the open seas. We couldn't tell in the dark if the ship was German or Allied. We finally figured out it was British, and they knew we were on the run from the Germans. They instructed the captain which direction to head to avoid confrontations on our way to Turkey. They suggested we go to Antalya, Turkey, and then make our way up through Turkey by land to Istanbul. The captain thanked him, and they gave us bread from their rations, which was a welcomed treat.

We landed in Antalya a week later to a whole new world. Antalya was a smaller town on the Mediterranean Sea. People were at market and doing their daily jobs. Turkey was not at war when we arrived. They entered the conflict in 1945, but by then the war was practically over. No Nazis checking papers. The fear we had been carrying for so long was not welcome in Turkey.

The captain was planning to stay in Antalya as long as he could and told us we could stay with him until we figured a way to Istanbul. We needed to make money, so Mother went to the market and offered to mend clothes. I found odd jobs to do at the market with her and the other vendors who would allow me to help them load and unload their things at the end of the day for a small tip.

Mother was in high demand in the market because she was a skilled seamstress. I know she was heavy-hearted and missed Father, but she worked as if her life depended on us getting to Istanbul. She thought her husband would be waiting for her. We finally bid goodbye to the captain, who we had been with by then for almost two months. We loved him for what he had done for us, and we knew we would probably never see him again; we didn't know how we could have stayed in touch with him. It was a crazy time in history. We thanked him, and though Mother had been offering him some of her earnings all along, he refused to take anything from her and made it clear he had plenty of wealth from fishing.

Mother secured a ride with a man who had been transporting items back and forth from Antalya to Istanbul. We rode in the back of his truck on the bumpy roads for the whole trip. He helped set up my mother in Istanbul with a booth at their bazaar, which was held on Tuesdays. She helped out by sewing pillows and other clothing items. Mother secured me a job making carpets in a factory in Istanbul.

The day we arrived in Istanbul, Mother and I darted to the Hagia Sophia, but Father was not there. The struggle we had gone through to get there, and no sign of him. We lingered for 48 hours, just to make sure we didn't miss him if he showed up at a different time. We secured a tiny room that overlooked the museum, so we could watch for him, but we never found him. My mother insists on remaining in Turkey, even today, believing he is still alive. I know it would take a miracle after all the death and destruction we have learned about since the war ended in 1945.

So, as I said earlier, today Israel became a state. I am trying to talk my mother into moving to Israel from Turkey. I am currently in Assisi for a few days and have sat at a local café to record this. My search for Father continues tomorrow.

33

THE SEARCH FOR CALEB

Rachel
May 15, 1948

Dearest Diary,

I am staying in a guest room on the grounds of the monastery at the insistence of Father Niccacci. When I arrived, he was thrilled to see I had survived. He figured out Father had hidden the box in the room but decided not to look for it, as he felt it must have been in a safe place. He said it saved him from having to hide it at his own house, since he couldn't find it when he searched the room after we had left. He laughed and said with the other refugees coming non-stop, there were likely hidden treasure left behind in every wall and that we were his hidden treasure. Such a humble man.

By the time the war ended he and his team of monks had rescued over 300 Jewish people through Assisi, right under the nose of the Germans. He told me countless stories of their town being searched and raided by the Germans. Someone convinced Hitler that Jewish smugglers had moved religious artifacts through Assisi, so he sent several waves of soldiers here to conduct searches for the entire length of the war. To the great credit of Assisi, not one Jewish person was found and sent to a camp while in their hiding places.

He asked me to show him where in the room the box was hidden and was overjoyed when it was still there. He even commented on the fact the box had fit perfectly in the space.

"God made a way," Father Niccacci quipped. He had no idea how true his statement was, or perhaps he did. I thought about telling him about our adventures in Bologna with Joshua but just nodded my head in agreement. I wasn't comfortable telling anyone about my encounter with Joshua because it sounded crazy, even to me, and I lived it.

I felt a slight invisible nudge from something on my side. Nothing I can explain, but something happened as soon as I touched the box. I held it up in the light to take a closer look and saw the design on the outside of the latch. I immediately recognized the design—it was the same symbol as my necklace.

Knowing Luigi had given me the necklace years earlier via my supernatural encounter with Joshua, I realized something was going on and I covered the necklace with my hand. Father Niccacci was very interested in seeing what was in the box.

I opened the lid to show him it contained my diary and old scrolls. Then I closed the lid fast and said they were just family recordings passed on through the years. I had seen the design on the box when I was a kid but had not realized until today it was the same design as on my necklace. It had seemed familiar to me, but I could never quite put my finger on where I had seen it before. It was clear something much more significant than I could imagine was happening.

I am not so sure what to do if Hitler, someone who used to be the most evil man on the planet, had been looking for this box. I am still holding out hope my father could show up in Turkey and figure out what to do. I am not sure how much longer we will be able to wait. Pain lingers as time goes on and we see the damage done by Hitler and his Nazis. I am planning on doing some research on what may have happened to my father after the train station while I am here in Italy. It has been publicized the Germans kept impeccable records so tomorrow I leave for Bologna to see if I can find more details at the government records department.

Angel Harper

Sweet Rachel is all grown up. I am so glad she figured out not to tell Father Niccacci about the necklace. I had to jab her in the rib hoping she would change the subject. What an ordeal it has been keeping the box hidden from the Germans. Even with the havoc-causing demon Marq hanging around. I'm not sure why his own father, Zagan, never led the Nazis to the treasure. I guess Zagan knew they could not get to the real contents without all the pieces of the puzzle. The Almighty has a plan; I just don't know what it is. I am on a need-to-know basis with the Almighty, and I don't need to know.

~~~

Rachel
May 16, 1948

Dearest Diary,

I am on the train to Bologna with renewed courage to begin the search for my father. I am hoping it's not hard to find the office in Bologna that might have details about Nazi operations there. I am melancholy on this particular journey, as I know it was the very same tracks I rode on with my father when I last saw him. I pray my mother is okay by herself, as she knows I am on this journey and it's hard to be alone waiting for news about her husband. I do have a sweetheart in Turkey who I know I will soon marry. He is a Jewish man from Denmark who also survived, and he is looking after my mother. We met at a local meeting for survivors almost two years ago. His name is Ethan, and he's working as a supervisor at a clothing factory in Istanbul. Since I left the carpet factory to help my mother make unique items for people to sell at the Tuesday bazaar, we decided I would be the best person to make the trip to pick up the box and see if Father had picked it up or if the church had found it.

I can hardly believe the box was where Father put it. The odds of someone else finding it after all this time were high, but there it sat. I am still in awe of my other findings.

The views along the train ride are stunning. It is hard to believe the stress we were under the last time we traveled on this route.

Rachel

May 17, 1948

Dearest Diary,

For the last two days Israel has been attacked by every one of its Arab neighbors. I pray it will settle down so I can move to our new homeland once I find my father.

When I arrived in Bologna yesterday, I started asking questions at the train station about what might have happened to him. Most of the people who worked at the station had only worked there since the end of the war. I asked around about rumors of where Jews they picked up in this station may have gone. One of the conductors mentioned Risiera di San Sabba in Triste, Italy. Another employee of the station said people have been coming there since the end of the war asking questions, and he knew they had opened the concentration camp in October 1943. We were at the train station on June 12 of 1943, four months before they opened the camp.

After digging around more, I learned from a local policeman that Father could have been put in holding until the camp opened or may even have been forced to work building it. Nobody knew much more about Nazi activity at the train station except perhaps that they took him to a transportation center and off to other camps in other countries. I found out their records department was not so detailed after all and there was not a central place to research what happened to our loved ones. It's a daunting task to track down the lost. We do know they are still trying to get an accurate count of how many Jews perished. I have one more day here to see what I can find before I have to make my way back to Turkey. I'm exhausted.

Rachel
May 18, 1948

Dearest Diary,

I have been to many Italian government buildings today asking as many questions as possible about my father. They all look at me with the same sadness. There are countless people looking for relatives and answers, and many of the clerks I have spoken to sound like actors who have rehearsed answers to my questions. Very few people know much. It is like all of Italy is in a daze and nobody knows anything. One clerk told me there are groups of people gathering information about the atrocities by the Nazis, but I have been unable to find one name or group. My mother is going to be so heartbroken when I return to her with the box and no information on Father. Tomorrow I start my journey back home.

Rachel
May 19, 1948

Dearest Diary,

I am on a boat on my way back to Turkey. No information regarding my father has surfaced. My greatest hope is that he was only sent to a work camp in Italy and released at the end of the war, as word on the street is many survived if they stayed in Italy. Being put on a train outside of Italy would be a death sentence. Details may not be available for years. I am not sure what to tell my mother. Many of our fellow survivors are moving to Israel. We may be safe in Turkey. However, the Arabs are very upset with the Jews for taking over what they call their land in Israel. In the future, living among Arabs may prove to be just as dangerous for the Jewish people as living among the Nazis. Even today the papers report the outrage of the Arabs toward Jews due to the new state created by the brand new United Nations. Egypt, Jordan, and Syria are still attacking Israel on all sides.

Rachel
May 21, 1948

Dearest Diary,

I caught passage on an old cruise liner. There are about 200 people on board, and I am hearing languages of all types around me. I am running quite low on funds and am ready to get home although I know it will be painful to return without better news. I think the captain of the ship may be an American. He is quite young to be a captain. I believe he likes me. I told him about Ethan, but he still wants to talk to me, so I guess he wants to be friends. I have always been an affable person, so I am not surprised. My English is not so great, and his Italian is even worse, but we manage to have a decent conversation. He is from New York and stayed after the war because he wanted to run a cruise ship he found in a shipyard in Venice. He says many people wanted to see Greece and Turkey and decided it would be a good route to run from Italy as people recover from the war. He also told me horrific stories of what they found in the death camps. I told him I was looking for my father. He said he was sorry for what the world had done to us. He claims most Americans didn't know what was happening over here until the very end. His parents finally started to believe what he was telling them in his letters, but only after seeing it on newsreels at the theaters. He explained most of the world was in denial or didn't want to face the truth.

I cried myself to sleep in my bunk last night after I heard him talk of the world not knowing. God knew. He could see our suffering, so why had he not rescued us? My mind races back and forth between God watching the murders and not doing anything and then to the awesome hand of God giving us land in Israel. The big picture must play itself out in a way too large for my mind to comprehend. I don't blame God. I blame people of free will making evil choices. Only evil could orchestrate such a thing. God is good. Evil is bad. It is that clear.

34

ISTANBUL

Rachel
May 28, 1948

Dearest Diary,

Today I arrive in Istanbul. We are cruising from Europe to Asia in the Bosporus where Istanbul sits between the two continents. The city is busy and bustling. People work in Europe and live in Asia, so they go back and forth daily. I know Mother will be waiting for me and is probably yearning for her husband to be with me. I am not looking forward to the look on her face when she sees I am alone. My trip was successful in that I recovered our family heirloom box with things I can't mention inside. But not finding news of my father or what happened to him makes me feel like I have failed. I know it is not my fault, but the knot in my stomach is causing me distress.

Rachel
June 15, 1948

Dearest Diary,

Much has happened since I arrived home. My mother was so upset the day I got home. She wept as expected when she saw the box. She believed if her husband were alive he would have gone and recovered the box by now.

My trip brought some closure to our lives. Mother has lost hope of my father still being alive and now we could just go wherever we wanted and send word back to Father Niccacci in Assisi of our whereabouts just in case. If Father is alive he will go to Assisi first, so we have decided to pack up and make our way to the United States. We think Israel is too dangerous and have heard New York is welcoming many Jewish people.

Living in Turkey has had its challenges for Mother with the language barrier. I picked up Turkish fast and helped her get up to speed when we first arrived, but now we need a place where the Muslims are not angry over the developments in Israel. Very few Muslims live in the United States and there is plenty of work for us in New York. I am excited to get the journey over with as I have done my fair share of boat rides. Mother is doing better than she did the first week after I got home.

Ethan and I are to be married next week and then we will leave for the U.S. Ethan said some of his employees are telling him it is time for him to go back home, to Denmark. Even his boss admits it is causing him a few problems to have Ethan in a leadership position over some of the Arabs. He is good at what he does, but there is unrest in the factory by those who would like to have his job. Ethan doesn't want to go back to Denmark. His few remaining family members who escaped Denmark are going to New York also. We are only staying here long enough to get married surrounded by friends we know from our survivors' group. Since we met in that group, we wanted to celebrate with them.

Rachel
June 20, 1948

Dearest Diary,

It's official! My new name is Rachel Cohen. Ethan and I went to a beautiful park on the shore of the Aegean Sea to exchange our vows and break the glass under the Chupa with 25 of our closest friends and family. In seven days, once the whole marriage celebration ends, we are leaving for the United States of America. I can't believe I am Mrs. Ethan Cohen. We are sailing to England first and then on to the U.S. We will all find work in the clothing factories in New York City. America has opened its doors to the Jewish community coming from Arab countries, and we are going to take advantage while we can.

These are the best of times and the worst of times, as

Dickens says. With Israel becoming a state, it is wonderful. However, the endless searching for lost family members is miserable. The numbers reported by investigators of the German atrocities is in the millions. I'm somber I must record this on my wedding day, but I felt compelled to write a few things down about what is happening in the world. Just like the day after Israel became a state and several different Arabs countries attacked Israel, we are still fighting for our freedom. The world does not make much sense, and I am getting married. It should be a joyous occasion. I just wanted to record that we will fight for freedom for as long as we have to. I pray we will be safe in the United States.

Rachel
June 27, 1948

Dearest Diary,

Today we boarded the ship to Liverpool, England. Being on the ship takes me back to the time I spent sailing with Captain Marseille to Turkey. However, this is a ship and not a sailboat. I learned so much from him. It will take us about ten days to get to England where we will stay for a day before we leave for the United States. The seas are high today, so I am beginning to get seasick.

Rachel
July 1, 1948

Dearest Diary,

The whole time we have been at sea, the seas have continued to be high. Many passengers have been sick, and it has caused others to be sick. Our second-class cabin is tiny, but at least we are not in steerage. Ethan learned from another passenger those people are getting more than seasick down there. Mother and I wanted to ride in steerage to save money, but Ethan would not allow it as we are on our honeymoon. Ethan has seen the box and asked about it, but I have not been able to bring myself to show him the contents.

35

THE SEAT OF HONOR

~Present Day~

Joel put the manuscript down on the desk. His Bubbe had provided so much information; he was not sure where to focus his attention first. He thought he knew what necklace his Bubbe Rachel was talking about and took a closer look at the box. The lid flipped open easily and the ironlike symbol on the top did look like her necklace. He examined it, fiddling with the metal design while wondering what Bubbe had done with her necklace. Endless possibilities ran through his head of what she might have known but never have the chance to tell anyone.

Joel had heard the stories of his grandparents coming to New York and how hard it was for them when they arrived. Bubbe Rachel became pregnant with his father on her honeymoon and in March of 1949 Ely was born.

Rachel lost her husband, Joel's Zayde Ethan, in New York in 1981, at a relatively young age. Bubbe was still alive today, but she had slipped into dementia a while ago and been spotty on many topics.

Joel wondered how much his dad had talked with his Bubbe Rachel about her diary. History had played out, and Caleb, Rachel's father, had been found under his fake name from Assisi recorded on documentation at a work camp in Italy. Most of the men in the work camp were shipped off to one of the other camps when they fell ill. The only trace found of Caleb over time was of him being in and building the work camp in Italy, but Bubbe Rachel never saw her father again. Joel had not contemplated long about his great-grandfather or the loss experienced by Bubbe and her mother who lost her husband in the horror of the Holocaust.

The Holocaust had long been over when Joel was born. Joel remembered pictures he had seen in school textbooks of piles of bones and shoes found near the gas chambers. As a young boy he knew he had lost family, but he had been too young at the time to allow the pain to seep into his heart. Now as Joel read he was experiencing the pain of a fifteen-year-old girl's anguish when she realized her father had distracted the soldier long enough to allow her to escape the enemy's snare. Joel contemplated how the hate was still present today with anti-Semitic countries that want to wipe Israel off the map.

The world had given Israel a state, but every day on the news he saw much of the population angry about it. Israel seemed to be center stage; the sliver of land given back to the Jewish people caused many to turn against Israel again over the last seventy years. The conflict was perplexing, and Joel had stayed out of the details of the Jewish homeland. He realized even more now the magnitude of the great suffering of the Jewish people at the hands of Hitler; God had brought a remnant through the Holocaust and provided them with a place to live and call home—the land they had not inhabited since Titus had marched on the Temple in 70 A.D. Joel had in his very hands a voice from that exact history, starting with Annas and ending with Rachel. The gravity of possessing such information hit him. He ached for the family he never had a chance to meet.

He missed Hannah and wanted her advice on the mind-boggling information. He had to decide if he was going to believe what Annas and his father had believed before they died, that Jesus was the Messiah. How could he not, with this first-hand witness and information he had before him? An eyewitness—his own family member who was the very person who pushed for an illegal trial to have Jesus crucified—had testified in this document that he believed Jesus was the Messiah. He needed to hide it in a safe place until he could work out some ideas in his mind. Where could he hide it? His father had kept it in the house, but for some reason Joel had a feeling this was not a safe place for it anymore. The thought of the two men in sunglasses at his father's funeral flashed into his mind. *Who were they?* He could not explain why, but he knew he was right. *Perhaps a safety deposit box or a vault?* He thought. Then he wondered about the woman who had interpreted it and where she might be. She had to be the only other person on earth who knew about the document. If the world found out about it, professors from major biblical archeological colleges would want to carbon date and verify it. They would want to take possession. *It is not a safe thing to have in the house,* he thought. He could see it being difficult to own if the world caught wind of the details. He suddenly needed to vomit as hundreds of different scenarios played out in his head.

Joel flew out of the bedroom toward the bathroom and lost it just in time in the toilet. His mother was sitting in the living room and came quickly to comfort him.

"Oh, sweetie, you okay? It will be okay," she said gently as she rubbed his back.

Joel kept heaving as frightening images flooded his mind. He saw hate-filled people on the streets spitting on him and his family. He saw his closest friends screaming at him to stay away. There were news reporters on the TV calling him a liar and a heretic. He could see several interviews of prominent professors from Harvard and Oxford discrediting him. Then he pictured visions of reporters, neighbors, and strangers swarming his house, berating Hannah as she left for work. He couldn't explain where these visions were coming from. When he finally stopped vomiting, his mother didn't say a word. She simply started to tear up. She had seen what this had done to her husband, and she didn't want the same for her son. She had no idea how to fix it. She knew it was a burden.

Joel sent her away. "I'm okay," he said as he waved her out of the bathroom.

After lying on the floor for a while, Joel got up and went to the couch in his father's office. He slept there for a few more hours. While sleeping, he had a dream.

In the dream, he was in a room with a large rectangular wooden table. Joel had an understanding in the dream that all his ancestors were seated at the table when he arrived. They looked at him in anticipation as he walked into the room. The only seats left were at the head of the table and just to the right of that. His ancestors were watching him to see where he was going to sit. Joel looked at each of them; they had visible scars from wounds they had experienced. He didn't recognize them, but he did see his father, Ely. He started to sit down next to Ely when he realized his father's wounds were fresh and bleeding. The blood was coming from his head and his heart.

As Joel walked to the seat near him, his father stood up and said, "Sit down and take your rightful place at the head of the table!"

"I want to sit by you," Joel said, shaking his head no.

"You have been asked to sit in the seat of honor. Would you say no to me?" Ely replied.

Then a cloudlike entity entered the room and picked up Joel and placed him in the position at the head of the table. The rest of the ancestors all stood on their feet and started cheering and jumping up and down in glee.

Joel woke up from the dream.

His mother came in with a cup of soup shortly after he awoke, and he told her about the dream.

She arched her eyebrows and said, "What a scary dream. The cheering is good, but your dad with a wound sounds disturbing. Perhaps your father or God is trying to tell you something."

"But what?" Joel asked.

"Well, God talked to Solomon in a dream, and Joseph. Why not us? Are we not his children, too?"

His mom had a point. It was an unusually vivid dream. He couldn't rule out the possibility of God communicating with him, considering what had been happening to him and what his family reported in the manuscript.

If God was talking to him, he had to find out. Joel always prayed the prayers led at the synagogue, but God did not 'communicate" with him, so to speak. He just prayed what he was taught to pray. Hearing from God in a dream was a bit off the radar for him. Not to mention, it was not something he had ever thought he would hear his mom say. He knew one thing—he needed God to tell him what to do with this box.

36

THE THIRD TEMPLE

Joel left his mom's house the next morning. Hannah had worked most of the week on a major project at the U.N. with the Consulate office. It didn't seem fair they made her stay, but as often with Israel, there was a major problem almost daily.

Hannah was pulled in many different directions at her job and seemed to be the only person capable of making decisions, Joel often thought. It just so happened this week the Israeli prime minister was in the United States speaking at the U.N., and Hannah was in charge of a security project for him. Hannah handled most head of state visits, as they wanted very few people knowing about the security procedures at the United Nations building. Hannah was one of three individuals with the knowledge, and the other two were on different assignments. *That means my wife is the only link to keep Israel safe*, Joel thought. A statement, which when reflected upon, could be true of Joel also as he carried the box in a suitcase into the apartment building. Joel was still unsure about sharing the information in the box with Hannah. She loved history and would be so excited to get her hands on something like this and she would agree it belonged in a museum. It sounded to Joel like a great idea, except it could cause a significant ripple in the Jewish community. Joel knew the revelation of Annas had the potential to change the way the world looked at Judaism and Jesus forever. He was still in shock.

When he walked into his apartment, Hannah was on her phone talking business and smiled at him, then pointed to the phone indicating she would not be very long.

He wheeled the suitcase in the front door, dropped his coat and plopped on the couch. Life was about to become even more complicated—and interesting—than he ever imagined.

"Hey, sweetie," Hannah said as she put down her mobile and came to where Joel was sitting.

"Hi, hon," Joel replied with a heavy sigh.

"How ya feeling?" she asked as she ran her fingers through his hair.

"Dazed and tired," he said as he pulled a pillow over his head and shut his eyes.

"How's your mom?" Hannah asked.

"Um, okay. Seven days is long enough for the fog to

slightly clear. She is still a stare bear but has had some moments of surprising clarity the last few days now," Joel said from under the pillow.

"I'll make her some food tonight and take it over and check on her while you rest. I'm sorry I haven't been able to be over there all week. It has been one of those crazy 'Israel consumes all' weeks," she said.

Funny she should mention that. *I feel the same way*, Joel thought.

She continued. "Everything is about to change for Israel. They brought plans to rebuild a Third Temple to the U.N. for review," Hannah said as she revealed her major security project.

Joel was barely listening. *Did she just say they have plans to rebuild the Third Temple?*

"What?" *This is too much in one day*, Joel thought.

"Yep, believe it or not, some young rabbi brought plans, research, and supposed proof that the Dome of the Rock is not where the original temple stood," she said as she stood up and took off her coat. She had just gotten home as well.

"No way. Someone had to have confirmed the location a long time ago, didn't they? I mean, did someone just go up there and guess where the original temple used to be? Who was in charge of that scouting party?" Joel asked.

"I don't know. Everyone just assumed the Dome of

the Rock is where the temple sat. The rabbi believes there is a spot between the Dome of the Rock and the Church of the Holy Sepulcher where the exact location inside the original temple is the true location of the Holy of Holies, which is where the very presence of God and the Ark of the Covenant was originally placed. He's saying the Dome of the Rock sits on the location of the Court of the Gentiles, so they can just leave their Muslim shrine in place because they are Gentiles anyway. It's all very confusing." Hannah surmised.

Joel was astounded at what he was hearing.

"Were the U.N. meetings on TV? What have I been missing on the news this week?" he inquired.

"Oh yeah, you've had no TV this week, have you?" She was feeling sorry for him. "Poor thing. It was brought up on a few newscasts, but honestly, I am not sure how that rabbi got the prime minister to allow him to even bring it up to the U.N. Most of Israel is not in agreement on rebuilding the temple and it wasn't on the agenda. For some reason the prime minister decided to submit it for review at the last minute. Probably to see how it would be received worldwide. Most people watching the U.N. meetings are reporters. I think many of them decided it wasn't newsworthy. There has not been a huge uproar, yet," she said.

"Hmmm, the key word is *yet*," Joel, said, in great shock the media didn't pick up on it. "They would have

OVER MY DEAD BODY 195

to have the Ark of the Covenant if they were planning on rebuilding the temple, right?"

"No, Joel, every Muslim on earth would have to be dead for them to be able to rebuild at the Temple Mount. I can't think of any way they could move forward with the plan. Who in their right mind would want to start animal sacrifice again? Why animal rights organizations have not been in an uproar is beyond me. Our security team was stunned; we weren't sure we heard the rabbi correctly. We were concerned about getting the prime minister back to the Consulate office afterwards. But when we left the building, it was like nobody was paying attention. The Palestinian protestors who are always there had the same signs about Israel occupying their land. I guess the protestors missed the rabbi speaking. I know what I heard; it was a huge topic for the world not to react," she said.

Joel's mind went on a wild horse ride with all this detail. *Should he tell her what he had in his suitcase?*

Hannah went to the bedroom to change, and Joel just lay there, his mind going a hundred miles per hour.

37

COURT IN SESSION

There was a sudden echo coming from the hall.

"Over my dead body!"

It sounded like a booming voice from a faraway place.

Joel looked around and thought it was coming from outside the apartment. He went to the door to peer down the hallway, but nobody was there. He looked out on the balcony to see if a neighbor was talking. No neighbors.

Hannah came back into the living room dressed in jeans and t-shirt.

"What do we want for dinner tonight?" she asked.

"Shhhh...you hear that?" Joel said.

"Hear what?" Hannah looked around.

"A conversation, did you hear a conversation... something about a dead body?" Joel's mouth fell open as his brain acknowledged the craziness of what he had just said.

Hannah looked at him and said, "You are tired."

"Yes, I'm tired, but I heard a voice say, 'Over my dead body.' Maybe it was outside?"

"Ah yes, an idiom. Someone is laying down the law. Perhaps the neighbors," Hannah said, slinging her arm down as if throwing a gauntlet. Hannah's cute, comical personality with plenty of wit was one of Joel's favorite things about her.

Joel sat up and rubbed his eyes while he chuckled at her. "This has been a rough week. I must be hearing things."

Joel decided he had no words or energy to tell Hannah everything about the box, manuscript, or Bubbe's necklace. He needed to rest and gather his thoughts.

"I am going to jump into the shower. It'll help me feel better," Joel said as he headed to the bedroom.

"Okay, so dinner is my pick. I will make us some pasta with a spinach salad," Hannah said as she headed for the kitchen, wondering if her husband was hearing voices.

Joel schlepped into the bedroom and made his way to the shower. He let the steaming hot water run over him, completely encompassing his body. His mind wandered to the topic of work. He wondered how behind he would be after being out for a week.

"He is ready, Lord," Joel heard a voice say. He snapped his head around looking for the source.

Joel started thinking about what his dad might have been facing. *Did he hear voices after opening the box, too?* He understood his dad not wanting to tell anyone. *Was this the angel again?* Joel was determined to get to the bottom of it with no fear. Out of nowhere, he was struck with awe and went down to his knees and then gently all the way to the floor as if being laid down by assisting angelic hands. The water continued to pour over him, and Joel released himself from fear and let whatever was happening just happen.

~Outside of Time~

"Joel, we are taking you to a particular time and place, so you can experience the heart of the Ancient of Days," the friendly pleasant male voice whispered.

"Who is the Ancient of Days?" Joel asked, barely finishing before he found himself floating through what looked like a funnel of layers and layers of beautiful green circular light waves. It reminded him of mirrors that went on forever and gave him a sensation of moving.

"Do you remember Daniel the prophet talking about Him?" the voice asked Joel as a flood of details from the book of Daniel flowed to Joel. Information about the Ancient of Days filled his mind with truths of heaven. Daniel had lived through several kingdoms set up and put into place, and in a vision Almighty God was seated on a throne with a garment as white as snow and hair like pure wool. The throne was made of a fiery flame and wheels of burning fire. Flashes of blue fire streamed from the Ancient of Days. Thousands upon thousands surrounded the Almighty to attend to his every need. There were also ten thousand times ten thousand standing before the Ancient of Days as He was reviewing verdicts for them as a court was in session. Ancient books were open before the Almighty as well.

Joel found himself standing in the very courtroom Daniel mentioned and he could not speak or move. He was awestruck as the water from the shower continued to trickle down his back. The thousands upon thousands ministering to the Ancient of Days stood in sheer awe of Him as He sat on his fiery throne. Joel's view was just to the right side of the incredible throne. He was near the flames yet could not feel any burning.

The Ancient of Days spoke and said again in a thundering voice, "OVER MY DEAD BODY!"

Then Joel saw a man who looked like a servant nodding his head at the Ancient of Days. The servant opened his mouth and said, "I understand, and I yield all to you." The man was standing before the throne and looked over at Joel. Joel looked next to him and saw a shimmering sphere with magnificent wings and then looked back over at the servant. Pure love filled the servant's eyes when he looked at Joel. Joel could not hold his gaze long and dropped his head as tears fell from his eyes from the perfect understanding of love coming from the servant's heart. Then in the next moment Joel realized he was sitting on what looked like a throne.

Joel wanted to understand the idiom. *What body?*

The servant knelt before the Ancient of Days and agreed to do something that didn't make sense to Joel.

More of the details from Daniel rushed into Joel's mind as if the servant's gaze had pushed through Joel's fear and put the particulars of the rest of Daniel's vision into Joel's mind.

"I was watching in the night visions, and behold, one like the Son of Man, coming with the clouds of heaven! He came to the Ancient of Days, and they brought Him near before Him. Then to Him was given dominion and glory and a kingdom that all peoples, nations, and languages should serve Him. His dominion is an everlasting dominion, which shall not pass away, and His kingdom the one which shall not be destroyed."

Joel's first thought was, *what am I witnessing?*

The servant thought back softly, *The Almighty Ancient of Days is defending you.*

Defending me from whom? Joel thought.

One who wishes you harm, he replied via thought like lightning.

"Who is the Son of Man?" Joel asked.

"That's me," the Servant responded.

Why am I on this throne? Joel's thoughts were moving very fast now.

It is my throne, and I am sharing it with you. Don't be alarmed, Joel. This situation is happening outside of time, in the courts of heaven. It did take place, but not inside the constraints of time. We are letting you witness it for understanding. Soon, the Ancient of Days shall step off the throne and allow himself to be a Son of Man.

Who are you? Joel asked in thought.

I am the I Am, the Servant responded. *I have stepped off the throne already but wanted you to experience the full Glory of my presence. I am one, yet my presence carries three separate aspects, all part of the Almighty. The Almighty exists of the Father, the Son, and the Spirit. We made you in our image. We are joined and in total unity, which is why you are allowed to sit on my throne.*

"But, that means you are Jesus?" Joel asked out loud.

"Yes," Jesus answered.

"I don't believe in you, so why am I given the right to sit on your throne?" Joel asked.

He smiled and replied, "You don't believe in me as of your last time on earth."

Whoa, so I do believe eventually? Joel's thoughts were running faster than he could react.

Yes, Jesus thought back, smiling and nodding.

Wow...it was easy for me to accept here. When in my time is this court taking place again? Joel thought.

"Joel, it's taking place before the foundations of the earth as well as currently in your time. Like I said before, we are not tied to time as you know it. We are allowing you to be in both places through your spirit. We wanted you to see that the entire sacrifice of my body was a decision made to defend you and all people who choose to be in covenant with the I Am," Jesus explained.

Am I seeing all of this because of the box? Joel asked in thought.

"Yes, you hold in the box wisdom for many people." Jesus responded.

"Wisdom?" Joel replied.

There is more to it, Joel. I made the box myself and placed the design and lock on the box. The key will unlock sacred proof for you and many people all over the world. So many don't have the wisdom to understand. I am trusting you with the revelation.

"You made the box on earth and brought it to Annas. I read that in the journal," Joel said.

"Yes!" Jesus said and smiled at his realization.

"You must have been a talented carpenter, even as a young man," Joel said. *Crazy to be making small talk at this moment,* Joel thought to himself.

Joseph was an excellent carpenter; I allowed him to teach me most of what he knew before I placed the metal ornament on the box to fit the key, Jesus thought back. "Also, I love small talk," He said.

He is listening to my every thought, Joel thought. *The creator of the universe is listening to my every thought.*

"I am also counting every hair on your head," He said out loud as He grinned.

In the next moment, Joel noticed the shimmering sphere was covered with eyes and hovering beside him. The angel, Harper, introduced himself to Joel but Joel couldn't take his eyes off Jesus, along with the Almighty and the Spirit, who were creating medallions that were keys forged from fire and metal. They poured the molten metal into molds. It was as if this vision of the making of the keys was sent directly to Joel's mind's eye while he was still inside the courtroom. Jesus took Joel in his mind to various situations to explain them, yet his physical body remained on the shower floor on earth.

The next obvious question is, where is the key now? Joel thought.

Jesus focused in on the key He was holding very close to Joel who looked at it and realized the key was Bubbe's necklace. He reached for the key and Jesus pulled it back from his hand. "It's very hot, and remember you are outside of time" he said smiling at Joel's eagerness.

"Oh, the key was given to Bubbe in Bologna! Bubbe still has the key?" Joel stated out loud sounding like he was sure, but unsure. Joel continued, confused: "But that guy's name was Joshua?"

Jesus nodded and answered him again, smiling. *Yeshua, Joshua, Jesus, the Almighty, the Ancient of Days... I have many names, Joel.*

Joel's mind rapidly switched to a new subject that had swirled around in his mind since he was young. "Where is the Spirit?" he blurted out, thinking he had so many questions and he had to get to them all before this ended.

"The Spirit is here with us as well, but you can't see Him. He is busy with the day-to-day operations and is outside of what you call time also, so He is always present. He is one with us. I walked the earth a mere 33 years as flesh and bones. He has always been busy in the universe with various outreaches."

"Like what? Not much was taught to me about the Holy Spirit other than it rested on Saul, David, and the prophets occasionally," Joel said.

"Just like Saul, David, and the prophets experienced Him occasionally, He now resides mostly within my people on earth. He is busy changing their hearts as a deposit from the Father and reveals the love of the Father for the Son. He enables all people to live. He helps them in their weakness, and hands out righteousness, peace, and joy. He is a hunter. Some call Him the Hound of Heaven. He yearns for your spirit that He created to want His Holy Spirit to live in your heart. He hides precious things to let you search them out, and by finding them He teaches you truth. I could go on and on about His benefits," He said with a soft look in his eyes.

I want to know Him, Joel thought.

"You will. He is My Spirit. Simply put, He is Me. It's odd, I know, since you have arrived here now from your current position in earthly time. However, when you see Me, you see Him, trust Me," Jesus said smiling. "Joel, you know Me very well. We have a relationship. You are one of my favorite people on earth."

Joel's heart ached—was it remorse? He had no memory of knowing Jesus.

"It's okay, Joel. It is time to go back. Our primary purpose in bringing you here is for you to see the magnitude of your assignment on the earth. You are called Joel. Your dream the other night about being at the head of the table is about you sitting in a seat of honor. You are invited to sit at the right hand of the Father because you are seated in heavenly places. You have all authority on the earth, that same authority I demonstrated by the power of my Holy Spirit while I walked the earth, and I have given you the key to the house of David. I need you to walk into your true calling. I have set you up with all you need, in order to accomplish what you have been called to do. My yolk is easy, and my burden is light," Jesus said.

"What about your body?" Joel asked.

"Well, Joel, all of this fuss is over my dead body. If my body had been in the tomb, none of this would be happening. But the fact is, my body was not there. I defeated death. So, it's not really over my dead body—that's just an idiom I use to remind Satan he can't have my followers. A throwing down of a gauntlet, if you know what I mean?" He said with a wink.

Joel chuckled a bit, as he knew Jesus saw Hannah's gauntlet joke from earlier.

"I use idioms and parables to drive home my points; I am particularly fond of this one since the truth is, my body is alive. Those in power were trying to prove I was dead. To them, my death proved I was not Messiah, but they ignored my resurrection and appearance, they always forgot about the thousands I appeared to for the forty days after I resurrected. But Joel, you have the witness of Annas," Jesus said.

Joel looked down in front of the throne and saw Lucifer's beady eyes squint as he peeked at Joel.

"He can't see you or hear our conversation, but he knows who you are," Jesus reassured Joel. "He will accuse you, but it is nothing to worry about. I've got you covered."

"What part do I play?" Joel asked as he slowly looked away from Lucifer's glare, trying desperately to focus on the conversation.

"I will give you all the direction you need. I can speak in many ways so be ready to listen. I walk in the Word, so I will meet you there, but I also speak through dreams and visions as I did throughout the Word, just like your mother said." As He finished speaking, His servant appearance left him as He turned to walk toward the front of the throne where Lucifer was standing. Behind Him was his robe, which filled the room with layers and layers of glowing fabric made of light. Joel had never seen the color before, but he knew it resembled purple. He recognized he was in the tangible presence of true royalty.

38

JOEL'S REVELATION TO HANNAH

~Present Day~

Before he realized it, Joel was being pulled back through stunning layers of light, and the courtroom scene was a distant circle of rainbow light moving further and further away from him. Joel found himself aware once again of being on the shower floor. He stayed there motionless as he became conscious of water falling on him from the shower. The water turned cold, and Joel started shivering but stayed because he couldn't get up. Hannah came into the bathroom.

"Joel! Joel! What on earth?" She shut off the water, panic-stricken as she saw him down on the floor.

Joel tried to talk but could not get much out except the word "Jesus." He began to weep inconsolably.

Hannah helped him up, wrapped a towel around him, and moved him to the bed. She tried to comfort him, but

Joel continued to sob and could not form words. Joel curled up on the bed like a child. As he wept, he could feel Jesus' presence even still. Hannah curled around him and they stayed that way the whole evening. The feeling of sadness continued - more than Joel ever thought possible - but soon he was experiencing joy. It was late evening, and Joel still could not speak. Hannah just waited for him to be able to gain composure. She knew something had happened in the shower—something more than just grieving for his father.

Joel woke the next morning with a slight brush of his cheek by something supernatural. Joel smiled, as he knew this was the Spirit of Jesus, the Holy Spirit.

Joel spoke, "Good morning."

"Good morning," Hannah answered.

Joel smiled as he rolled over and held her tightly in his arms. She was perfect for him.

"Are you okay?" she asked as she rubbed his arm.

"Yes, yes, better than ever," Joel replied.

"I am worried about you. What happened in the shower last night?"

Joel did his best to put the experience into words for Hannah. He started with the box, the scroll of Annas, his Bubbe's diary, and what had happened since his father died. Then he tried to explain to her what had occurred in the shower and that he needed to make a visit to Bubbe anyway and would track down the key. She was silent until he finished.

Joel could tell Hannah was not sure how to react, and her mouth opened, but nothing came out. It was not like her to be speechless. She was an opinionated woman.

Finally, something came out: "What does all of this mean?"

"To me, it means I have to explore the glaring truth. Jesus is real, and I want to be used to my fullest potential, whatever that may look like," Joel said.

"You believe *what?*" she asked.

"I think I believe Jesus is who He said He was; I think it's true what my ancestor Annas wrote about Him and what many of my other ancestors thought, including my father."

Hannah didn't say a word.

"I'm not going to keep this a secret, Hannah. I have to reveal all of this publicly somehow, so the world will know the first and primary person who pushed to crucify Jesus was eventually a true believer in Jesus as Messiah," Joel added. "Jesus showed me a vision of him making the key to the box. He gave it to Bubbe in Bologna. Now I have to find it," Joel said as he jumped up to head to the living room.

Hannah didn't follow him. Joel found his suitcase, pulled out the box, and brought it back to the bedroom.

Hannah was stunned when she saw it; Joel gave it to her to hold. The moment her hands touched the box, she knew her life would never be the same and it left her speechless. Joel thought just a couple of weeks ago about how his life with Hannah was excellent but could become mundane if the newlyweds settled into their marriage. Now, all of a sudden, he was excited about something, about being part of something bigger than himself. He had a burst of strength he had never known before.

"Hannah, I can't do this without you by my side," he told her as he held her shoulders firmly and looked into her eyes. Joel's eyes were still puffy from the constant tears of the night before. Hannah could see he was serious about pursuing this train of thought. She was hesitant but didn't want to let on her concern for him.

Finally, words spilled from her mouth as she sat on the bed: "Where do you think Bubbe hid the key?" Joel jumped on the bed next to her and started to rifle through the box. There was nothing on the bottom and no hidden spots he could visibly find. He played with the symbol on the front of the box, but it didn't move.

"Maybe it's not a physical key. Perhaps it's a spiritual key," she said, trying to be helpful.

Joel knew now Hannah was backing him up no matter how crazy it sounded. Here she was, trying to solve the riddle. Not one word yet on the topic of being a Jesus believer. Joel would not push her; he would just take it one moment at a time. He knew she had to believe the magnitude of what had happened to him because he had the evidence right before her eyes. He could tell she was excited and was truly his helpmate in this new adventure. *If Jesus can appear to me to prove who He is, He can show up for her too*, Joel thought. He would leave the convincing up to Jesus.

"Baby, believe me, it is spiritual, and we're going to figure it out," Joel said as he pointed to the symbol on the front of the box.

Hannah could see the excitement in his eyes when he called her baby. She ran her finger along the embossed symbol on the outside of the box. "What does this mean?" she asked.

"I don't know... I'm not sure it has a meaning. We'll have to do some research on the key of David. I'm trying to figure out why Bubbe gave my father the box without the secret key," Joel said. "I suppose the other possibility is the translator, Leona, knows something. I am not sure how to find her. Father said in his letter she was a Hebrew professor. She has known about all of this for a long time. He must have sworn her to secrecy," Joel said.

"That could be it. I wonder if Leona knew the implications," Hannah replied. They were already on the same page together, and in his spirit, Joel received a gentle reminder from his wedding, "the two become one." The Holy Spirit was revealing a truth to Joel about marriage and how when one gains wisdom and knowledge the other gets it in their spirit even before their mind understands.

"Do you know what the implications are?" Joel asked in wonder, hoping Hannah had a plan in that brilliant mind of hers.

"Not really, but I do know it has something to do with Israel and probably something to do with end times," she replied.

"How would you know that?" Joel asked

"I have been working with Israel for a while, and I knew something extraordinary had to come along sooner or later. It is no coincidence I am directly involved with top officials in Israel. I am not sure about Jesus, but I know you, Joel, and I believe what you say has happened to you is the truth. This box is phenomenal, and I know we have to do the right thing."

She gets it, Joel thought. "What is the right thing?" he asked.

"I don't know, but we need some direction for sure," she replied. "Maybe I should contact the prime minister?"

"No, let me call my mom and see if she knows anything about the translator of the scrolls before you take this thing that high."

Hannah agreed.

Joel called his mom and asked her several questions about Leona, the person who translated the text from

Hebrew and Italian to English. His mom said she didn't have any idea who Leona was or what Joel was talking about. He tried to explain to his mom who Leona was without discussing what was in the box, but she insisted again she didn't want to know anything. She told Joel she was feeling fragile and sensitive and didn't need to hear about that woman on the phone. When she said, "that woman," Joel knew he had better drop the subject. She sounded hurt. It was clear she knew who Leona was and did not want to talk about her. Joel decided to make a trip to see his Bubbe.

39

BUBBE RACHEL

~Present Day~

Joel got dressed and told Hannah his plan to visit his Bubbe. Rachel had not been well enough to attend her son Ely's funeral and had been unable to communicate with the family for some time. It was heartbreaking to Joel that Bubbe's son had died before her. Children were not supposed to die before their parents; it was not the natural order of things in Joel's eyes.

Joel arrived at the nursing home and signed in at the front desk. When the receptionist called Rachel's doctor, he came out to talk to Joel and give him an update. The family had decided not to tell Rachel about Ely's death because she would have no way to express her grief and she was already going downhill at this point, plus they were unsure about her level of understanding. Up until a month earlier, she had been able to communicate with eye blinks - one blink for no and two for yes. Even that activity had stopped; they thought it was because Ely had stopped visiting her when he became ill. Ely used to visit her every few days to check on her. When he didn't come, she stopped communicating. Joel had been so busy taking care of his parents while Ely was in the hospital, he had not prepared himself to face Bubbe with the news.

When Joel went into her room, she was sleeping. He looked at her soft, thin-skinned face and imagined her a fresh young lady crossing the Atlantic Ocean. She had quite the life. Joel decided to take a look around her room while she was sleeping. They had moved all her most treasured things with her when she moved out of her house five years earlier. She couldn't take all her belongings from a three bedroom flat to a small efficiency apartment and in the nursing home it was paired down even more. Joel browsed the room for any keepsake or jewelry box; there were a couple of them. Inside them were some costume jewelry and broaches but no sign of the necklace. *It has to be here!*

Disappointment was just starting to settle in when Joel noticed it—there, around Bubbe's neck. He had seen it there many times before but never asked her what it was, never had a reason to notice it. Now he could plainly see it was an exact match to the symbol on the box. Excitement bubbled up inside him. As he went to reach for it, his Bubbe started stirring. They looked at each other, and a large smile spread across his face.

"Hey there, Bubbe," he said.

Her eyes were tired, yet they lit up when she saw him as if someone had turned on a flashlight from the inside. Joel had not seen that look in her eyes in quite a long time.

"Bubbe, it's me, Joel. You were sleeping so I was just looking around a little bit at all your beautiful things."

Joel pointed to the necklace.

"Bubbe, I remember you wore this necklace all the time when I was little. I love it."

Her eyes lit up even more, as though she knew what was happening. She couldn't speak, but Joel knew if she were in there she would realize he was interested in the necklace because he had the box. Joel tried to judge her reaction. She had aged quite a bit in the couple of weeks since his last visit. She was a good Bubbe, and Joel loved her. He wanted to take the necklace, but wanted her permission. The last thing he wanted her to think was he was trying to take her stuff.

Suddenly, tears started to form in the corners of Bubbe's eyes as she blinked twice, and Joel knew she was in there. She may have figured out her beloved boy Ely had passed away. Joel realized talking about the necklace might have been a clue. He wasn't sure what to do since the family had decided not to tell her. On the other hand, Ely was her son and she had a right to know. They just never knew if she was all there, but *he* knew. This was his Bubbe. He knew she was sharp in her thinking most of the time, even if she could only blink yes and no. If she had stopped communicating since Ely stopped visiting, she was back today.

"Bubbe, I saw this same symbol on the box from Dad. Is this the necklace mentioned in your journal?" Joel asked. Bubbe blinked twice again. Tears streamed down her face.

Joel began to tear up along with her and went to hug her. He held her tight and told her Ely had died from heart problems and complications. He told her Ely had been sick and in the hospital for a while and they didn't want to upset her because she had been so ill and stopped communicating.

"I'm sorry, Bubbe," he said as he looked in her sweet eyes. He continued to hold her as she wept for her son.

"Can I have this necklace, Bubbe? I think I need it for something significant," Joel asked.

Bubbe blinked four times: "Yes! Yes!"

Joel realized she knew what was happening. She looked relieved and relaxed as certain peace came over her. Oh, how Joel wished Bubbe could talk and tell him more about her incredible story. Joel knew from her diary she had a relationship with the living Jesus.

"Bubbe, I know you know Jesus."

"Yes," two blinks and a softening of her eyes almost to a smile.

Joel's eyes continued to well up as he told her everything that had happened to him. He talked to her about her diary and how special it was to read about her life and adventures. Joel realized this was a miracle, to have all of her mind and attention for however long this lasted. She just listened for a long time while Joel told her everything. He told her he wished she could show him how to use the key and she blinked once. Joel found that odd; perhaps it was something he had to discover on his own.

When Joel had been there a couple of hours, Bubbe suddenly cleared her throat and moved her mouth and sound came from her throat.

"Can you talk?" Joel was thrilled that she might be able to speak.

"My father Caleb…" she said in a whisper.

"What about Caleb?" Joel asked.

"He was hiding artifacts from Hitler," she said. "Hitler knew a Jewish family had the box because he made a deal with the devil. He killed all those innocent people. He was looking for the artifacts to complete the deal. Caleb kept him from fulfilling the deal."

"How do you know that, Bubbe?" Joel asked.

"He sifted the entire Jewish race looking for the box and the key of David, but my father found the best hiding place for the box and I had the key," she said as huge tears rolled down her face.

"Who else knows about this, Bubbe?" Joel asked as he grabbed a tissue and wiped her tears.

She stopped talking and shut her eyes. Rachel was tired and started to drift off to sleep.

Joel decided he'd try again tomorrow. It was an easy conclusion to think Hitler was possessed, but he would have to press her for more details later. Joel was thrilled to hear her voice. On the other hand, the topic of their discussion was disturbing. The danger surrounding the box was becoming more and more clear to Joel. He had heard of people making a deal with the devil, but thought it was just a figure of speech. Bubbe believed her father Caleb had sacrificed himself to save the Jewish race. Joel told her while she was sleeping that he believed her story. He told her goodbye and that he loved her deeply. He kissed her forehead and left her room with the key of David.

On his way out, Joel stopped by and reported to the doctor that she had been talking and perhaps she was improving. The doctor said he must have been hearing things, because there was no way she could talk after the dementia and strokes she had experienced. Joel realized at that moment he had witnessed yet another miracle.

Demon Marq

She told him. How in the world was she able to talk? That irritating sphere angel was not present, but others were here. I had not noticed the cohort of healing angels hovering over Rachel or I would have reported it immediately for backup. I see she passed on the key to Joel. We are going to have to work overtime to secure it for our purposes now. I can't believe she told him Hitler was looking for the key. Very few people on earth have that information, and I have no idea how Rachel knew. I will have to report it, so we can sow some doubt amongst Joel's thoughts. Some fiery thoughts of unbelief and lies are in order. If this gets out, it's going to ruin everything. The fact that Joel knows this is unfortunate.

40

LIONS AND COFFEE AND THUGS, OH MY!

Joel could hardly wait to tell Hannah the news of his Bubbe speaking and that he had the key, but Hannah didn't answer her phone. Maybe she went to check on his mother, he thought.

Joel arrived home to a broken front door and deadbolt. Alarmed, he called Hannah's cell phone, and it rang in the apartment. Joel ran to the bedroom where it rang, and her purse was on the dresser. He looked around, and the box was gone—along with Hannah. Overcome with dread, Joel dialed 9-1-1 as panic rose in his throat. What could have happened to her and the box?

When the police arrived, Joel explained to them what he had touched and the only thing missing was his wife and a wooden box he had inherited when his father passed away. He explained there were old journals and scrolls in the box that belonged to his family. He told the officer Hannah was wearing a red sweater and blue jeans with brown leather boots. The police asked him hundreds of questions and had him call the family to see if she was there. Joel called his mother and Hannah's family. Nobody had seen or heard from her. While the police were still there, an unknown call came into Joel's phone on the caller ID. They directed Joel to answer the call. It was Hannah.

"Joel, they're looking for the key," she said.

"Hannah, thank God! Are you okay?" Joel asked.

"No, they're looking for me now. I got away. Joel, they know you have the key. I'm trying to stay hidden at the Starbucks on Astor Place. I borrowed a stranger's phone," she said.

"I'm on my way. Stay on the phone if you can. Who are they? Do you have any idea?" Joel asked.

"No, I can't stay on the phone. I'm going to hide in the bathroom and give this guy back his phone. I don't want them to see me and this place is all windows. I'll be in the ladies room with the door locked, waiting on you," she said.

"The police are here right now and will send their closest patrol car to your location. Any idea who they are?" Joel asked.

Joel wrote down the location for the police and they called it in on the radio.

"I don't know who they are," Hannah said. "I was just getting ready to walk out the door, and they pushed their way into the apartment. They asked me where the box was and just saw it on the coffee table and took it. Then they mentioned the key and decided to take me hostage until they could get the key. I told them the box was not locked and flipped open the lid, but they insisted on getting the key," Hannah reported.

Joel's heart was sinking. His dad had protected the family, and now that the box was Joel's responsibility, his family was at risk after only a week.

Hannah continued, "They had me in an alley about to take me into a building. I fought them off and started weaving in and out of people and ducked into the coffee shop. I can hear a siren right now. Oh my God, please hurry up."

"Stay on the phone with me, Hannah...Hannah?" Joel said.

"Um...the police just arrived, and your wife is in the ladies room, sir," Joel heard an unknown man's voice say on the other end of the phone.

"Is she okay?" Joel asked

"She seems to be quite panicked, and her nose is bleeding," he said.

"Thank you for letting her use your phone," Joel said.

Joel and the police headed for the door to make their way to Astor Place.

"Sure, she probably needs an ambulance too," the man said.

"She needs an ambulance," Joel told the police officer, who called it in immediately.

"Thank you. Any suspicious people around there?" Joel asked him.

"Nothing that I can see. She must have done a good job of dodging whoever beat her up," he said.

"Thank God for that; be right there," Joel replied. There was a growing fear in his heart, which reached up to his throat when he heard the guy say someone had beat her up. Hannah was a pistol in a fight, but she was still his wife.

"K," he replied and then hung up.

When they made it to the coffee shop, the ambulance was already there, and Hannah was giving a statement to the police.

Joel began to understand what may have happened to his father. He started to panic as he thought something much worse could have happened to his wife. He began to realize more and more this was a dangerous situation and someone was willing to do whatever it took to get the box and the key. It dawned on Joel that Hannah may have told the police more than she should. He ran to where she was giving a statement and gave her a huge hug.

"Oh, thank God, you're okay," Joel whispered in her ear as he held her tight. "We can't tell them everything, baby," he continued to whisper.

Hannah hugged him back tight. She was shaken but tough. She worked in security and knew how to handle herself. Hannah acknowledged Joel's lead on withholding information by nodding.

Joel knew they needed some protection if the people who took Hannah somehow knew he had retrieved the key from Bubbe. This situation had just become much more threatening than he could ever have imagined.

"Can I have one moment with my wife, please?" Joel asked the officer.

"Sure, but keep in mind every minute we wait the less likely we are to catch them," he said.

"Hannah, are you okay?" Joel asked as he held her out to get a good look at her bleeding nose. They hugged tightly again, and she put her head in the nape of his neck and melted into his arms. He held her close until she stopped shaking.

Joel spoke in her ear, "If the people who took you know I have the key, they're watching us right now. I think we're in grave danger and I'm not sure if we should tell the authorities."

Joel could feel the strength come back to Hannah as she realized the situation they were in. "We need some help, Joel. What are we supposed to do?"

Out of nowhere a massive scream sounded from across the street.

People were running and yelling "Lion! Lion!" Joel looked and sure enough, as big a lion as he had ever seen, with a large, glorious mane, was walking nonchalantly down the street. Stunned for a second, Joel grabbed Hannah by the hand and took off running alongside all the other people who were running for their lives.

"What is a lion doing right in the middle of New York?" Joel blurted as they ran as fast as they could away from the scene.

Hannah was beside herself but was keeping up with him; she had already been through enough today. "You were looking for an excuse to not tell the cops everything!" she yelled back.

The thought occurred to Joel this could be a stunt by the people who were after the key... or perhaps something from heaven ...or the zoo. Who knew, but it had given them a chance to get out of explaining anything else to the police.

What it didn't do was put Joel at ease. The only thing he could think to do was make their way to the Consulate office and see if they would protect them.

"Hannah, call work and tell them we're on our way," he told her as he handed her the phone.

"Good idea. We have the best security on the planet, and maybe we should talk to Levi. He's an expert on historic Israel," she said catching her breath as they hopped into a cab.

Hannah had blood on her shirt, and the taxi driver was hesitant. "It's just a nose bleed," she reassured him. She was already thinking fast on her feet. Joel loved that.

"What exactly did they do to you?" Joel asked her in a whisper.

"They mostly just dragged me with them once they saw the box. One hit my nose with his elbow when I was trying to escape. You should have seen the other guy's face," she said joking. "Honestly, the thugs didn't seem like real criminals. It was like this was the first time they'd ever done anything like this. They were New Yorkers, and I would almost say they were Jewish if you can believe that?"

"Why and how did they know I had the box and the key?" Joel asked quietly.

"They had to have been watching your father and Bubbe," Hannah said.

She was right, Joel thought.

Angel Harper

Okay, that was close. I was just hanging around the box and minding my own business when these two guys burst through Joel's door. They startled me. I immediately reported to the Almighty what was happening, and the local angelic hosts were dispatched to help Hannah. Joel had left, but the box was with Hannah, so I am glad I stayed put. Anyway, that powerful little woman Hannah knows how to brawl. She landed some punches on those guys with a little help from my friends. I have to admit I was a bit confused when she ran into Starbucks. But then again, Americans love their coffee and I thought about grabbing a cake pop for myself. It was a good move, so she could call Joel and hide. Meanwhile, the Lion was my idea. I was so excited when Jesus said yes. I mean, it's not often that the Lion of the tribe of Judah walks down a New York City street. However, He created enough of a distraction to help them escape. I love it when I have an idea, and the Almighty likes it, too. He loves to work with our creativity.

41

LEVI

When they arrived at the Consulate office, Hannah made her way to her office. Her nose had stopped bleeding, but it was evident she had been through something, and the security guard greeted her with concern. "You okay, Hannah?"

"Yeah, just a nose bleed," she replied.

He looked at Joel who had to put on his "yep, just a nose bleed" face in agreement.

Hannah barely got herself cleaned up before she hopped into action. This woman was more than a helper; she was Joel's exact opposite. What Joel lacked, she had. She moved into combat mode fast. Joel was grateful for her.

Out of nowhere, Joel had second thoughts about talking to Levi.

"Hannah, are you sure we should pull Levi into this?" Joel piped up.

She stopped dialing the phone for a moment. "We have to come up with something fast, honey. These people just tried to kidnap me."

"I know. It's just that my father kept me safe all those years by not doing anything. Now, I have the box, and our lives are in peril. Anyone else brought into this will be put in jeopardy as well. Levi is going to be helpful from the historical aspect, yes, and he's trustworthy—but are we willing to put him at risk?" Joel asked

"Levi is the closest thing we have to an expert and has been a great friend. Not to mention he is heavily involved in investigations of security situations here and in Israel. If anyone could help us sniff out who took the box, it would be him. I thought our goal was to get the box back? Plus, he would be offended if I didn't go to him first. He'll be able to help with the ins and outs of dealing with Israel as well, if we decide to go that direction," she said.

Joel hesitated for a moment to think but couldn't come up with a better plan. So, she called Levi.

Levi was a squirrely looking guy. He suffered from male pattern baldness and his hair was jet black, so it was noticeable. He and Hannah had worked together a long time and had helped each other out of some tight situations over the years. Joel had never been a big fan of Levi's, because he got to spend more time with Hannah than Joel did when you added up all the late-night security detail operations they had participated in over the years.

Levi was a few blocks away at the U.N. but said he would be back in about twenty minutes. That gave Hannah and Joel a chance to discuss what had just happened.

"If they were watching Bubbe and my father, they have been watching us, too," Joel told Hannah.

"Yeah, I've been thinking about that. I wonder to what extent. I mean, they could have our phones, our homes, and our offices..." Hannah stopped talking and motioned to Joel while pointing around her office.

She started looking around the room for bugs. "No, that's impossible. This building is secure," she said as she shook her head no and pointed around the room while she mouthed, "*Look for a bug.*"

They started combing the office for bugging devices under lamps and her desk. Hannah silently mouthed to Joel, "*Say something,*" while gesturing with her hand in a circular motion.

"Yeah, well, you *are* part of the security team, so you should know," Joel said with a lost look on his face.

"For sure," she said as she kept looking around and then shook her head no.

She froze as Levi opened the door to her office. "Hey, Levi," she said, "I just dropped my pen. Ah, there it is," she said as she stood up.

They had a big problem. They didn't know if people were listening and Hannah had a suspicious look on her face.

"What is the problem, Han?" Levi asked. "Hey, Joel, so sorry to hear about your father," he said as he extended a hand and gave him the awkward pat on the back, a fake man-hug.

"Aw, thanks," Joel said as he accepted Levi's acknowledgment of his loss. Joel didn't know Levi well, other than what Hannah had told him over the years. Levi's favorite topic was the history of Israel. Joel would see him at various office holiday functions, but Hannah worked with him day in and day out.

"Hey, Levi, sit down. We have a little problem here," Hannah said as she went to sit at her desk.

Joel was not sure how his wife was planning on not sharing the details with Levi, yet getting his help—this would be interesting. Joel tried to come up with a plan and blurted, "I got an inheritance we think might belong in a museum." Joel decided if they just approach this as an old heirloom box and not bring the key into the discussion, perhaps Levi would give them the needed insight without knowing the whole story.

Hannah caught on quickly to where Joel was going with this, and she interjected, "Yeah, it's an ancient box. We think it may be from first century Jerusalem."

"Really?" Levi said.

Joel noticed Levi seemed a bit unsurprised, for someone who loved historical Israel. Suddenly he felt something put an unseen hand on his head. Joel looked up but saw nothing. He realized the angel was there; he could feel his presence. At that moment he began wondering where the angel had been when Hannah was taken, and he thought about how angels guarding the box had failed. The box was gone, and Joel had no idea how to track it down.

"So, where is this box?" Levi asked.

Hannah looked at Joel again. He could see she wanted to tell Levi. Joel decided they were already too far into this conversation to back out at this point. People were probably monitoring their conversation and Heaven, or at least Harper, was watching. Joel nodded in agreement at Hannah to go ahead and tell him.

"The box was stolen from our house this morning by a couple of Jewish-looking men," Hannah said.

"I think they might have been the two guys I saw at my father's funeral," Joel said out loud as it had just dawned on him. "They have probably been watching us," Joel said.

"Really?" Levi said, again unsurprised. The guy was a bad actor.

It suddenly dawned on Joel why the angel was warning him—he was guarding the box because it was somewhere here on the premises, or somebody here knew where it was.

Joel looked at Hannah and hoped she could see from the look on his face what he was thinking, but of course, she probably didn't feel the angel's presence. One thing Joel knew was that the angel guarded the box, so it must be close. Levi knew something.

"Yeah, it is an ancient artifact that will be one of the most surprising discoveries since the Dead Sea Scrolls," Joel said, laying it all out there. *Like taking a Band-Aid off*, he thought. Just do it quickly, because the anticipation of Levi's reaction was gnawing at Joel.

Hannah gave in to the fact that they were going to have to tell the whole tale—bug or no bug.

When Joel referred to the box as an artifact, he noticed Levi lean back as if someone or something had tried to punch him in the face. A strange look came unexpectedly over his face—it was disgust. Levi was seething. Fear started to rise in Joel, but he pushed it away as he realized this guy knew something about the box, enough for Joel's comment to make him angry.

"How would you know that?" Levi asked, trying to quell his frothing anger upon hearing it referred to as an artifact.

"Let's just say what is in the box is just as explosive as the box itself. So where is the box, Levi?" Joel asked through clenched teeth. Joel had a hunch and decided to take a chance he was right by confronting Levi.

Hannah gave Joel a look that said, "*What are you doing?*"

Levi shrugged his shoulders, "Why are you asking me?" He quickly erased the disgust from his face as it morphed into another bad acting scene from a B flick. "Hannah, you called me for help and your husband here is accusing me of something?"

"Levi, I'm sorry. I'm not sure what's wrong with Joel." She shot Joel a look.

"You know something, Levi. Where is the box?" Joel stood up in front of Levi and leaned on Hannah's desk. Joel wanted Levi to look him right in the eyes when he lied.

"I have it in a safe place," he said, looking up and down Joel's clothing. Joel knew he was trying to spot the location of the key, which was in Joel's front jean pocket.

"Where is the key?" Levi asked as he raised his eyebrows, smirking.

"What key?" Joel said as he thrust Levi's chair back with his foot. He watched as Levi toppled backward to the floor, trying to steady himself with one hand and reaching for his gun with the other. Joel put his foot down hard on Levi's hand as he was going for the gun. Hannah rushed over to help Joel.

"Hannah, run, get out of here!" Joel yelled.

"No, Joel! What is going on? Levi, what is happening?" She could not comprehend this guy was crooked.

"He is involved in your kidnapping, and he knows where my box is. What is the deal with the box, Levi?

It belongs to my family. What is your problem with it?" Joel demanded an answer as he added his weight to Levi's hand pinned to the floor.

"I know what's in the box," Levi said, seething again. "I was assigned to keep an eye out for signs the box was passed on to you. I knew you had it when your father passed away."

"How?" Hannah asked.

"Joel's family has been on the watch list since the eighties when an anonymous person who saw the documents brought a copy here to the Consulate office and gave it to the receptionist. It was a woman who must have had access to it through your father," Levi said. "Since your dad never did anything with the documents, we just watched him and figured we could secure it from you once he passed away. We decided to go ahead and get it just in case you decided to do something stupid like exposing the documents."

"Leona, the translator…" Joel said looking at Hannah.

"Why would the documents put us on a watch list?" Hannah asked.

"Oh, come on, Joel just said it was as important as the Dead Sea Scrolls. You know why. I read the translation, and I know if the original person pushing the story of the death of Jesus came out and said Jesus was the Messiah it would cause mayhem in Jewish communities all over the world. We are just trying to protect our communities. Jesus could not have been the Messiah. One of the main things the Messiah will do, according to our belief, is rebuild the Third Temple. Jesus can't do that because he is dead. We just want to keep the box safe, and we're going to have to ask you to give up the key as well." Levi said.

Joel mustered up courage and scrambled to get the gun—successfully. He pointed it directly at Levi.

"How dare you come after my family and tell me what to do with my inheritance! Where is the box, Levi?" Joel screamed.

"Joel, you can't have it back," Levi replied.

"It seems to me I am the one with the gun. You are acting just like Annas. The Jewish leaders in the community are at risk of giving up all their power, so they're going to try to squelch truth. You want them to continue believing the only way to salvation is through the Day of Atonement?" Joel said. "Hannah, wasn't there a group of people here to talk about rebuilding a Third Temple? By the way," he said, looking Levi in the eyes. "Jesus is not dead." Joel realized what he was saying. He was defending Jesus.

"Let's all calm down. Yes, that rabbi said they had proof the exact location of the Holy of Holies was between the Dome of the Rock and the Church of the Sepulcher and they wanted to rebuild the Third Temple in that spot," Hannah filled in the details.

"Lies, lies, lies; they are making all of that up. They have no real proof. Besides, they need the rest of the things from the First and Second Temple to rebuild the Third Temple...the Ark of the Covenant being one of them. But also, other things that were taken and hidden long before Titus sacked the Second Temple," Levi spouted.

"Yes, the list Annas mentioned in his journal," Joel said.

"Exactly," Levi said, "and nobody knows where the list is, so it doesn't matter if they get approval to rebuild the Third Temple anyway. It will do no good," Levi said.

"You are going to call the thugs who took my box and get it back for me. And if you refuse, I am going to call the major news stations and get the story of Annas's box out to the public. Hannah, call the main person in charge of the group who wants to rebuild the Third Temple. Levi, where is your mobile phone? Call the thugs who hurt my wife, now. Hannah, also grab the numbers to your contacts at ABC, NBC, CBS, CNN, FOX, and MSNBC," Joel directed.

Levi moved at a snail's pace as he got up off the floor. He pulled his phone from his back pocket and handed it to Joel.

"From what I recall, the Ark of the Covenant was not there during the Second Temple, so they don't need it for a Third Temple either," Joel heard himself say, not knowing what he was talking about, but speaking with authority for some reason. This comment came from an unknown source as if being led by the Holy Spirit.

"Joel, let's think this through," Hannah said.

"No, I get it, honey. There is more information to be recovered and your friend Levi here knows what it is. Why else would they want the key? Joel asked.

"I am not telling you anything else. If your father didn't tell you, that's your problem." Levi was using hurtful words as a weapon, hoping Joel was sensitive about his relationship with his father, as most men are.

That was enough to silence Joel—his father was a sacred topic. Joel could figure this out without Levi.

"Besides, I'm not calling anyone. You're bluffing," Levi continued.

Hannah was on her computer pulling up her list of contacts at all the news stations. She had personal friends at each of the outlets she could reach, as she worked with all of them for all things Israel. The whole planet had always had their eye on Israel.

"Here are my contacts' mobile numbers," she said as she pulled the list off the printer. "I also have my press release service and a massive email list that will hit every major website and news outlet interested in Israeli news. I could send information to that list too if you prefer?" she said with a sideways smile at Levi.

"Okay, okay I'll call them," as he took his phone back

from Joel and started thumbing through his address book on his phone. "Hannah, your husband is a Christian, did you know that?" He was trying to start trouble.

Joel looked at Hannah for her reaction; Levi wanted to get her to rethink her position. Joel had rapidly changed his position on Jesus but did not realize it until a minute earlier when he found himself saying Jesus was alive. She had not had the same experience Joel did in the throne room. Joel knew Jesus was alive. Joel told her everything but wondered how she was going to react now.

"He is planning on single-handedly tearing your religion apart piece by piece," Levi continued, "not only for you, but there will be a crisis of faith for millions of Jewish people if this information gets out. Hannah, I thought we were friends. We're on the same side here," he pleaded.

"Levi, Joel is a smart, logical man. He is my husband. I don't understand everything he has been through over the last couple of weeks, but I trust him, and he believes the Jewish people can think for themselves," Hannah replied. "I don't have all the information yet, but I support him. You, on the other hand, have been lying to me since the day we met, which tells me your character is questionable."

Joel had won her over with his character.

42

FLIGHT TO ISRAEL

After Levi dialed the number, Joel grabbed the phone from him. The voice on the other end answered and said, "Hey, did you secure the key?"

"Not yet," Joel said quickly, hoping the person would think he was Levi.

"Well, hurry up, we're on our way to the airport now. The plane leaves in three hours," the raspy voice on the other end of the line said.

"I'm on it," Joel said and hung up.

"Where are they going, Levi?" Joel asked him as he put the gun to the man's face.

"You figure it out, traitor. I am done sharing information with you," Levi said, spitting in Joel's face. Joel wiped it off and looked over at Hannah.

"Hannah, get on the airport websites and figure out what planes are leaving a few hours from now and where they are going. I guess we're going on a trip." Joel's thoughts went toward Israel. "My guess is Israel. See if any flights are leaving for Tel Aviv in the next few hours from either airport."

Hannah verified a flight leaving for Israel from JFK in exactly three hours.

"Joel, the group who brought the Third Temple idea to the U.N. are back in Israel already, so that will work out nicely if they're taking the box to Israel," Hannah said.

"I hope we can get to it. If not, maybe that group can help us get it back," Joel replied.

"It's a possibility," Hannah said, looking at Levi for his reaction. Levi looked away and didn't say a word.

They were going to Israel and now had to decide what to do with Levi. He wasn't going to give them any more information without torture, which was not a viable option. So, they decided to bring him with them to the apartment to collect their passports and a few things.

Hannah called a limousine service to pick them up, as they could not take the chance of Levi blurting to a cab driver to call the police.

Once the limo arrived, they secured Levi in the back seat and had to figure out how to get to the airport—with or without him. When they got to the apartment all three of them went upstairs.

Joel could tell Levi was still looking for the key as they walked into the apartment. Joel thought Levi figured he could get away from them whenever he wanted.

Joel was right. Levi was going along with them until he could come up with the key or a better plan for getting the gun. Levi knew Joel wasn't a threatening person, and also noticed he was not efficient with a weapon either.

Hannah was sure she could identify the guys on the plane by calling their mobile phone again from Levi's phone once they got on the aircraft. They would be watching for Levi but would also recognize Hannah when she boarded the plane. Joel also knew it would be quite dangerous. Since none of them could bring a gun on board, there could be a scuffle on the plane.

Maybe a U.S. marshal on the plane would help us, Joel thought. The outcomes of this endeavor were endless and starting to boggle his mind.

Joel wondered where Harper was now—he hoped on the airplane guarding the box or maybe even causing trouble for the criminals who took it and were probably on their way to the airport.

Joel told Levi to have a seat while Hannah went to the bedroom to grab a few things. Joel's suitcase was already packed, from being at his mother's house, so he just threw a few things into a backpack. He was thankful she had washed all his clothes, so he was ready to go.

Before Joel knew what was happening, Levi kicked over the coffee table, and as Joel went to grab it, Levi went for the gun. Joel scrambled toward Levi, fighting to get it away from him. Levi kneed Joel hard in the stomach. Joel doubled over, the wind knocked out of him, as the gun fell out of his hand and skidded across the floor. Levi lunged, snatched up the gun, and pointed it steadily at Joel, who was still trying to catch his breath.

"Give me the key, Joel," he said flatly.

Joel shook his head no. He could not talk.

"Give me the key," Levi's voice rose in intensity as he moved the gun close to Joel's face.

Joel shut his eyes tightly and kept shaking his head no as he still could not breathe. A gunshot rang out, and Joel thought he would be dead in an instant. When he opened his eyes, Hannah had shot Levi in the back of his thigh, and Levi instinctively grabbed his leg, dropping the gun.

"You shot me!" Levi yelled in disbelief.

"You had a gun to my husband's head. What did you expect?" Hannah said, defending her right to bear arms.

Joel grabbed the gun back and pointed it at Levi. His adrenaline was running high, making his hands shake. Hannah grabbed a towel from the kitchen to apply pressure to Levi's wound.

"It's a clean shot. The bullet went straight through. You'll live," Hannah said while she applied pressure to his leg and grabbed a scarf from a desk drawer.

Levi wailed in pain when she touched it and looked down at his leg in disbelief.

"Grab him some bourbon," Hannah said.

Joel jumped to attention; Hannah seemed to have a plan. He opened the liquor cabinet, grabbed a bottle of bourbon, and handed it to Levi. He drank it like water while moaning in agony. Joel wondered if anyone would report the sound of the gunshot to the police. Then he decided if the police show up he'd just say the kidnappers came back and they defended themselves.

Hannah wrapped up the wound with the scarf and Levi kept on drinking. He was going to be quite drunk soon if he kept it up.

"What're you going to do with me?" Levi asked once he stopped guzzling.

"We're going to drop you off at the medical clinic on the way to the airport. They can give you pain medicine and get you to the hospital," Hannah said.

It was a good plan, as the hospital would have cameras everywhere and with Levi a bit drunk, maybe no one would listen to him until he sobered up. Joel offered him more bourbon at the thought. Levi grabbed the bottle and took another swig

"Let's go," Hannah said as she pointed the gun toward Levi.

"How am I supposed to walk on this?" he asked.

Joel propped him up and, and they made their way down the elevator and into the limousine. The driver was a bit suspicious, but Hannah gave him some excuse, and he bought it as Joel shoved Levi into the back seat.

By the time they arrived at the busy medical clinic, the liquor had kicked in and Levi was about to pass out. Joel and Hannah helped him into the lobby and grabbed the paperwork from the receptionist. They filled out as many documents as they could for him, then left him there leaning against the wall in a chair with his paperwork.

People were eyeing them, wondering what was going on, but Hannah had stopped the bleeding before they left the apartment and had cleaned and wrapped Levi's leg. According to Hannah, all he needed were some stitches and antibiotics to prevent infection.

Joel and Hannah hopped back into the limo and headed to the airport.

"Not a bad plan, but we'll have to see how it works out," Joel said.

"I feel awful shooting him like that, but he had a gun to your head! What choice did I have?" she asked.

"Thank you for saving my life." Joel said as he hugged her tight. "I just hope he will be okay."

"He'll be fine. He has no phone and is in no shape to call the police. The people at the clinic might call the cops, but Levi drank a lot of bourbon. He won't be coherent enough to pull himself together to come after us or even call anyone to come after us—I hope," she said hesitantly.

"What did you tell the driver?" Joel asked.

"I told him Levi fell and broke a mug and a piece of it cut his thigh pretty deep, so we needed to get him medical help."

"Good one. He seems to have bought it," Joel said as his mind wandered to the airport. "We have to get the box back and figure out how this key works," he said, pulling it out of his pocket to show Hannah.

"Wow, that's a key?" she said, taking it from his hand. "I remember seeing Bubbe wearing this, but I thought it was just a cool necklace with a contemporary design," Hannah said.

"I wish I would have asked her more questions about it sooner while she was more in her right mind. The story she just told me has me a bit concerned for our safety," Joel said.

"What're you talking about? Did she talk to you?" Joel had forgotten Hannah did not know the rest of the story Bubbe told him.

Joel told Hannah what Bubbe had said about Hitler pillaging Assisi, looking for the box and the key together.

"They were never together because Bubbe didn't get the key until after they were in Bologna, according to her diary. Plus, if Hitler was willing to pillage the entire Jew-ish population looking for it, I could only imagine who is after it now. It's a bit stressful, don't you think?" Joel said to Hannah.

"Uh, you think?" she said with a deep sigh. "What the heck have we gotten ourselves into here?

Hannah's mind was going a million miles an hour. She could barely stop the flood of possible scenarios of what might happen to them from running through her head.

Joel could see she was getting anxious and started to get knots in his own stomach thinking about it. Their lives were in danger, and they were walking onto the airplane without a plan. It was exciting, yet nerve-racking at the same time. Joel put his arm around Hannah in hopes it would help calm them both.

Joel gathered his thoughts enough to call his mother to check on her before they got to the airport. He wanted to tell her what was happening but knew he could be dealing with a bugged mobile line too, so he just called her and acted as if nothing had happened.

Joel was a better actor than Levi; he had to be because their lives depended on it. She still sounded sad, but Joel made it short and told her he loved her and said goodbye before she picked up on any problems in his voice.

They had reached the airport and the driver dropped them off at the terminal. By the time they checked into their flight, they only had about forty-five minutes to get through security and on the flight.

"We need to keep an eye out for anything suspicious," Joel told Hannah. "Watch for people watching us."

They moved through the airport with great ease, eyeballing every person within view. On their way to the boarding gate, rather than walking down the main concourse, they decided to weave their way through seats from gate to gate to see if Hannah could recognize the two thieves from a distance. The plane started boarding, and people began to line up. They stayed put a couple of gates away, watching.

"Who knows what would happen if they saw us and not Levi?" Joel said. "They must be curious at this point and looking for Levi. We should have considered disguises," he told Hannah.

She nodded her head but did not take her eyes off the people in line.

"I see them!" she whispered urgently, reminding Joel a little bit of an undercover detective. "Quick—face the other way. They're sitting watching the line too and every person who walks up." Hannah turned around to hide herself from the gaze of her unknown enemies. Then she laid her head on Joel's shoulder and whispered into his ear, "What's our plan?"

Unfortunately, he did not have one. He decided to

pray. He put his other arm around Hannah and whispered back in her ear, "Lord, hide us."

His heart was racing, and his whole body felt the heightened sense of danger. He held Hannah in his arms. She relaxed a bit after he prayed. Prayer just seemed like the right thing to do, and then he whispered to his wife, "No matter what, I love you."

She hugged him back and whispered, "I love you too."

Hannah turned to look at the line again; it was close to ending. The thugs had not seen them and stood, mission incomplete, at the end of the line. The flight attendant had just announced the final boarding call as the two men entered the jetway.

Joel and Hannah hustled to the desk before they announced their names over the loud speaker. Joel told her to rustle through her purse for the boarding passes to allow the two men time to get their seats. If they were going to see them, he wanted it to be after they were buckled in and the door to the plane already closed.

Joel wanted to ask the flight attendant if there was a U.S. marshal on board, but he thought it might set off a red flag, so he just kept quiet. They had no idea what lay ahead as they walked down the jetway to board the plane. They had no plan and knew the men would recognize Hannah as they walked down the aisle.

Joel's mind was saying, *This is crazy, just call the*

authorities, but his heart was saying, *Peace, be brave and courageous*. Joel decided to listen to his heart.

As they boarded the plane, Hannah spotted the two men in first class, pointing them out to Joel. They'd been watching the door intently, waiting on Levi. The minute they spotted Hannah, Joel saw their faces change. *If looks could kill*, Joel thought and shot the same look back at them straight in the eyes. He decided he was going to let the courage in his heart shine on his face. It may have been a cheap poker move, but the guys were not going to intimidate Joel. When they saw his face, Joel recognized fear in their eyes. Hannah and Joel being there meant Levi was out of the picture, and the two had likely now bitten off more than they could chew. At least Joel hoped that was what they were thinking.

Joel glanced at the compartment above their heads and wondered if his box was there. They knew what he was thinking. Joel and Hannah kept walking to their seats in coach. They would have to figure out how this was all going to work out in the air. It was dicey at best. The plane door was shut behind them immediately. Now they had ten hours and twenty minutes to figure out a plan for once they hit Israel. Joel was sure none of them were going to sleep on the flight. The good news was there were no weapons on board, so they were relatively safe for now.

"They saw us," Hannah said after they got settled.

"I know. I'm sure they think we killed Levi or something like that. They were surprised. I detected some fear. How about you?" Joel asked.

"Yeah, I saw that—it was unexpected. I wonder why?" she replied.

"Not sure. Maybe it scared them that you got away and we were brave enough to come here and confront them," Joel said.

"Just keep that necklace hidden," Hannah told him.

"It's in my front pocket," Joel said as he patted his chest. "Believe me, they will not be getting to it. Do you think someone will be waiting for us in Tel Aviv?" Joel asked, already knowing the answer.

"Probably...we are talking Israel here. It's a good thing I know the prime minister. The only problem is, we don't know what side of the issue he's on. Levi knows the prime minister too. It's so hard to figure out who Levi may be working for and why," Hannah said.

The thoughts were maddening as they tried to hash out a plan to get the box away from the two men and out of the airport. Nothing seemed plausible. Then it occurred to them—Hannah could use her security status to try to get the box. They decided to enlist a flight attendant's help. Hannah made her way to the back of the plane to use the restroom and to talk to the flight attendant and explain something of high value was on the aircraft that belonged to Israel. Hannah was part of the security team on board to guard the article. The two gentlemen in the front of the plane were transporting it, and Hannah was security. She showed the attendant her identification badge from the Consulate office. Hannah convinced the attendant to allow her to move to the now empty seat Levi would have occupied in first class.

Once Hannah was up there, she looked for an opportunity to grab the box, knowing it was probably in the overhead storage. They knew they could not have a gun on board and with the general public around, what could they do?

Joel remained in coach and still recognized the peace that had calmed him earlier. He thought about the angel guarding the box and decided to see if he could get some details somehow from the Holy Spirit. Joel had never actually tried to have a conversation with God directly.

Since he had a long flight ahead of him, Joel began to think on everything he remembered about God and thought of the story he had heard once about how God spoke to everyone after they all escaped from Egypt. Then they had all cried and said, "Moses, you talk to him," because they were afraid. After Joel's experience with Jesus, he was no longer afraid. He felt as if he could talk to Jesus face-to-face. He had called out to Jesus earlier that day and at that moment knew something within him had changed. He had heard talk of a personal relationship with Jesus by Christians. He recalled a Christian friend speaking to Jesus as if he was just someone in the room. Joel thought he should try it now.

"So, Jesus, where is this angel Harper you assigned to the box?" Joel whispered.

The noise of the airplane drowned out the sound of his voice, so he felt a little bit more comfortable just speaking out a prayer. Still, he felt a bit crazy to ask out loud and hoped the people around him didn't think he was talking to them. Just then Joel detected an unusual sound rising above the airplane's noise—it was sweet, the sound of many voices singing as one, sustaining a single clear note in mid-air. It was the same note he had heard in the throne room. He felt a gentle tap on his right shoulder and looked over but did not see anything. Calmed and moved by the supernatural sound and touch, he wanted to know more and was filled with courage and peace all at the same time. Joel knew heaven was watching and singing. It occurred to him that perhaps all of heaven knew the outcome of this adventure. Being outside of time put everything in perspective for him and he longed to experience that again. Joel was not afraid of what was going to happen here, as he knew he was being protected.

Hannah tapped him on the head and said, "Hey, sleepy head, I'm glad to see someone is getting some sleep."

"I am so sorry. I prayed for you and then fell asleep. I know we are protected, so we don't need to worry. What is happening up there?" Joel wondered.

Hannah looked at him confused and thought *did he really say that?* She paused for a split second unsure what to say about him mentioning prayer and continued on with her report.

"They noticed me move up there, of course, and were agitated but played it cool. Then one actually turned around and asked me about Levi. I calmly explained to them that Levi was fine and that they were going to give us the box back. I explained the Israeli police were contacted before we left and would be waiting for them as they got off the plane. I also told them to go ahead and give me the box back. They didn't seem to believe me so now it's a game of chicken."

Hannah's guts and confidence are incredible, Joel thought.

"Wow, great job, Han," Joel said.

"Thanks. But my eyes are so heavy. I decided to stretch a bit and come back and check on you. I'm glad you're getting some rest. I can barely keep my eyes open, and the two of them seem to be taking turns sleeping." Hannah said, hinting for Joel to take a turn as she sat down next to him.

"Oh, Han, go ahead and stay here and sleep. If they're going to give you the box, it's not going to be until we get off this plane. You should stay back here until we're ready to land. You could get a good four hours in," Joel said as he rubbed her shoulders and put his coat under her head for a pillow.

"Good point," she said as she drifted off to sleep.

Joel laid his head against the pillow and drifted off to sleep as well. Peace like a blanket fell over them once again. Harper covered them with a heavenly blanket.

43

LANDING IN TEL AVIV

They woke suddenly to the captain on the loud speaker.

"Ladies and gentlemen, we are starting our final descent into Tel Aviv. The weather is bright and sunny, and we should be on the ground in twenty minutes."

Hannah jumped up and ran to her seat in the front of the plane. Their plan was that as soon as they landed and were cleared to use their mobile phones, Joel was to call Hannah's contact in Israel to see if he could get some help at the airport to hold the two men. It was the only plan they could come up with.

"They might have time to send someone to the airport to help us. We have to clear security and Customs, which will take some time. I'm not even sure they'll help us, but we have to try," Hannah had explained before she darted to the front of the plane.

Joel was not sure how Hannah was planning on detaining them but had no better ideas.

The plane came in for a landing and Joel got on the phone and called Hannah's friend, Nathan.

Nathan was part of the security team in Israel for the prime minister. Joel was unsure what to say to get him to help without actually telling the whole story. Joel called Nathan's number as soon he noticed phone service on his cell. Nathan answered the phone, "Shalom."

"Nathan, this is Joel. Hannah Cohen's husband from the United States."

"Hannah Cohen, yes. How can I help you, Joel?" He sounded confused, and with good reason.

"Nathan, Hannah and I are on a flight that just landed at Ben Gurion Airport. I know this is an unusual request, but we need some assistance with a couple of criminals who have stolen a valuable family heirloom. These two guys are on this plane with us. They broke into our apartment in New York City and kidnapped Hannah. She managed to get away, but we tracked them to this flight and were able to secure seats, and we are just landing. Is there any way you could send someone to the airport to arrest the two men as they disembark, or can you assist us in any way?" Joel asked.

The other end of the phone was quiet, and then finally a response, "Um, I am with the prime minister at the moment. However, I could contact security at the airport for you and see if they would assist. They are all former Israeli military and quick to respond if contacted by the office of the prime minister. I'm not sure what I would tell them to do... Has the United States sent a request for us to detain them?" he asked.

"No, I contacted the police in the States, but they lost track of them. Hannah and I happened to figure out they were on this flight and we were able to follow them," Joel replied.

"That sounds dangerous. I will contact security for you, but I have no idea how they will handle it. Can you text me a picture of them? We would also need to hear from the U.S. State Department to detain anyone at the airport. What is the flight number?" he said.

"Flight number 3-3-3-5, and like I said, we just landed," Joel said.

"Flight 3-3-3-5, got it. I will make a call. I'll be back in contact on this number," Nathan said and hung up.

As soon as the seatbelt light turned off, Joel ran up the center aisle to first class where Hannah was and took a picture of the two men with his phone; he was sure now these were the men at his father's gravesite. Both had bags with them, but only one had a bag big enough to hold Joel's box. Joel tried to grab it from him, and the stranger scuffled, trying to hit Joel. The other passengers were dumbfounded as the two men tried to get at Joel with

Hannah in the middle.

Behind Hannah, and seeing what had just erupted, stood the flight attendant who had helped Hannah earlier. Before the flight attendant could react, Hannah looked at Joel and said, "Let him carry it." Then Hannah turned to the flight attendant and said, "They're so competitive about who gets to carry it onto Israeli soil." Then back toward the men, "You guys behave!" She was quick-witted.

The only problem, as far as Hannah and Joel could tell, was that the men would be some of the first ones to disembark and could make a run for it as soon as they were off the plane. As the cabin door opened, people began filtering out of the aircraft. Hannah and Joel followed very closely as the two men beat them off the plane and to Joel's surprise, started sprinting up the jetway. Joel didn't understand - they had been the ones chasing Hannah in New York and Joel was not all that threatening.

"I got ahold of Nathan," Joel said to Hannah as they exited the jet, running and trying their best to tail the two men while they looked around for security.

The two men darted toward the doors to Customs, with Joel and Hannah following close behind. Joel was sure they were trying to figure out how to get through Customs without him and his wife making a scene. When they arrived at Immigration, the two thieves were able to go through the shorter Israeli line. Joel and Hannah looked at each other—they were not expecting that.

The two men were not from the U.S., but instead were citizens of Israel. The queue was set up to herd all other citizens through a long line. All Joel and Hannah could do was let them get away and hope for another opportunity.

It occurred to Joel he had not texted Nathan a picture of the two men.

"What did Nathan say?" Hannah asked.

"He requested the flight number and that I text a photo—that was about it," Joel said as he looked down at his phone to text the picture. "It didn't occur to me they were Israeli citizens."

"I know," she said with a confused look on her face. "Maybe they'll stop them at Customs, and we'll catch up with them. They have to show the box in Customs—maybe someone will get suspicious."

It was a long shot. Hannah and Joel made their way to Immigration. The officer saw Hannah's passport and called over his supervisor. The man approached and asked Hannah and Joel to come with him.

"Hannah, welcome to Israel. I am Amir, the supervisor. I got a phone call from the prime minister's office to help you?" he asked it as a question, rather than a statement. The man had a thick accent.

"Thank you. This is my husband, Joel. The two suspects are citizens and went through the other line quickly. Were you able to stop them at Customs?"

"I am sorry, Hannah. We did not have enough information about who we were looking for. Nathan asked me to find you to get the details and we would see if we could find them. If they are citizens, they may have already left the airport. Do you have names?"

"No, no names." she said, frustrated.

"Can you give me a description?" he asked.

"One is about five-foot-eight, with short dark brown hair and brown eyes, wearing a white shirt and jeans with a brown leather jacket. The other is a couple of inches taller, about five-ten, also with short dark brown hair and brown eyes, and wearing a navy jacket and jeans. I did not notice any tattoos or anything like that, but they spoke perfect American English, so I thought they were U.S. citizens. I was surprised when they went through the Israeli citizen line," she said.

Joel held up his phone for them to see the picture. "They stole a family heirloom that has been in my family for generations," added Joel. "It's an old rustic box that looks like a small trunk or chest about two feet by one foot," Joel said as he motioned the size of the box with his hands.

"They could have dual citizenship. What would be their height in metric?" the officer asked as he got on the phone and called the Customs area.

Joel wished at that moment he had paid attention in

science class, as Hannah looked at the conversion app on her phone. "1.524 meters?" she said.

"He is not very long, is he?" Amir said.

Hannah and Joel chuckled to each other at the accent and the misuse of the word long instead of tall. Joel used his hand to motion about how tall in comparison to them the two men were, and the officer notified Customs what they were looking for with the box.

"They will search the bags of anyone who meets your description," he said. "Come with me, and perhaps you can identify them if they haven't made it through the lines yet."

Joel and Hannah followed him but noticed the other people filtering through were people from the back of their same flight. The two men were long gone. Joel and Hannah felt dejected.

"I think they are gone," Joel said. "These people were sitting back by me, so they had to be ahead of them."

Hannah and Joel both watched as everyone else filtered through the lines. The perpetrators were not there. They had hoped they could get some more information about the men, like names and details of anyone on the flight, but privacy laws would make that impossible. They decided to leave to find a hotel and regroup.

"Nathan said he would call us," Joel told Hannah.

"Those men will find us—remember, they still haven't

gotten what they wanted. We have the key. I'm not sure why they were running scared anyway. It's not like we are threatening," she said. "They must have had a reason to believe we had the upper hand here, but as citizens of Israel they knew they would get through immigration faster than us."

"They know you work with security forces here. So, they were probably sure you could pull some strings and stop them at the airport," Joel guessed.

"They may be watching us anyway and following us, so we need to be alert. Let's try to get to a more private location but one that is still somewhat public, so we can see if they're watching us," Hannah suggested.

Joel and Hannah contacted the closest airport hotel and jumped on the shuttle. It was empty except for them and the driver. As soon as the shuttle took off, they noticed a car start to follow them from the airport. They could see three men inside the car, following less than a few car lengths back. *Anyone could see the name of the hotel on the shuttle*, Joel thought, *so why would they bother following so close?*

"Let's take over the shuttle," Hannah whispered in Joel's ear.

"What? That sounds like a horrible idea," Joel said, but in his mind quickly thought, *this girl has guts*. He knew that about her when he married her, but he didn't know to what extent she would go. Hannah Cohen was a non-stop risk taker—perfect for him in every way.

"Well, I think our friends and your box are all in that car," his beloved spoke. "They are chasing us, but we need the box as much as they need the key. There's got to be a way we can put the fewest number of people at risk and somehow get our hands on the box," she said.

Hannah's phone rang. It was Nathan calling back. She answered and caught Nathan up on everything that had happened to this point. She explained the people they were trying to catch were now following behind them and mentioned they probably had some gun power now, as someone had picked them up at the airport. She gave Nathan the name of the hotel she and Joel were headed to and gave him a run-down of what had happened in the U.S., along with a description of the other man in the car, from what she could see. The call ended with her thanking him for his help.

"What did he say?" Joel asked.

"He's sending a car to the hotel to pick us up," Hannah said.

"To take us where?"

"He wants me to come to the Knesset where he is with the prime minister."

"That's their legislative building, right? Sounds like a safe place," Joel said. "But what about the people chasing us?"

"Yeah, it's where they make their laws. We have to just go to the hotel and hope our ride will get there before something else happens. I don't know what else to do. If we get to the prime minister, he'll help us figure out how to find the box and get it back. All we have to do is keep these guys at bay long enough," she said. "Or we could commandeer the shuttle as I suggested earlier."

The driver was an older man who looked like he'd been through plenty in his life already. Joel was hesitant to put him in danger and Hannah recognized what Joel was thinking. Being the only two people on the shuttle, they decided it was possible to simply ask the driver to take them to the Knesset.

"Could we pay you to drive us somewhere other than the hotel?" Joel asked.

The driver looked in his rearview mirror at Joel with a bit of confusion, as he slowly comprehended what he was asking.

"I would not be able to leave my route, sir," he said.

"What if we told you there are people following us to try to kill us? Could you then go off your route?" Hannah asked.

He looked in the mirror again and, squinting his eyes a bit, asked, "How do you know that?"

"It's a long story sir, but a few cars back you will see a gray vehicle following you. In that car are three people who are chasing us. We have a car meeting us at the hotel to take us to the Knesset to meet the prime minister, as this is an Israeli security situation. I am with security from the Consulate office in the United States," Hannah replied as she pulled out her security badge, glad she had packed it since she had to use it twice already. "If we didn't have to switch cars and you could take us directly to the Knesset, it would protect us from being exposed while changing vehicles."

He looked in his rearview mirror once again at Hannah. They watched the driver's face as his eyes darted back and forth between them and the car. He believed her.

He started shaking his head no, "Ahhhhh, never a dull moment in Israel," he commented, chuckling.

They shared a nervous laugh with him but continued to look in the mirror at him hoping he would say yes. One could see that what the driver thought might be a dull day had now become a chance for adventure as he maneuvered the shuttle into a sharp right turn. He watched in his rearview mirror as the gray car turned as well. "Hmmm, they do seem to be following us," he said.

It seemed the jury was still out as he weighed his decision, then picked up his radio to call the hotel dispatch and said something in Hebrew.

Joel and Hannah both smiled in the mirror. Joel could tell the driver was pleased with his decision for adventure.

"The only reason I'm doing this is because I love America. If not for America in 1948 voting yes for Israel, we would not be a state. For this, I love America," he said.

A response in Hebrew came over the radio.

He replied in Hebrew and turned the radio off. He had decided to put his job and life at risk for a couple of Americans he didn't know.

Joel reflected on what this guy may have been through in his life, as he was probably alive during World War II. Joel was unsure how other Israelis treated Americans, as he had never been to Israel before. Joel never thought about what the Israeli people thought about Americans. What he did know was that some people in the world did not like Americans. Joel was thrilled to have run into someone who was grateful.

"They know you've turned off the route," Hannah reported as she was watching out the back of the shuttle.

"I will drive calmly, and they can follow, but I will get you to your destination," he said in determined, shortcut English.

"How far is it?" Joel asked.

"Forty kilometers," he answered, which was about twenty-four miles.

"I'm so sorry, I haven't even asked...What is your name, sir?" Joel said.

"I am Ben. Yours?"

"I'm Joel and this is my wife Hannah. We are most honored to make your acquaintance."

"Likewise."

Joel turned to Hannah and whispered, "We only just met this guy and we could cause him to lose his job."

"We don't want you to lose your job or your life—this is very dangerous for you," Joel said to him.

"Life here is dangerous. Most days it's fine. Then once in a while, something happens, and you have to decide what to do... just live a boring life or participate. I am a widower and my children are grown. I am happy to take you to your destination. This city has been attacked fifty-two times, besieged twenty-three times, destroyed twice and captured and recaptured forty-four times. I have lived here since World War II, after my family all died in Europe. America helped me have a place to call home in my homeland when the rest of the world was spitting on us. I will do for you what you need. I knew one day I would have a chance to help Americans, so this is that day," he said.

"I lost family in Europe too," Joel said, lowering his head.

"Where?" Ben asked.

"Italy," Joel explained. "My grandmother survived and went to New York in 1948."

"Yes, many of us did go to America and others came

here," Ben said.

"Where in Europe were you?" Hannah asked him.

"Poland, in the Warsaw Ghetto. I was rescued by Jolanta at the age of five," Ben replied.

Hannah gasped, "Oh my, what a wonderful person she must have been! I've heard about her. I believe she rescued over two thousand children from that ghetto."

"Yes, twenty-five hundred, to be exact, and she got us papers and helped us escape. She was an amazing woman. They should have made a movie about her because she saved more lives than Schindler," he said.

Joel had not heard of Jolanta. "Who was she?" he asked.

"She was a Christian woman, named Irena Sendler we called Jolanta, who would come into the Ghetto to check for typhus and put babies and children under a sheet or in a sack saying they were dead and push them out, to freedom. She stored details of their parents in jars and buried them until after the war to help the children find their parents. Not many parents survived," Ben said with a soft sadness in his voice.

Joel hung his head low, listening to Ben talk about her. The magnitude of the stories so many people here must have about World War II weighed heavy on his mind. *Why did all of that have to happen?* Joel thought.

"Thank God for those who helped so many Jewish

people escape. So few people cared, but the stories of the few who did are humbling nonetheless." Hannah said.

"Wow, that was so risky! Christians also rescued my family at a church in Assisi, Italy," Joel replied. He was glad he knew the details from Bubbe's diary. "They filtered many through St. Francis of Assisi's Catholic church. The priests hid them in a secret room while the local printer made new papers for them to get out of the area."

"Yes, I have heard many stories of Christians risking their lives for the Jewish people," Ben said.

The car behind them was drawing closer. As they arrived at the Knesset, Ben brought the shuttle to a gentle yet quick stop, and the two grabbed their things and jumped off. They were determined to make their way to the front door without incident. They bid goodbye and thank you to their new friend and driver Ben.

The men who'd been following them also leapt out of their car and trailed them into the building. They were all halted at security as they entered the building. There was no way one of the men would pull a gun on them with all the security around, so Joel and Hannah decided to take their time and sign in and prepare to go through the procedures.

As they arrived at the security checkpoint inside the building, Hannah spotted Nathan standing just inside, which put her at ease instantly. They put their things through the metal detectors as they watched behind them.

The two men followed suit with calm demeanors. For some reason they were no longer chasing them. Joel and Hannah made their way to Nathan as Hannah pointed out the two men to him.

As Nathan turned around to look, they all fell silent as they watched the screen—the box was going through the metal detector and they could see a complete X-ray layout of its contents. Joel and Hannah stared in awe at what the X-ray revealed on the screen.

They could see items in hidden secret compartments in the box. Nathan saw it also. Chills went up and down their spines. They were about to get to the bottom of this mystery soon.

44

LIFTER OF MY HEAD

"Nathan, those are the men who kidnapped me," Hannah said, pointing at the criminals.

Nathan nodded his head toward a security detail. The officer took the box off the conveyer belt and brought it to Nathan. The two thieves did not appear ruffled but simply followed the box.

"That box belongs to me," Joel claimed. "It is a family heirloom. We chased these thieves from New York City to return it to its rightful owner."

"Let's find a safe room to discuss this," Nathan said as he motioned all four of them to follow him toward a small office down the hall. As the two men complied, Hannah and Joel looked at each other and realized they had fallen into another trap—Nathan knew these men.

Joel's mind was reeling about what could be in the hidden compartments in the box. He started to realize he should call a lawyer or someone who could help him, as things didn't seem to be working in his favor.

As that thought raced through his mind, he felt a hand on his shoulder. He turned to look but nothing was there, and he realized again that he was not alone. Either Harper or Jesus was with him. The touch he experienced from the spiritual world emboldened Joel so much that he stood taller in his stance and said, "This is a joke!"

Out of the blue, Joel started laughing loudly. The group looked at him like he was crazy, including Hannah. His laughing picked up speed and intensity, and Joel was rapidly losing control of his ability to stop. His thoughts raced in the midst of this laughing fit. He couldn't believe they had escaped the men and then followed them all the way to Israel, only to fall into another trap.

The laughing fit became so hysterical he could no longer walk, and his stomach already felt like it had done fifty crunches. As Joel fell to the floor right there in the hallway, the rest of the group started laughing too at Joel's outburst. Joel realized the angel's strategy was that laughing was contagious. His eyes began watering. Hannah was laughing at the insanity of Joel's laugh. The rest of the group chuckled, while trying to maintain their composure, but soon all of them were outright laughing as if they had heard the funniest joke on earth. Before long they were all rolling on the floor in uncontrollable laughter—the two thieves, Nathan, the security officer, and Hannah. Joel picked that moment to muster control of himself, grab the precious box, and take a shot at a run down the hallway. Hannah realized what he was doing and followed him, still laughing, but right in step with him. The grown men were rolling around on the floor trying to gather their wits about them as Hannah and Joel made their way out the front door.

Unsure of their head start, they darted as fast as they could. Joel knew they had supernatural help to escape, so in his mind there was no fear of being caught. After running a few blocks at top speed and dodging a few corners, they ducked into a small deli and grabbed an inconspicuous seat in the back. Joel was quick to pull the box from underneath his coat and tuck it into his backpack, safe and sound.

"Wow, how in the world did you pull that off?" Hannah asked, breathless.

"It was not my idea! It appears the angel that guards the box came up with the idea. Have you ever heard me laugh like that?" Joel asked. "No, that was not my doing. It was quite a remarkable experience for sure, and you followed me effortlessly," Joel said as he kissed his wife's soft cheek.

"Yes, that was the best laugh I've had in weeks! Maybe ever! My gut and my face hurt," Hannah said, still enjoying the after-effects of her laughter.

"I know, but now what do we do? I'm finding it hard

to believe every turn we take someone knows more about this than we do. If they know about the box at the Knesset, then we are in a huge mess here. Did you see what I saw on that X-ray?"

"Yes, oh my gosh! It really does have hidden compartments. And I think the Israeli government is after it," Hannah exclaimed.

"What do you think those things we saw in the X-ray were?" Joel asked. "Bubbe would not write it down, so it has to be major."

"Something powerful," Hannah answered, shaking her head. "One thing is for sure—we need to be in a secure place before we even consider opening it."

"But where? No doubt they'll be scouring the city for us," Joel stated as he continued to catch his breath.

"We may need to get out of the city somehow, find a way to get undercover or something," Hannah suggested.

Just then, a group of tourists started piling into the deli. They were taking a break from their tour for lunch.

"We will be here for one hour before we continue our trip," the tour director announced.

The woman pointed to the guy behind the counter. "This is my friend Daniel who has a few options ready for you for lunch. Please order one of the three items on the list we gave you on the bus. I recommend the shawarma— it's an amazing Middle Eastern dish everyone should try at least once. Daniel is prepared for a large crowd. We like this place because we can be in and out in an hour. We have a scheduled tour at the Church of the Holy Sepulcher we will have to make by one o'clock sharp. Remember, we have been given special access and want to honor my friend there who has agreed to give us a behind-the-scenes tour of the church. So, we have to stay on task and have everyone back on the bus by twelve-thirty to get through traffic," she explained.

She was a pretty lady who carried herself with dignity and poise as she spoke with kindness to the people who gathered around her asking questions about the tour. Others who were hungry lined up in obedience to order one of the three meals available.

The tour group was good news for Joel and Hannah. They didn't have food on their minds, but they realized they could mingle with the tour group.

Hannah perked up when the woman mentioned the Holy Church. She and Joel looked at each other with the same thought: the church was as good a place as any to try to hide.

Joel leaned over and asked Hannah inquisitively, "Remind me again, what is the deal with that church?" Hannah knew plenty of tidbits about Jerusalem and happenings in the city, thanks to her job.

"That is the church that sits on the site where they believe the Romans crucified Jesus. They call it Calvary or Golgotha in Greek. It means "the place of the skull." Some also think it's the place where David buried the head of Goliath," she whispered.

"Wow, too bad we're not on vacation. We need to come up with a good plan ... maybe we could blend in with the group as they leave, or board the bus with them somehow?" Joel said.

Hannah had an idea. She popped up from the little two-seated café table to talk to the woman who had brought the tour into the deli. Joel stayed put with his back to the door just in case the Israeli security came into the deli. He put his head down on the table and started to pray. "Lord, some way around this fiasco would be altogether fantastic and appreciated," he whispered.

Prayer was becoming a habit now. Joel felt compelled to at least ask, after what they had just experienced. He glanced at Hannah as she spoke to the woman, and they both glanced back at him. Joel nodded and smiled as Hannah continued to talk to the tour guide. A few minutes later, Hannah came back to the table and sat down.

"Okay, all we have to do is pay the woman, and then pray that for the next hour the security detail does not come into this deli," she said as she rifled through her wallet in search of some money. "Cash is the best option. We never know if they will be tracking credit card purchases. How much do you have? I wonder if they'll take U.S. dollars? We need about a hundred and fifty for the two of us."

Hannah took the money and went over to the tour guide with a confident smile on her face as if the woman could never turn her down. Joel had seen Hannah do this before. She had a confidence about her that would make it hard for anyone to turn down.

"Lord, a little help here? Please?" Joel mumbled under his breath, as he dropped his head again in prayer. He noticed he sure was being chummy with the God of all creation.

Joel heard a small voice from inside, an internal source not from his brain, but from his heart say, "I am the lifter of your head." Joel looked up toward Hannah.

The woman was shaking her head at first and pushing the cash back into Hannah's hand. Joel saw Hannah offer her an extra hundred. The woman pushed it back. Hannah offered her another hundred, and the woman pushed it back again as she looked at Hannah and then looked above Hannah's head. She was looking at something above her head.

Joel thought to himself, *Wow, this woman is a hard sell, not accepting an extra two hundred bucks?* Hannah went for her wallet to pull out a card, and the woman whispered in Hannah's ear and pushed her wallet away.

Hannah nodded and came back to sit with Joel and whispered to him, "Follow me."

They grabbed their things and walked past the crowd

of people. They climbed on the bus and went to sit in the very back by the restrooms. The windows on the bus were tinted so nobody could see them inside.

Angel Harper

What an adventure today. I had so much fun working with the Almighty to show Joel and Hannah a way out with a little tickle. The Lord's joy will strengthen them for the journey ahead.

Just wait until I tell King David about this experience of hiding in Jerusalem. He brags so much about hiding in caves back in the day, but this hiding in plain sight is much more impressive. I am so glad that tour director saw me—or was it the Archangel Michael she saw? He has been showing up out of the blue to check on us since he is often in the vicinity of the Holy City. Also, Joel heard from the Almighty just like David heard the voice of the Lord speaking to him. I wonder if Joel realizes he has started on a grand adventure with the Almighty, one that will change him and his eternity forever?

Demon Marq

It's not right the way that throne angel flaunts creative means of rescue. A laughing fit? Disgusting. I was caught off guard. Laughing is not part of my repertoire. I had a difficult time getting them all back on the task of getting their hands on the box. They were rolling around on the floor for five minutes while Joel and Hannah escaped. I don't get embarrassed, but I watched them all get embarrassed, which sparked humiliation. They should feel humiliated they lost the box, but often humiliation can lead to humility, the enemy of pride. I just can't work near humility. Strangely enough, humility can even affect me; it's like kryptonite. It can jump on me without notice. Since I am a spirit of bitterness, it would be my ruin if I allowed it to invade my spirit. I often wonder what would happen if I just let it invade? I suppose I would be worthless to Lucifer if I allowed such a thing to happen. I believe the reason humility can come after me is that half of my spirit is from my mother's human spirit. The fallen angel side of me is a powerful adversary to my human spirit, but nonetheless, the temptation to know if the Almighty could or would forgive me since I am half human has been a long-standing curiosity for me. But, I would have to humble myself. Not a likely scenario for the likes of me.

45

NAOMI THE TOUR GUIDE

"What happened back there?" Joel asked.

"She changed her mind and was amazed I would offer her extra money. She couldn't accept dollars and when I reached to give her a card she just pushed my wallet back and whispered in my ear, 'The Lord has revealed to me, I am to let you go ahead and climb on the bus.'"

Hannah's face was lit up like Joel had never seen it before. He knew Hannah could not believe all of this was happening to her.

"I am shocked!" Hannah continued. "Does God talk to people about someone in a deli?"

It was a valid question. Joel cleared his throat and said, "He never used to, but it seems He does now. I thought I heard a voice say, 'I am the lifter of your head' at that exact moment when I looked up and saw that woman look up above your head. I can't explain how, but I guess we are

288 KELLY FITZGERALD FOWLER

going to the Church of the Holy Sepulcher," Joel said with a chuckle, shaking his head and trying to understand how all these miracles could be happening to them.

"What is going on here, Joel?" Hannah asked as she began to tear up. "How do these people hear from God? Why is He talking to them and you but not me?"

"I was praying for the Lord to help us. Maybe my prayer was answered," Joel said. "I have no idea," he said, shrugging. "I'm new to all this too, my love," he said as he put his arm around her to comfort her.

Hannah sighed heavily. "It is so unlike anything I have ever experienced. God is not real," she said, speaking out loud what was in her heart.

As soon as it came out of her mouth, she was unsure of the statement and put her hand over her lips. She bowed her head. Hannah knew about God but never knew Him despite her time spent at synagogue services throughout her life.

"Is He real?" she asked Joel. "Why would He do this for us if we don't believe He's real? I mean, yes, we grew up in our Jewish tradition, but we were just doing what our parents taught us. I never actually believed—I just went along with the crowd and followed traditions. God does not talk to us. How could He talk to that woman who is leading a group of Christians on tour? She's a Christian. Why is God talking to the Christians and not the Jews? It is so confusing to me, Joel."

She was heartbroken and jealous as she continued. "Did I miss something? Did my parents miss something? My grandparents? How is this possible?"

Joel didn't have the answers but attempted to empathize with her. "Honey, my family missed it too," is all he could come up with. "As you can see from my ancestors, they had the same crisis of faith. It's tradition or truth, religion or relationship. I don't understand it all, but I know I now believe Jesus is Messiah. You are experiencing now what I encountered in the bathroom the other day. He is real, and for some reason, He's helping us," Joel said.

There! Joel thought. *I said it out loud to my wife. Jesus is Messiah.* She looked at him and was shaking her head no as Joel was nodding his head yes.

"It's true; I believe," Joel said as he continued to nod.

She looked him in the eyes and knew he meant it, and slowly she began to nod her head yes too.

"You are saying yes, Hannah. Do you believe, too?" Joel asked.

Still crying and looking more beautiful than he had ever seen her, she said, "I have to believe... how else can you explain why we're sitting here on this bus while the Israeli Defense Force is hunting for us? Only God could hide us like this by using a Christian."

Joel hugged her and held her close. It was as if something encircled them as their hearts joined in the belief

Jesus was who He said He was.

It was hard for Joel to pinpoint, but he could feel a tangible and pleasing weight of peace surrounding them as they held each other. Hannah experienced what she would call a concentrated dose of pure joy. They both knew this meant their friends and family would persecute them and judge. It meant the community they grew up in would reject them, but they didn't care. They had joy and peace.

They wiped the tears from their eyes and both turned their attention to the box inside the backpack. They were in a safe location and had a short span of time to try Bubbe's key on the box. Joel pulled it out and placed it on his lap, then pulled the medallion from his pocket.

Just as they raised the necklace medallion up to the box near the embossed symbol, the tour director walked onto the bus. They hurried to hide the box as she walked toward the them carrying a paper sack.

"Here you go; I thought you might be hungry. We're going to be busy on this tour all afternoon and won't have any other options for food or drink after now, so I wanted to make sure you were well-fed," she said as she handed them a bag and introduced herself. "My name is Naomi."

"Oh, my goodness, I am so sorry. I didn't even tell you our names when we spoke in the deli. I'm Hannah, and this is my husband Joel," Hannah said as she extended her hand to Naomi. "Thank you so much. You are so kind to do this for us."

"You're welcome. It is my pleasure to be on assignment for the Lord," Naomi said as she started to rifle through her bag. "I was wondering if you would like to exchange some of those dollars for some Israeli shekels? I have some here. I can always trade the dollars in later. You'll need to have shekels to do anything here."

"Oh wow, that is so generous of you! Yes, thank you so much," Hannah said as she pulled out all the cash she had and gave it to Naomi.

Naomi had a relationship with "the Lord," as she put it. Joel knew that was not typical lingo.

Joel cleared his throat and asked, "So, what do you mean, 'on assignment for the Lord'? Can you explain to us how the Lord told you?"

"Oh, I saw a huge angel standing behind Hannah, and the Lord spoke to my inner spirit, to my heart. You two are on an important assignment," she said.

"So, you saw the angel?" Joel asked, excited.

"I'm not sure what you mean by 'the angel,' but yes, standing right behind Hannah," she explained.

"Oh, I saw you look behind her and was wondering what you were looking at when you looked up. Do you see angels often?" Joel asked.

"Oh yes. I mean, I live and work in the old city here in Jerusalem at the holy sites where spiritual activity is rampant, so I do see spiritual beings often. This one was an unusual angel—mighty. He appeared to be a very high-ranked angel. He was tall, with dark brown hair. I only caught a glimpse, but he could have been Michael. There were tons of other angels surrounding you as well, in the back of the café," Naomi said, nodding to Joel.

Hannah and Joel were astonished. Even after his experience in heaven, Joel was having a hard time realizing there was really a hidden spiritual world people interact with.

"Have you seen one?" Naomi asked Joel.

"Yes, but in a vision. I have also been able to feel a presence. It's all new to me," Joel replied.

"It is a very high-ranking assignment you must be on to have all that angelic activity around you. I saw tons of weapons with them," Naomi said.

"How can *we* see it?" Joel asked. He was glad he could come up with a useful question.

"That's up to the Lord. Ask the Lord to let you see," she said.

"Naomi, my wife and I were just sitting here and realizing for the first time that Jesus is the Jewish Messiah." Joel thought, if God sent her, then he was going to get as much information from her as possible.

"Oh, amazing! I love the grace of God!" Naomi exclaimed. Then she laughed with a deep joyful, delightful smile on her face. "That is so wonderful. I guess I thought you two were old pros with that huge angel protecting you. How amazing! You two must be on an incredible journey if the Holy Spirit has just revealed the truth to you. Welcome to the family!" she said as she reached to hug Joel.

She embraced him as a sister would a brother and did the same with Hannah.

Naomi started to tear up with joyful tears and a beaming smile on her face, then said, "Did you ask Jesus to forgive your sins and be your savior?"

"No," Joel said looking at Hannah. "We did not know that was something we had to do."

"We are amazed and dazed, as we both grew up in traditional Jewish homes," Hannah said.

"Oh, me too, sort of," said Naomi. "My dad was Jewish, and my mom was Christian. My mom was a praying woman and used by the Holy Spirit for signs and wonders. Her spiritual life was so strong, it made my dad and I so jealous that we both became believers in Yeshua. You two are in for a treat and a challenge. Your life will never be the same. Joel, it's not so much that you *have* to do it, but rather your realization of the truth means you have the ability to acknowledge Jesus is Lord. If you are like me, praying was not my strong suit before I learned the truth."

"Tell us how to do this," Hannah said, and Joel agreed.

"Ok, just use your own words to ask Jesus, Yeshua in Hebrew, to forgive all your sins and vow to turn from future sins with His help. That's really all there is to it, but you can start the conversation by telling Him how grateful you are to Him for being your Passover Lamb and dying on the cross for your sin. Express your gratitude for revealing to you through his Holy Spirit the truth that Yeshua is Messiah and ask Him to be your very own Lord and Savior."

Right there on the bus, Joel and Hannah bowed their heads and each expressed what Naomi had said in their own words.

"Oh my, you probably have some major questions," Naomi encouraged them as she sat down across from them.

"Yes, we do have questions. How do you hear from the Lord?" Joel asked, since Hannah had been so upset about that particular topic.

"Well, you just heard from the Lord if He revealed to you Yeshua is Messiah. He will speak to you in many different ways. He talks through his written Word, which is the Torah, and the prophets, as well as the New Testament, which teaches all about the life of Yeshua and then the birth of the church and how the truth of Yeshua was spread all over the world," Naomi said.

She continued, "For me, I read the Word every day, and over time the scriptures gave me a moral compass. It told me if God would agree or disagree about certain things. It's like when you know someone well, you almost know what he or she would think. That's one way the Word of God works. So, you'll want to get a copy of the whole Bible, the Old and New Testaments, and start spending time soaking it up."

"The other way you can hear from the Lord is from what I think of as a small whisper. My theory is He speaks to your heart. Did you know there is a tiny brain in your heart? When He talks to you, you can tell it's Him because it seems to come from a different place than your mind. Plus, if you read his love letter to you, which is the Bible, then you'll recognize Him because He will never ask you to do something contrary to the Bible," Naomi explained.

Hannah and Joel just sat and listened. Joel was now fascinated at the thought of reading the Bible. It had never occurred to him to read the Torah after age thirteen. The rabbi would study it and tell everyone what to think. Joel didn't know anyone who would consider reading it beyond Sabbath traditions for themselves.

"Another way He will speak to you is a dream or a vision," Naomi continued.

Now that piqued Joel's interest even more. Jesus said the same thing about his dream of being invited to the head of the table.

"Do you have dreams you remember?" she asked Joel.

"Not often, but I did have a dream the other night that seemed so real, I will never forget it. And I have recently had what I would call an encounter with Jesus. Not a vision, an encounter," Joel said.

"Oh, yes, we call that a visitation," she said with eager excitement in her voice. "I have heard about an increased number of visitations, particularly in the Middle East, to the Muslim people, but also more and more Jewish people have been sharing visitation stories with me. It's so amazing to hear and enjoy every detail. Some of them are quite personal, so I won't ask you to share with me unless you want to but hearing about visitations are one of my favorite things!" Naomi said, glowing. She carried sincerity in her smile. However, no matter how sincere she seemed, Joel wasn't ready to share the details with her. It was entirely personal, and she picked up on his hesitation.

"So, it is a common thing, visitations?" Joel asked. "I can't believe I have never heard of it happening to anyone."

"Well, it is on the rise, a sign of the times I suppose," Naomi said, "and there will be an increase of dreams and visions just like the prophet you must be named after, Joel, said:

'I will pour out my Spirit on all people.
Your sons and daughters will prophesy,
Your old men will dream dreams,
Your young men will see visions.'"

"So, do you know anything about a group of people who plan on rebuilding a Third Temple?" Hannah asked.

"As a matter of fact, I do," Naomi replied. "I'm a close friend with one of the top rabbis involved in that project. Rabbi Jacob is one of the founders of the group. Did you know they introduced the idea to the U.N. recently?"

Hannah and Joel looked at each other in surprise. "I was there! I work for the Consulate office. We know all about it. We were shocked the world didn't respond in uproar. What did your friend Rabbi Jacob have to say about the lack of media coverage?" Hannah asked.

Naomi shook her head, saying, "He was amazed, but I wasn't. I had been told in a dream most people wouldn't pay attention to the announcement. The fact they got the prime minister to allow it was mind-blowing. The prime minister and most of the secular people in Israel have been against rebuilding the Third Temple. The truth is our bodies are now the Temple of the Lord. The Holy Spirit lives in us, so we are the Temple. Rabbi Jacob hasn't been able to bring himself to believe Yeshua is Messiah, so he's on this quest. I am praying the Holy Spirit will show him the truth one day."

They started to hear sirens closing in from behind the bus. Hannah and Joel tensed up. Naomi stood up to look out, and the vans sped past the bus.

"Nothing to worry about. They passed us. So how else can I help you?" Naomi asked.

"Well, I think we need to get in contact with your friend Jacob," Joel said.

"I can do that. Let me call him right now. His office is in the Old City, so I could have him meet us at the Church of the Holy Sepulcher," she said as she pulled out her mobile phone.

"That would be great," Hannah said in agreement with Joel's idea. *Perhaps Rabbi Jacob could help them with the box,* she thought.

"Let me get him on the phone and go check on my group really quick," Naomi said as she disembarked the bus.

Angel Harper

What an exciting moment in heaven when Hannah and Joel proclaimed their belief in Yeshua! Wow, the cheering by the cloud of witnesses, elders, and us angels was deafening! It is a big celebration to say the least, and the Almighty was smiling ear to ear when Hannah was in agreement with Joel. He loves unity. Ely, Joel's very own daddy, is now part of the cloud of witnesses and saw the whole scene. If humans could see the warfare surrounding their decision and how the amazing Holy Spirit of Jesus is their only saving grace it would be eye-opening. He knocks on the door, and through their own free will, they either open it or they don't.

46

ARTIFACTS REVEALED

As soon as Naomi got off the bus, Joel and Hannah, alone again, got back to their task at hand. Joel carefully pulled out the box and Bubbe's necklace. They were determined to get to the bottom of what was in the hidden compartments.

As Hannah watched with nervous anticipation, Joel took the necklace and matched it up to the symbol on the box. It was an exact match. His hand shook with excitement as he pressed down on the symbol using the necklace, which caused the outer portion of the box to shift open as if peeling on all four sides, revealing hidden compartments, just as they had observed inside the X-ray machine at the Knesset. Inside two of the compartments were small scrolls, and the other two compartments held two ancient nails and a small spearhead.

Breathless, Hannah picked up the tiny scrolls to unroll them as Joel leaned in to catch a glimpse of their contents.

The first scroll revealed a list, written in ancient Hebrew. Joel opened the other scroll and it was written in another language, one he didn't recognize.

"What are you thinking?" Hannah asked as they both eyed the scrolls.

"These are from the crucifixion of Jesus," Joel said as he held up the nails. "Remember, I told you Annas mentioned the soldier who pierced his side gave him these items."

"It would make sense," Hannah said, her eyes as big as saucers. "It's no wonder people are after these—they could be worth a fortune."

Joel's mind was reeling.

"Bubbe said Hitler sent soldiers to Assisi looking for artifacts. Maybe Bubbe's dad Caleb, when he was captured by the Nazis, somehow sparked them to scour Assisi."

"This day keeps getting more and more bizarre. No wonder people want to kill us. If these are what we think they are, they are some of the most valuable artifacts in Christendom, and perhaps Judaism, on earth today," Hannah said.

"Plus, if these scrolls are what I think they are, we may have access to even more artifacts based on the Annas scroll. He mentioned a list of Temple treasures. I bet this is the list. Take a look at the writing on this other scroll; some of the characters look like Bubbe's necklace symbol. It's some other ancient language," Joel said as he put the items back inside the box and closed it, using the necklace to lock it. Thoughts of paranoia set in and he began to get nervous and started shaking at the thought of having such responsibility. Joel felt the full weight of their discovery. By the look on Hannah's face, she was in shock as well.

"We have to find a safe place to hide until we get to the bottom of it," she said as she grabbed Joel's hand to steady him. She wanted him to know he was not alone.

Just then they saw Naomi walk out of the deli with a few of the people from the tour following her, coming toward the bus. It seemed an hour had passed in only minutes.

Hannah and Joel stuffed the box back into the backpack and began eating and looking nonchalant as the people started finding their seats on the bus. Naomi boarded the bus shortly after the others and came back to talk to them as the others began to file out of the deli.

"Rabbi Jacob will be available to meet with you at the end of the tour. He has appointments all day, but said he would meet us near our drop-off place, so it looks like you can just mingle with our group for the afternoon if that is okay with you?" Naomi said.

"Perfect," Joel said as he tried to gain his composure.

"I look forward to teaching you many amazing things about Yeshua," she said as she headed to the front seat.

Hannah and Joel looked at each other and shrugged as they took long breaths at the same time. They were unsure what else to do. The Lord had sent someone to help them. They didn't say a word to each other regarding the items in the box, as they knew the danger if someone on the bus overheard them talking.

The bus filled up with tourists, and they were on their way. As they drove to the Old City, Naomi sat in the front of the bus explaining each and every thing they drove by on both sides of the bus.

Hannah and Joel were exhausted from all the discoveries. Hannah laid her head on Joel's shoulder. He was grateful for their current safety. As they watched the landscape roll by through the bus window, Hannah and Joel talked about all the sites from Judaism they were familiar with as they passed by and wondered about the sites from Christianity they had never thought much about until Naomi pointed them out.

They arrived near the Old City in a parking lot where they filed off the bus. Naomi brought them tour lanyards, so they blended in well. They both kept their heads down and tried to stay in the thick of the crowd as they headed through the gate.

The city was bustling and people were everywhere. They were shoulder to shoulder with the tour group and other tourists who were making their way to various places in the city.

The streets were made of uneven old stone bricks, each of them narrow and tight, so they had to look down to pay attention to every step they took in the natural as well as the spiritual, so they would not fall. There were shops filled with oils, herbs, scarves, and carved olive wood crosses from Jerusalem set up on both sides of the narrow streets.

Naomi held a red and white umbrella up high, so the group would be able to see her from far off if they lagged behind. Once they made it to the Church of the Holy Sepulcher, they gathered around to hear Naomi discuss the significance of the location, one of the holiest sites in Christendom.

As they all filtered into the amazing old building, Naomi explained it was one of the believed sites for the crucifixion as well as the burial and resurrection of Jesus.

"Six different sects of Christian churches run the building," she said.

One of the people in the group questioned Naomi at length regarding how all those different sects manage to get along.

Joel and Hannah studied the maps in the brochure while Naomi gave people the option to go with her trusted local guide or use the map to explore the church on their own.

"So, what do you think?" Naomi asked.

"I've always wondered why some depictions of Jesus have blood coming out of his rib and others don't?" Hannah asked as she pointed to a painting of the crucifixion.

Naomi explained, "Oh, I suppose it depends on what time during the crucifixion the artist is depicting. For all crucifixions they would break the legs of the criminals, so the criminal would not be able to use their legs to ease the pain of their body weight hanging from the nails at their wrist. If you break the legs, they will die sooner also. But when they got to Jesus to break his legs, He already appeared dead, so a soldier pierced Jesus in the rib with a spear just to make sure. Some artists don't like to depict the brutality and others chose to paint Christ before his side was pierced. It also fulfilled a couple of prophecies about the Messiah. If you read what King David wrote in Psalms 22 and 34, he described what appears to be a crucifixion scene, roughly 800 years before the Romans used crucifixion as a capital punishment."

"That is fascinating! I've never read Psalms," Hannah said.

"That's astonishing," Joel said. "More evidence hidden in plain sight!" he commented as he ran his hand through his hair in disbelief at how so many of their ancestors had missed the truth.

"Well, don't be discouraged," Naomi said. "You haven't even scratched the surface. There are so many confirmed Messianic prophesies Jesus fulfilled, it would make your head spin. The chance of Him fulfilling just a few of them is so rare, yet He fulfilled well over 350. I have yet to find one He didn't fulfill unless you count some of the prophecies of the Last Days. It truly is confirmation He was who He said He was."

They walked around the church for a while and marveled at the history. Joel and Hannah watched as others on tour reacted to the sights and sounds. They presumed the rest of the group were Christians, so it was interesting to observe their reactions to the rock of Calvary and the actual place believed to be where they scourged Jesus. It was a sacred journey for the tourists, and many of them didn't speak; most of them were somber.

Joel was unsure what to think of most of this stuff. He had heard about some of it around Easter time but never paid much attention. They had Passover to pay attention to, and the Christians had Easter. Joel pondered what Naomi said, that the Passover Lamb was Jesus.

As the tour was ending and time drew near to leave, Naomi got a call from Rabbi Jacob.

They were to meet just outside the Jaffa gate in a small café. Joel had no idea what to say or do with this rabbi, but he had a feeling Rabbi Jacob and Naomi may be their only allies in the city.

47

RABBI JACOB

Rabbi Jacob came through the front doors of the café and greeted Naomi, who then showed him to Joel and Hannah's table. He was young and astute-looking, with classic dark hair and thick black-rimmed glasses. He stood no taller than Joel and was about his same age. Joel expected him to be ancient, someone who had spent years studying the prophets and carrying a heavy burden for Israel. Not Rabbi Jacob—he was young and vibrant. It surprised Joel but not Hannah. The rabbi had what appeared to be a permanent smile on his face, and his eyes lit up like he knew the secrets of the universe. He sat down after they all greeted each other and ordered some Turkish coffee.

Hannah recognized Rabbi Jacob from his recent trip to the U.N. She leaned over to whisper in Joel's ear as soon as she saw Rabbi Jacob walk in.

"He was under the tight watchful eye of Levi and

his security team while he was at the U.N. What are the chances we would run into Naomi and meet this guy?" she said, a bit freaked out over the whole situation. "I didn't have access to him for some reason. I guess I was busy with the PM."

They needed to decide now if they were going to trust Rabbi Jacob or not. Current information and logic would say Levi was assigned to him at the U.N. to keep him away from Hannah, but they didn't know what he knew. They had to tread lightly in their conversation until they had some sign he would be a safe ally. The rabbi didn't act as though he recognized Hannah, but as it goes, security people are supposed to blend into the background.

"My friend Naomi said it was urgent I make some time to meet with you. When Naomi sees high-ranking angels, let's just say we pay attention," Jacob said as he sipped dark muddy coffee from a tiny cup.

Joel smiled; the enormous angel accompanying him lent him significant credibility with Rabbi Jacob. It was laughable to him that he would ever hear anyone say something like that in his lifetime.

"Yes, Naomi mentioned the angels to us. We can't see them…well, I have seen something, but barely, and just enough to make me think I was seeing things. I am more likely to feel them nudge me," Joel said.

"Well, it is exciting times here in the Old City, my friends, exhilarating. We are taking it one day at a time.

So, tell me, what has brought you to inquire so much about the Third Temple and why are the authorities chasing you?" Rabbi Jacob asked.

"We are curious about the progress on the Temple because of something my father left for me when he died. It sparked our curiosity, and we decided to seek out someone who knows what is going on with the project. Hannah here works at the Consulate office with the U.N., but we are not here on official business. It's personal." Joel informed.

"I thought you looked vaguely familiar when I saw you; perhaps we saw each other when I presented at the U.N.," he said as he nodded his head toward Hannah.

"Yes, I remember seeing you, but I was on security for the prime minister, while my friend Levi was part of your detail," Hannah said.

"Oh, yes, Levi. He was serious about his job while I was there. He expected some major uproar in the streets, but for some reason, there was little to no problem regarding the rebuilding of the Temple. Levi did act disappointed when there was no backlash from any Muslim organizations. It was as if the world ignored it. But I knew the world was not going to take us seriously," the rabbi said as he shook his head. "So, tell me, what questions can I answer for you?"

"You are a founding member of the group? You are so young! I expected someone much older," Joel commented, reluctant to discuss his findings.

"Well, my family spoke of this for generations. But I am the first generation to outwardly pursue rebuilding the Temple," said Rabbi Jacob. "My father and grandfather just dreamed about it. I decided on my 13th birthday to do something about it. I was at the Wailing Wall for my Bar Mitzvah celebration, and it occurred to me that what was happening with Jewish people only having limited access to the Temple Mount was not right. Let's face it—Abraham went up there to prove his dedication to Yahweh. I was compelled to at least try to make a way for us to have more access to the area. So, I've been working ever since to build up finances and manpower to rebuild the Third Temple."

"Wow, what a mission at age 13," Joel said.

"Yes, sometimes people just know what they are called to do at a young age. I am years into this dream and may not attain it in my lifetime, but I started the stones rolling, so to speak, and we will accomplish it," Jacob affirmed.

"So, Naomi here is a longtime friend of mine. She told me a few things and asked me to meet with you in urgency upon your request. She tells me you two have a new belief of Yeshua being the Messiah." He put his head down as if trying to use words that would not offend. "Ummm," the rabbi cleared his throat, "Naomi and I disagree on this topic, but our friendship is so precious to us, we move beyond the arguments and agree to disagree. Not to mention she has been making me jealous with her supernatural adventures for years, but I have yet to experience seeing angels."

"I see," Joel said smiling "We're new to the faith of Yeshua being the Messiah. Most of what we know about Christianity is what we learned today from Naomi. We lived around Christians all our lives, but who pays attention if it's not your religion? I barely paid attention to my own religion. Naomi shared how difficult it can be for Jewish converts, but we are sure of what we have decided," Joel said grabbing Hannah's hand as a show of unity.

"It's indeed a tough stand to take, not only here in Israel, but anywhere you go," the rabbi said. "The Jewish people are not thrilled about what the Christians have done to them over the years, and many are offended at the very thought of a cross. So many Jewish people suffered at the hands of so-called Christians," he said as he cleared his throat.

"Yes, I am familiar with some of those arguments, now that I think about it. The Crusades were an ugly time for everyone," Joel said.

"Well, yes, and the expulsions from England in 1290, France in 1393, from Berne Switzerland in 1427, and Spain in 1492, to name a few more examples. Then there is, of course, the Holocaust in our era," he commented. "We could talk about that topic for days." Rabbi Jacob didn't skip a beat as he continued the accusations, now focused back toward Muslims. "Did you know that Arafat's little PLO Intifada was a terror war that murdered 1,000 Israelis? Then in 2002 and 2003 several Israelis left the Gaza Strip in an attempt at peace. However, terrorists launched rockets and bombs anyway. Then in 2005, there were more Israelis from the Gaza Strip kicked out of their homes. They pushed them out of 21 settlements, which was about 10,000 Jewish people kicked out of their homes. It cost our government $500 million."

Naomi softly touched his arm, and he relaxed a bit.

"Oy vey! It is a never-ending saga here," the Rabbi had decided he needed to take a breath, and threw his hands in the air.

"True, why do you think our people are so hated?" Joel asked.

"I can't speak for every person who hates us, but I would venture to say the root of it would be jealousy. Not many religions claim to be the chosen race by the one and only God," Rabbi Jacob answered.

"Many Jewish people are Jewish in heritage only and don't even believe God exists, so why would it bother them so much?" Joel asked.

"Because, I believe, God put a piece of Himself into each person and deep down, even though they doubt, they believe He is real, but won't admit it. Let's face it—the story of Noah's Ark is a huge stumbling block for many people. It sounds so far-fetched, and to this day, even possible findings of the Ark are weak at best. Noah's Ark is just one of the many reasons people don't believe; there are others. So, they fight the thoughts of unbelief and defend their right not to agree with our God," the rabbi said.

"So, do you believe the story of Noah's Ark?" Joel asked.

"Everybody calls it a story like you just did. It's clear in history there was a flood and animals and humans survived. I would like to see real evidence, not just a satellite photo from the sky. Some of those scientific photos of a snowcap with the picture of a boat drawn over it so if you squint your eyes you can see it are a joke. They don't know where it is. I never knew this, but I read recently that even Hitler had some strange flying machine he used to try to find it. The theory in the article was that the Nazis had gained knowledge and technology from demonic beings and they were on a quest for occult secret knowledge. It's bizarre what people have done to try to find Noah's Ark. God mentions it, so it's entirely possible," Rabbi Jacob said as he came to this conclusion.

"I guess if people could believe in Noah's Ark, maybe they could believe Jesus was who He said He was also. Maybe that 'story' of Noah's Ark is what's holding everyone back from believing the Messiah already came to earth as a man and there is something keeping the world from coming to that conclusion?" Joel asked.

The air got thick, but Joel knew his encounter with Jesus was real and the details he had in his possession were not just for the Jewish people to rebuild the Temple. Perhaps this rabbi just needed some proof. Joel needed to decide if he was going to reveal the contents of the box.

Hannah dropped her head, either knowing Joel was unsure how to proceed or freaking out because he was confident about Jesus and she was not used to it. She realized the question had to be presented and this rabbi was a great person to ask. He must know all the details of the Third Temple. They needed help deciphering the new scrolls as well as some protection for them and the box.

Joel felt the invisible presence behind him nudge his shoulder.

"I saw that," Naomi said.

"Huh?" Joel said.

"I saw an angel nudge you on your shoulder. Not the big angel I saw earlier—this one is a sphere," she said.

It made Joel wonder if Naomi was just trying to change the subject, so the rabbi would not leave in anger. He was calm but seemed a bit irritated at the conclusion Joel was leading him to.

"Really?" Joel turned to his side and wondered why he couldn't see Harper. "I can feel the angel," he said.

"Yes, it's there by your shoulder," she said, pointing.

Rabbi Jacob raised his eyebrows and chuckled. Hannah looked beside Joel and, charmingly, squinted to see if she could see anything.

"I felt it, but what do you think it wants me to do?" Joel asked.

"Seeing another one huh, Naomi?" said the rabbi. It had worked to get Jacob on a different subject.

"You know me," she said as she smiled. "He's used to it. I've been seeing in the spirit realm for a long time," she explained.

Joel tried to change the subject. "So how close are you to pulling together all you need for the Third Temple?" he asked.

"We are so close. We have most of what we need as far as the priests being trained and we're working out the issue of the animal sacrifices. We know the location of the First and Second Temple wasn't where everyone thinks. All the materials are ready with artisans lined up to build at a moment's notice. Permits are submitted as well—granted, they are not yet approved," the rabbi said and continued.

"There are arguments by some people about the location of the first two temples being right where the Dome of the Rock sits. However, we laid out a map of the actual location showing the Dome of the Rock is located exactly where the Court of the Gentiles used to be, which is what

I presented to the U.N. So, we wouldn't have to touch the Muslims' beloved monument. As you know, Muslims are simply, well, Gentiles. We're just waiting for a significant move of God to help us with the approval and reveal the whereabouts of a few stashed items from the Third Temple, so we can proceed," the rabbi explained.

"So, what items are missing?" Joel asked.

"Mainly a little challenge called the Ark of the Covenant," Jacob chuckled in his reply. "The Temple operated without the Ark for years, but we want it back and believe it is within our grasp. We have re-created the few known other items everyone believes were hauled off to Rome by Titus in 70 A.D., like the candelabra. We don't want to have to wait for Rome to decide to give them back before we move forward with the Temple."

"Does anyone have any idea where it is?" Hannah asked. "Like Harrison Ford?" she said with an unintended snort followed by embarrassment. They all laughed, and it felt good, but Rabbi Jacob stayed serious, although Joel thought his eyes lightened up. You could tell he had heard that joke a hundred times.

"There are some theories, but we believe the things we need will show up at the right time in the right place. Our job is to handle all the other preparations," he answered.

"What if I told you I think I carry a piece of the puzzle?" Joel asked.

"I would say today is a great day if it were true," the rabbi answered.

Joel wasn't sure what to do. He mentioned it, and now he was expecting some indication from the spiritual world, something real to give him the sign to go ahead and tell Rabbi Jacob.

Hannah grabbed Joel's hand and nodded her head in agreement. Joel wasn't sure why she urged him, but it made him feel loved and supported and so he decided to tell the rabbi. Was this a safe place and could the rabbi be trusted? His hesitation drew attention to his indecisiveness.

"You seem troubled. Please tell me of your trouble, and I will try to help in any way possible," the rabbi said.

Joel looked around the café and noticed there was little to no activity. Yes, the angel was protecting them, but Joel knew if he told the rabbi and Naomi, they too would be in grave danger.

"Before I say anything, I want you to know it's unsafe to know what I know. I would not share this with anyone, except we need some help translating something to get to the bottom of a great mystery. The only reason we would show you this is if we were being led by a supernatural force to believe you may be a safe person. We've already made the mistake of sharing some of the information, and it has put us on an out-of-control spiral for the last 48 hours. We're tired and weary and need some direction. If you're willing to accept the danger, which may come to both of you, then we will share. We want to give you an opportunity to say no thanks, and we will be on our way," Joel said.

There, Joel had put it out there. It was no wonder his father didn't want to deal with it. He had already put Hannah at risk and he needed both Naomi and the rabbi to understand this was a dark and dangerous hole.

"If this is an assignment from God, then I am here for you," Rabbi Jacob said. "I have always known life is a struggle. Look where I live. People fear traveling to Israel. It's the world stage, every news cast every night is focused on Israel. We are a small country and a peculiar people, yet the world watches us with bated breath. I want to help in any way I can, especially if this has anything to do with the Third Temple. It's part of my destiny, and I accept the danger willingly." Naomi nodded in agreement.

Joel took a deep breath then spilled the beans.

"I have a journal from the High Priest Annas from when Titus marched on Jerusalem." Joel did not want to reveal everything yet. In his mind, the items hidden in the secret compartments were hidden for a reason. Joel needed to see how helpful the information in the journals would be before he revealed the nails, spearhead, and other tiny scrolls. Hannah and Joel looked at each other and understood they would not mention the other items. Then they both looked at the rabbi.

Rabbi Jacob sat silent for a pregnant pause, Naomi the

same. The rabbi put his hand on his chin and thought for a moment.

"Where is it?" Rabbi Jacob asked as he lifted his eyebrows and looked at Joel's backpack. Then they *all* looked at Joel's backpack like it was a ticking bomb that at any moment might explode.

Joel smiled at him and nodded. He looked at Naomi, looked around the shop, and then back at the rabbi.

"We need to get to a private location," the rabbi said.

They all stood up and headed for the door.

"Where are we going?" Joel asked.

"Just follow me," Rabbi Jacob said.

The rabbi got up and walked out the back door of the café, the other three following close behind him. They made their way through narrow alleys of ancient stones, winding and bending several times. Hannah and Joel hustled to keep up but they had no idea where they were. Naomi followed as well. Within ten minutes they arrived at a home with a beautiful wooden red door and windows on either side with flower boxes in the front.

Very quaint, Hannah thought.

Rabbi Jacob knocked on the door, and a young woman with thick dark hair swept up into a bun opened the door. He spoke Hebrew to her for a few moments, and she pointed him to a side garden gate. Jacob entered the gate and walked to the back of the house to a small

bungalow hidden behind the home and let himself in, as
Naomi, Joel and Hannah trailed him like little ducklings.
The inside was rustic with exposed beams and very cozy.
A simple wooden table stood in the middle of the room,
and nobody seemed to care he had let himself in. There
were bookshelves lined with interesting-looking ancient
books begging to be opened, as well as a small sink, stove-
top, and refrigerator. Along one side of the room was a
single bed.

"This is one of the many places I come to study Torah,"
Rabbi Jacob said. "I have made many friends and enemies
on my mission and have had to be creative about finding
places to work. I have several supporters in the city who
offer me space to study and get away. Lots of people know
who I am and don't agree with what I'm doing," he said.
"Please sit, I'll make you some tea."

Naomi, Hannah, and Joel sat down at the table. Joel
put his backpack on his lap and pulled out the box, plac-
ing it on the table. Rabbi Jacob's eyes were fixed on the
box as he was preparing the kettle for tea. Naomi was
silent as well, watching Joel's every move. As Joel turned
the box around to reveal the symbol on the front, Rabbi
Jacob's mouth dropped open.

"Naomi, look at that symbol,' he said.

"I am," she spoke with her mouth ajar.

"Do you know this symbol?" Hannah asked.

"Yes," Naomi replied, as she put her hand to her mouth in disbelief.

"Do tell," Hannah said.

Rabbi Jacob set down the kettle and walked to the box and placed his hands on the wood.

"It's acacia," he said.

"Yes, it is," Joel replied.

They all looked at Naomi to gauge her reaction. Her eyes were welling up with tears as she spoke. "I have seen this symbol one other time in my life. It was in a dream Rabbi Jacob and I have discussed at length. The dream was very vivid, and I remembered every detail when I awoke. It had this symbol in it, as well as others." She looked behind and above Joel again at the angel as she had in the café, and took a deep breath.

"That's where I saw this angel before, in that dream. Jacob, remember I told you about the angel in the dream. It's the same angel protecting Joel and Hannah," Naomi exclaimed. "This symbol is the combination of two letters that are part of an angelic alphabet. They are the first and last symbols combined in the alphabet I saw in the dream."

"I know," said the rabbi, "that's what I thought when I first saw this from the symbols you had written down for me after we had discussed your dream. I would recognize any of those symbols immediately. That dream of yours must have some significance in leading us to what we need to complete the Temple."

"So, Naomi, what do you think this means?" Joel asked.

"I think these symbols have the equivalent meaning as the Alpha and the Omega, except they are an alphabet from heaven," she said.

"Alpha and Omega are the first and last letters of the Greek alphabet, right?" Hannah interjected.

"Yes, however, the two together are used as a name for God in the book of Revelation," Naomi said. "It's in the last chapter of the book of Revelation. God says he is the beginning and the end, the Alpha and the Omega."

"So, are you saying this is a symbol that means God of Heaven?" Hannah asked.

"Based on my dream, I would say yes, that is exactly what it means," Naomi confirmed.

Rabbi Jacob sat down and flipped the lid open the way Joel had opened it the first time. Joel felt in his jacket pocket for Bubbe's key and pursed his lips tight as the rabbi pulled out the typed document and scroll from inside the box. Joel wasn't ready to show him everything quite yet and felt anxious.

The rabbi took the scroll out and started to unroll it carefully and slowly. "I should have gloves on."

Joel had been thinking the same thing the first time he

had held the scroll in his hands. The rabbi read to himself the Hebrew writing right to left, then looked at everyone and began to read a portion of it out loud in English:

"I must tell the beginning from the end and the end from the beginning."

Joel, Hannah, Naomi, and the rabbi all looked at each other in awe, as this was another reference to the Alpha and the Omega.

"God's name again!" Hannah exclaimed.

Everyone could feel the room electrify.

Joel had read the translated manuscript, but he was not about to stop Rabbi Jacob from reading the scroll out loud to verify what he had read and see if the translation was accurate. Joel reached into the box to pull out the manuscript, so he could follow along with his translation.

The rabbi continued from the beginning: "I recall the first time I saw Yeshua Bar Youssef of Nazareth." The translation was very close as he read through the letter from Annas.

Rabbi Jacob was mesmerized and translated each word with care to assure he was getting the full meaning.

"I told you it was acacia wood," he said when he got to that part.

He continued reading about the atrocity of the murder of the innocents in Bethlehem as well as the reference to the prophet Mica speaking of the Messiah coming from that tiny town not even fifteen minutes from their very location. Rabbi Jacob continued reading, as Annas laid out his argument from the prophet Hosea that Messiah would also be from Egypt.

As he continued reading, the rest of them sat on the edge of their seats as the presence of something larger than themselves slowly unfolded. Joel knew in his heart of hearts how much Annas' writing had changed him.

On the plane ride over, Hannah and Joel had read the New Testament account of the trials of Jesus. Now Joel had a clearer understanding of who Annas was.

Rabbi Jacob stopped reading for a moment. He looked over at Joel, stunned. "If this document gets out, there could be a rise in anti-Semitism."

There it was. Out there in plain sight, for everyone to hear. The rabbi hit a chord in all of them at that moment. The last thing any of them wanted was to cause a rise in hate crimes against Israel.

Demon Marq

I was growing weary of trying to attach to flesh. Hannah's not bitter, but this conversation could be of some help. This was one of the best lies out there to use against Israel and exactly the type of emotion we used to turn the world against them during the Spanish Inquisition, the

Crusades, the Reformation, and most recently the Holocaust. That is right up my alley with the deep bitter root.
Perhaps this Rabbi Jacob would allow some bitterness? I
know nothing of his past, but something painful is welling
up inside of him. If only Joel were as easy to harass as his
father was. Wait—why is Archangel Michael here? I am
not equipped for that. I am waiting outside.

Angel Harper

There they go again, swirling around Joel. If you even
mention anti-Semitism the demons show up; Marq does,
anyway. My Archangel friend Michael is here with Joel,
so they don't have a chance right now. Michael is not omnipresent, so he can't be with the box nonstop. But like I
said before, I report to the Almighty, and Michael shows
up most of the time, unless there is some unknown dilem-
ma. The box is a well-known assignment in the ranks, so
I am sure all Michael has to do is say "the box" and every
other assignment is on the back burner. The box had not
been a busy task for quite some time until Ely got pro-
moted to heaven. Now it appears to be time-consuming
for Michael.

~~~

Naomi spoke up at this point. "All of humanity is responsible for the death of Yeshua. He died for the sins of the world before the foundations of the earth were established."

They all three looked at her as they processed her statement.

"My friend Rabbi Jacob, are you more concerned about what your people might think and do rather than the truth? You must have faith in your Creator to have a plan. His plan for humanity to be saved is Yeshua. He chose your people to save the whole world. Yeshua is a descendant of David," she said encouragingly. "This ongoing anger toward the Jewish people is a frothing lie from the pit of hell. Jesus left his throne by his own choice and allowed his death on the cross. He decided to allow it; believe me, nobody could have killed Him if He didn't allow it. The Romans were the ones who thought they killed him. You know how the church is called the body of Christ? Lucifer is still trying to kill the body of Christ, but he has forgotten about the resurrection. There was no dead body in the tomb! The devil is thinking he will be able to wipe Jesus - the body of Christ, the church - from the face of the earth by making people hate Israel. That loser Lucifer is on his last grasping rope to destroy Israel by thinking that will put an end to Jesus. But don't you see? Israel's rejection of Jesus is what allowed Gentiles to be accepted into the family of God. Lucifer is after all of us. Have you not heard it said, "'first the Jew then the Gentile' or 'first the Saturday people then the Sunday people'"? We are all one, and we must come together as one to defeat evil."

Rabbi Jacob's face softened as he took a deep breath. His mind was reeling over all this information.

Naomi continued, "Jacob, Israel preserved the Word of God just long enough to allow us Gentiles a chance to enter the fold. The rejection of the Messiah by Israel allowed Peter, Paul, and the followers of Yeshua a chance to reach the rest of God's beloved lost, the Gentiles. Now it's the job of the Gentiles who are part of the fold to wake up and remind Israel who Yeshua really is. Imagine how fast evil will fall when we are all in unity. Lucifer will do anything to keep Israel from waking up, but I contend you should be jealous and want what I have in my relationship with Yeshua. I can see angelic activity; I can hear and talk to God directly through his Holy Spirit. Before Yeshua was human, his Spirit only rested upon people—it didn't dwell indefinitely within even the prophets. I want you to want what I have!"

Joel had the advantage of Yeshua appearing to him, so to see the look now on the rabbi's face was incredible to witness. Tears welled up in the rabbi's eyes. Joel could see his heart melt. Naomi saw the same thing and realized what was happening in the rabbi's heart. She laid her hand on his shoulder. When she touched him, he began to weep deeply, and she hugged him and held him close. They all three watched in amazement at this strong-willed man who appeared to melt like butter.

"God-Elohim so loved the world that He gave his only Son, Jesus-Yeshua, so whoever would believe would be given life everlasting. He took on the sin of the world as the sacrificial lamb, the Passover lamb, rabbi. All he asks of us is to confess we are sinners and believe it is true, then turn around and walk with Him."

Hannah handed him a tissue. Rabbi Jacob continued to wipe the heavy flow of tears from his eyes.

He dried his eyes and said, "How do I do this? I hear and see all of this evidence, but I still doubt," he said with his head down. "I need something more, a sign, a miracle, an angel, or Noah's Ark. I just have to have something more tangible than your words."

"Just ask like this, 'God, if Jesus really is You, then make Him real to me' then wait and see," Naomi encouraged him.

48

AIR RAID TEST

Naomi could not believe, with all this evidence, Rabbi Jacob was still asking for more. She was sad but not broken. She knew it was not her job to pressure—it was the work of the Holy Spirit to gently complete what had been started.

Rabbi Jacob started talking about the prophecy of Daniel for building the Third Temple and how many rabbis he had spoken to were worried about rebuilding it. Some rabbis had even used the fact there was no Temple to prove Yeshua was not Messiah. Naomi elaborated on the information from Annas's writings about how the fabric in the Temple was ripped from top to bottom on the day Yeshua died.

Rabbi Jacob sat like a school child, as if all sorts of truths were being revealed to him for the first time as Naomi explained the facts of fulfilled prophecy in more detail. She even went so far as to joke that Yeshua may have asked the prophets to stop saying Messianic prophecies, so he didn't have to run all over the place trying to fulfill them.

"What exactly were the chances of one person fulfilling them all?" Hannah asked.

"Some would say impossible, but He is the God of impossible!" Naomi said.

"Listen," Rabbi Jacob said. "Ezekiel had said God would make a covenant of peace with them and it would be everlasting, and there would be a sanctuary in their midst always, and His tabernacle would be with us. This Temple I am working on appears to be an avenue of fulfilling yet another prophecy even for Yeshua."

"I am all for rebuilding the Temple. I am not too happy about killing innocent animals because Jesus was the Lamb from God who takes away the sins of the world. God provided his own sacrificial lamb, just like He did for Abraham on Mount Mariah. The temple Ezekiel is speaking of is within our bodies, not a building. Ezekiel says he will take your heart of stone and make it a heart of flesh so his Holy Spirit can dwell within us," Naomi said.

Rabbi Jacob was perplexed and thinking how much time he had spent working on the Third Temple and concluded, "It's clear, God will make a way to rebuild the Third Temple, even if it turns out Yeshua is Messiah and sacrifice is not necessary," he stated.

Naomi nodded her head, unsure how he still did not believe.

The rabbi took a deep breath. He had seen and heard so much evidence but was still asking for more. "I know I don't work in vain," he said. "My perspective has shifted. I have no idea how I will tell the rest of our committee what I discovered today. We must decide where to go from here as a group. Perhaps, with this information, all of Israel will turn and believe, and I will be the last fool standing." he said. "After all, there is no way I ever thought I would even consider such a thing."

Naomi smiled at them, knowing it was only a matter of time.

"I am honored to be a part your journey, Rabbi Jacob. Now, we need to figure out where to hide these two and what to do from here," Naomi said. "We need to get them to safety and try to figure out exactly why the Israeli government is after them. It's clear they know about the box, which is probably the culprit, and we know we are not only wrestling against flesh and blood here—this is a spiritual battle."

Demon Marq

Exasperating. How am I supposed to handle this assignment with this type of backup? Someone didn't do their job and bring in reinforcements. We almost lost the battle over Rabbi Jacob. I am not sure where the breakdown in communication is, but this is not going well. That was way too close. If I had lost him, who knows what would happen to me? I am NOT taking the blame for this.

Angel Harper

Oh, so close. The tides are turning. Surely it won't be long. I did my job as a watcher. I am not going to fret over Rabbi Jacob. The scales are always in our favor; I know that much is true. All of Heaven works together for every soul. There is not a victory without a fight. I am going to have to stress-eat some manna!

~~~

At that moment, an air raid siren started. Hannah and Joel jumped, while Jacob and Naomi both looked down at their watches.

"It's the national test," Naomi said.

"Yeah, we should move to the bomb shelter," Jacob said.

Hannah and Joel looked at each other with a hint of fear, knowing this was not normal life, but for those in

OVER MY DEAD BODY   333

Israel, it was their daily reality. They all gathered their things and moved to a shelter behind the main house in the backyard. It wasn't a large shelter, so it was tight and a bit claustrophobic. Joel thought about who might be in the main house with the young woman, but they did not show up.

"So, where is the woman in the house?" Joel asked.

"They have a basement shelter as well as this bomb shelter. She would stay inside with her family," the rabbi replied.

"Oh, so why do they have one outside as well?" Hannah asked.

"Well, you can never be too prepared for these things," Naomi said. "Many people have these in their yards around here, as the entire nation has been dealing with bombings since 1948. Plus, I think people got tired of being in their shelter and strangers pounding on their door to let them in. You can imagine how scary it is to hear someone pounding on the door for you once you're already secure in your shelter. The government started getting people to put these bomb shelters up in their yards to allow people out and about to pop into one if there was a raid."

The shelter was a small square building with iron walls and concrete on the outside of the building. It looked sturdy but was tight for the four of them. There were no chairs; it was basic.

"How long do we stay in here?" Hannah asked.

"Drills usually last ten minutes, then the Israeli army will text citizens when the coast is clear and to have a nice day," Naomi answered. "It shouldn't be too long," she said as she patted Hannah's shoulder.

"They text, 'Have a nice day'?" Joel asked with a slight chuckle.

"Yeah, they have a sense of humor, don't they?" Naomi said laughing as well.

"Well, when you've been dealing with terrorism this long, I guess the humor helps the stress," Rabbi Jacob added.

It was nerve-racking just sitting there. Growing up Joel had heard about the bomb shelters in Israel but being there for a drill lent a whole different perspective to what these people had been going through for the last seventy years.

49

BLACK AIR SHIP

An hour had passed since the drill began and they were still in the shelter. Discussion started shortly after the first twenty minutes as to what could delay a text from the Israeli Defense Force.

Rabbi Jacob took a look outside the door while Naomi wanted to get out from under the metal, so she could potentially get a blocked text. As the rabbi opened the door, they all realized the sun had practically set, or so they thought. It felt early for the sun to be setting.

As they emerged from the shelter, they all looked up into the sky and saw something very strange indeed—something solid and black was covering the sky, obliterating any sun. It looked like a military air ship, some sort of modern technology. It startled all of them as they cowered back into the shelter. No, the sun had not set—this monstrosity was blocking its light. The structure was immense—black on the bottom and hovering over the entire Old City.

336 KELLY FITZGERALD FOWLER

"What was that?" Hannah asked, on the edge of hysteria.

"I don't know," Joel said equally spooked.

Rabbi Jacob and Naomi had gone out to get a better look at it and ran back to the shelter. Naomi's phone was not getting service, just as everyone else's.

"It looks like something from outer space!" the rabbi said.

"Let's be calm; try not to panic. Have you ever seen anything like this before, rabbi? Perhaps it's a military drill with some new technology we've never seen?" Joel said.

Rabbi Jacob was speechless and holding onto Naomi, who was a bit shaken. She was praying out loud in a foreign language. He shook his head before Joel had even finished the question.

"Don't panic—we are protected right now by the angel and Yeshua," Joel said.

Joel looked at Hannah's face as she comforted Naomi. He looked into her eyes and repeated, "Don't panic, it's okay. Breathe. Everyone, listen to me and take a deep breath."

All four took a deep breath in unison.

"We've got to think clearly about what this is and how to protect ourselves. We won't be able to do that without being calm," Joel said.

"He is right," Naomi said. "Let's all pray for protection and know the Lord our God is with us." She had calmed down with the deep breath.

Then they all agreed with her as she led them in a prayer.

Joel had never heard such an elegantly worded prayer.

Then, within seconds, thoughts started running through his head about what this thing could be. Joel had never seen something so huge, even in science fiction movies, but had heard about some new technology that enabled hovering the way this was. They were in Israel, after all; they were on the cutting edge of security and defense in the world.

"What do you think we should do?" Joel asked the group.

"I vote for waiting until it leaves," Hannah said.

"I was thinking that also," Joel agreed.

Rabbi Jacob and Naomi were nodding their heads in agreement. There were two options, stay here or go outside. Outside was not ideal in their minds.

"How long should we wait here?" Joel asked, trying to limit how long he would allow fear to rule the situation.

"What would you say about trying to get back into the house?" Naomi asked, "At least then we might have a chance at phone service to see what the news is saying."

"True," Joel said.

They all looked at one another, but nobody went for the door. They heard what Naomi said, but nobody jumped at taking a chance.

The ship was colossal and black as night. Joel's mind went wild with possibilities, mostly trying to explain it away as an Israeli secret weapon or from a country looking to take over Israel with this massive weapon they somehow built in secrecy. Joel couldn't allow his mind to even go to the space ship option. He was not willing to accept that, even with all the Star Wars movies and being a Star Trek fan; it was just science fiction. Total fiction.

For the next hour, they all discussed different possibilities, but none of them made a move for the door. Finally, after another hour they felt brave enough to approach the door with a plan to try to get back to the rabbi's room.

This time as they emerged from the shelter, it was actually dark. The sun had set. They couldn't see the black blob as clearly as they had during the day, but Joel shot a few pictures of it with his phone as they ran back to the room. Not that it was safer than the shelter but having no idea how long they would be under the massive black object, they decided the shelter was a tight fit and no better than the room.

When they got back to the room, Joel started playing with the pictures on his camera using a flash filter to lighten them up. Joel and Hannah huddled around to see a close-up. As Joel lightened up the picture and zoomed in on what he had captured, he noticed the pattern on the bottom of the ship looked familiar to him. As he zoomed in closer, it hit him.

"It's the same pattern on your Bubbe's necklace!" Hannah cried in a hushed tone.

"Yeah, it does seem similar to that, huh?" Joel said, trying to get her to keep it down. They had still not shown the others the necklace or what was in the rest of the box.

"It's the exact symbol on the box, Joel," Hannah said, then tried to change the subject.

"What's that?" Naomi asked as she peeked over his shoulder.

"I zoomed in and lightened it so I could get a good view. Here, take a look," Joel said as he handed Naomi his phone.

"It appears to be metal or iron," Naomi said. Then she put her hand to her mouth as she recognized the symbol from her dream. "That is the same symbol from my dream again!" she exclaimed.

"Let me see," Rabbi Jacob said as he reached for the phone. He held it close and zoomed in, trying to focus on what he was seeing. "What do you think?" Jacob asked, looking around at the group.

"I think this has something to do with the box," Joel said, flabbergasted.

"It has to have something to do with it," the rabbi said, looking at Naomi.

Joel pulled out Bubbe's necklace and held it next to the phone. "Check it out," he said.

Rabbi Jacob and Naomi both looked at the necklace and made the connection immediately. They were looking at a mirror image key. Hannah was quiet, and Joel's heart started racing when they realized this thing over the city could potentially be coming for him.

"I think we need to find a safer place," Joel said. "I believe this is what is called the key of David."

"The key of David? How would you know that?" Naomi asked.

"Jesus showed me in a vision I had of Him in heaven forging the key," Joel answered.

"Did you match it up to the box?" Naomi asked.

"Yes," Joel said.

"Well, what happened?" Rabbi Jacob asked anxiously.

"This." Joel took the necklace and locked it into place, and the secret compartments were exposed. As they opened, and Naomi saw what was inside, she gasped in merriment. Jacob just looked and marveled at the way the box glided open. He was curious about the mechanics of the box. Then he saw the two small scrolls, nails, and spearhead.

"Do you know what all this is?" Jacob said, looking at Naomi. Her eyes were huge—she began to tear up.

"Oh, my!" Naomi exclaimed. "Think about it. This box belonged to Annas. He mentioned a list of hidden items in his journal. Jacob, this could be what you have been waiting for...a key to the remaining items for the Temple and the nails and the spear could be—" She stopped talking. Everyone knew what she was thinking.

"May I touch this?" Jacob asked as he pointed to one of the two scrolls written in ancient Hebrew. "This language I recognize. That one must be for you, Naomi."

The other scroll had symbols similar to Bubbe's necklace.

"I guess. I don't know what to do with this, so any ideas you might have on helping us figure it out are welcome," Joel said. "I'm at a loss, and now I think this huge thing outside is here for me," he said as he took a huge breath and continued. "I'm sorry in advance for any danger I have put you both in. I guess we are just on our own here and hoping to do what is right."

The rabbi picked up the scroll, unrolled it, and began reading.

"Twenty-four basins of gold, twenty-four basins of silver, twenty-four bowls of gold, twenty-four bowls of silver, and the list goes on, listing some other twenty or so vessels of gold and silver," Jacob said. "This is the most significant finding regarding the Temple I have ever seen, Joel. Do you know what this means?"

"Not really," Joel replied.

"It means we can begin the rebuilding process; this list has been a legend for years," Rabbi Jacob said. "I mean, we have to find where these items are hidden—maybe that is in the other scroll? Yes, they may be after you, and no, I have no idea what to do next."

The rabbi put his hands on Joel's shoulders, looked him in the eyes and continued, "This has been one of the greatest days of my life."

Rabbi Jacob continued, "I am speechless and have no fear over that thing in the sky. We will figure out a way around all of this, as the truth will set us free." Tears started rolling down his face. "I can't believe the peace I am feeling in my heart at this moment even though we are under attack."

His heartfelt thankfulness touched all of them and they banded together in a group hug.

"I always thought the key of David was a spiritual key, not a physical key," Naomi said. "We didn't get to that part of the Annas journal yet," Joel said, "Annas stole this key from Herod, then Jesus took it from Annas and gave it to my Bubbe who gave it to me yesterday."

"Well, it seems spiritual to me," said Hannah.

"The key was mentioned by the prophet Isaiah and

in the book of Revelation by John, one of the disciples of Jesus. It said what Jesus opens no one can shut and what He shuts nobody can open. It opens a door to the spiritual for everyone to walk through if they choose to do it. Perhaps the ship outside is not a danger to us if it has the same symbols on it, or it has the angelic alphabet because the angels using it are fallen angels?"

"Well, the people chasing after us in New York were sent to stop us, and the government here is still looking for us. We need to proceed with caution," Joel said.

50

ANGEL ALPHABET

Naomi's phone beeped with a text message. She grabbed it up, "Maybe it's the IDF."

Naomi looked down and read: "Please stay calm. We are trying to communicate with those who are currently illegally in our airspace. Stay in your homes and shelters until further notice. Do not panic! As soon as we have more information, we will inform you. Again, for everyone's safety, please remain inside your shelters and homes at this time."

"That's not much information," Joel said.

"I think we should try to get to an underground location, Joel. This seems like a volatile situation for all of us," Rabbi Jacob said. "We have a workspace in the tunnels under the Temple Mount where we were able to do our research, which is not far. I'd feel better if we were there, but I need to do a bit of brainstorming on how to get there unnoticed."

"What about just going out there and confronting the ship?" Hannah said.

"Really?" Joel said. "You think I should just do that? I guess it's pretty clear it has something to do with the box. If it were angels, my guardian angel here would agree with me," Joel said, trying to communicate with Harper but getting nothing.

"If you go out there, I'm going with you," Hannah said.

"No, that doesn't seem like the right option here," said the rabbi. "Who knows who or what they are? As Naomi said, it could be fallen angels. It looks like that thing can wipe us out. Let's admit—it is pretty huge and daunting."

Another text beeped on Naomi's phone. She read it out loud: "The Israeli Defense Force are looking for two Americans in the city of Jerusalem connected with the large vessel hovering over the city. Male, 30 years old, 1.68 meters in height, dark hair and brown eyes. Female, also in her 30s, with medium-length brown hair. Their names are Joel and Hannah Cohen. If anyone has information regarding these two persons of interest, please notify us immediately."

They all looked at each other wide-eyed and knew things were going to get difficult. Joel felt a sense of dread.

"You can just turn us in. Eventually, we're going to get

caught," Joel said to Rabbi Jacob.

"Do you think someone is communicating with the ship?" Hannah asked.

"They have to be. How else would they have your names and descriptions?" Naomi said.

A third text came in on Naomi's phone. She read it out loud: "We are offering a 3.5 million Israeli shekel, or one million US dollar, reward for information that may lead to finding Joel and Hannah Cohen. Please circulate this picture among your friends and family to inquire if they have seen this couple in the city of Jerusalem."

Naomi held up her phone, which showed a picture of them in the Knesset from earlier that day as they went through security. They had to come up with an idea, and fast.

"We have to go somewhere else—I don't want to put my friends here in danger," the rabbi said.

"You stay here, rabbi," said Joel. "Just give us an idea where we could try to get into the underground tunnels. We were near there today. I remember Naomi pointing them out to us as we drove by on the bus as a great site to visit for tourists. If you give me an idea where we could get in, we can try to make a run for it. That way you won't be caught with us and get in trouble. Unless you just want to turn us in and collect the money. We may get caught anyway. I prefer you get the reward rather than someone else. I mean, we still have no clear idea why the prime minister or Israeli Defense Forces are after the box," Joel said. "Yes, major artifacts perhaps and a damaging journal, but why the heavy warfare outside? They are using something the world has never seen. That thing is either from space or a weapon of war, and they decided to pull it out today to track us down? It just doesn't compute."

"Joel," Naomi said, "Rabbi Jacob says there are items for the Third Temple on this list. Do you know what is on the other scroll inside the hidden compartment? Was there a translation anywhere? It appears to be the alphabet from my dream."

Joel shook his head no. "Other than the vision I had of Jesus creating the key and that it has to do with the key of David and an alphabet from heaven, I would say you were also given clues through your dream to solve the mystery. It's no mistake that we ran into you, Naomi."

It was becoming clear to Joel they could solve the mystery by interacting with angels, which happened to be Naomi's specialty.

"Naomi, you said it was an angel alphabet, right?" Joel asked.

"Well, it looks similar to what I have seen only in a dream. It's nothing I could confirm, and I can't decipher what it says," she answered.

"Yes, but you can see angels, and we know there is one or more guarding the box," said Joel. "We have to get that angel to tell us what is going on."

"Sounds logical to me," Naomi said with a nervous laugh. "I may see angels, but I don't talk to them unless they talk to me. I just observe them."

They all half chuckled and started to think they might be able to figure this out after all. Everyone started looking around the room, as if this angel was going to just appear to them right then and there, because they didn't know what else to do.

"How did you know the symbol was representing the Alpha and the Omega?" Hannah asked.

"There's just something that happens in dreams where you have knowledge about what's going on," Naomi said.

"Let's see if you have knowledge on any of the rest of the writing," said Joel as he held up the scroll.

"I know Greek, Hebrew, and ancient Hebrew," said the rabbi. "That is none of those languages."

"Just write down the A's and the Z's if those are the only ones you know," Joel said hurriedly.

They had to get out of there before the woman who opened the door to the house realized the people with the rabbi were Hannah and Joel.

Naomi sat down and tried to make out what the scroll said but got nowhere. They were getting antsy and started looking around again for the angel, who was missing in action at this point.

"Do you see any angels here now?" Rabbi Jacob asked Naomi.

"No," she said, disappointed.

Hannah was watching out the window, "I see a few people milling around out there in the street. Do you think we should try to go to the tunnels now? I'm concerned about pulling any other people into this situation and putting them in danger," she said.

"I know. Let's try to go out and see if we can make it to the underground tunnels," Joel said.

"Wait, I will go with you," Rabbi Jacob said. "I know my way around all of the underground options in this city. I want to use my expertise to help you out. If we get caught, we get caught. Naomi, maybe you could take a picture of this scroll with your phone and see if you can get anywhere with the angelic alphabet or the angel. Call me if you get any details."

"We don't want you to get into trouble, Rabbi," Joel said.

"Joel, I have to go. As I said, I know all the underground areas. There is no way you will make it without me. You need to walk like you know where you are going, or it will draw attention. Besides, this list of Temple treasures is something I have been searching for my whole life. This is my true calling, to protect the list and help you in the meantime. You wouldn't want me to miss my true calling, would you?" the rabbi asked with a smile.

"No, of course not," Joel answered.

"Then it's settled," Jacob said.

Joel and Hannah packed up the box and Naomi took a picture of the other scroll. She agreed to stay and try to find a way to decipher the message and let Rabbi Jacob know as soon as she had a breakthrough.

51

HOLY OF HOLIES

Jacob, Hannah, and Joel headed out the door. Hannah pulled her hair down around her face and tried not to look up as they walked outside. They didn't know if the airship had some type of facial recognition.

They only passed a couple other people on the streets. With this scary aircraft hovering over the city, the few people they did see were running to different locations and not paying attention to them.

Rabbi Jacob couldn't help from looking up a few times as they were running through the narrow, puzzling maze of streets that were the Old City. Joel realized right away there was no way he could have maneuvered the city on his own. He was moving fast through the slender stone streets, dodging from one curve through another. They would turn a corner, and there would be steps. Then turn another corner to a street full of vendors booths left unattended. People were scarce, and the vendors must have left for cover when the aircraft showed up. Nobody was paying attention to unattended booths. Joel thought about looters and realized only the necessary people were outside—not even looters. This thing even scared thieves.

They kept moving until they came upon an opening in a rock, which looked like a burial tomb. Rabbi Jacob slipped into the opening and followed a tunnel downward until it was pitch black, his entourage close behind him. They pulled out mobile phones to light the way as the rabbi continued to move through the tunnel. When they got deeper inside, they noticed water leakage along one wall. Just past that, into a curve, they could see a light in the distance—a welcome sight for Joel and Hannah. They continued toward the light, and soon were inside a long, straight tunnel with wall lights on one side and huge stones on the other.

"We are walking on the streets Jesus and Annas would have walked on in 70 A.D. below the Wailing Wall," Rabbi Jacob said.

There were little stops along the way with plaques explaining where they were along the wall. The stony paved floor of the tunnel was uneven just like the streets of the Old City, but now the stones were huge rectangular blocks. Joel's thoughts wandered back in time to consider Jesus and Annas having walked this very road. Annas and Jesus may have seen each other as they passed on this street for the holy days. Joel pictured Annas with his entourage surrounding him and Jesus with his family at ages 13, 16 and 18, coming to the Temple and walking along this same way. *Annas may have paid Joseph for the box in this very spot. They may have politely greeted each other on the street through the years,* Joel thought.

"There are probably other people down here," the rabbi said, "so make sure you keep to yourselves just in case they got the same text messages Naomi got with your pictures. That's a lot of reward money. I'm sure someone would like to turn you in."

They came across a tour guide who stopped and talked to Jacob directly in Hebrew. Hannah and Joel continued walking to the next plaque and pretended to read it as the rabbi conversed with the female tour guide. The woman was scared, and the rabbi seemed to calm her before moving on to catch up with them.

"What was going on?" Hannah asked.

"She was saying they were trying to keep the tunnels clear, but tour guides and people who know the city well are using them to get around. I told her who I was and that we were headed underneath the Holy of Holies to pray. I could tell she was scared but trying to do her job. She said, if you are led to pray, get going."

"Good call," Joel said

The rabbi started moving faster through the tunnels. The wood beams ran along the wall for support, and it

356 KELLY FITZGERALD FOWLER

was well lit at this point, so they could maneuver quickly.
They ran across a couple of other people who worked in
the tunnels, but Rabbi Jacob told them all the same thing.
They were headed straight to the location where the Holy
of Holies would have been.

The rabbi stopped, turned around, and said, "This is
the closest spot to where they think the Holy of Holies
is, but through my research, I know it's in a different
location."

"Really?" Hannah said.

"Yes, I have figured out the exact location. Follow
me," he said.

They turned down another tunnel that was less well-lit
and less used. When they got there, Jacob stopped and put
his hand on the ceiling.

"This is the place. If you go straight up to the surface
from this location, that is the actual place where the Holy
of Holies, the most sacred location where God dwelled
in the Temple, was located. Not many people believe it—
only about half of our Third Temple group," the rabbi
said. "And not one Muslim agrees," he said in a joking
manner.

It was a cleared, simple alcove. Three locked trunks
lined the rustic stone walls. Rabbi Jacob invited them to
have a seat on the trunks.

"Even after you presented this at the U.N., nobody

believed you." Hannah said shaking her head.

"No, it was as if the translation at the U.N. was not accurate. Like I said, Levi and I expected riots in the streets after my presentation, but it was nothing more than usual. Those are all paid protestors on the streets anyway. They had not been trained on how to think about the topic," Jacob said, with a hint of irritation in his voice.

"I know, I discussed that with my colleagues on the security team," said Hannah. "We were surprised as well, but there had to be a reason why the world news didn't react to your presentation. I thought the topic would have been on every major network."

"Maybe it was for our protection," Joel said.

The rabbi, Joel, and Hannah all agreed they didn't have time to figure this out right now. The three had to decide what to do next. They could hole up down here for a while, but eventually, they would have to make their way out again. They decided to be quiet, pray for guidance, and perhaps rest.

Rabbi Jacob pulled out a key and opened one of the trunks to give them a couple of blankets. He spread them on the floor for Joel and Hannah. Then, he stood on one side of the room, in the location he had pointed out as the Holy of Holies earlier, and started to pray in Hebrew.

Hannah and Joel were lying on their stomachs on the blanket, heads facing each other; they were exhausted.

Hannah was so beautiful—Joel wanted to remember this moment. She had always been a strong woman, but Joel admired her even more now. Her support meant everything to him, and he knew many others would not participate in this crazy adventure. Joel kissed her nose and drifted off to sleep as they had been running on U.S. time. In the midst of all the trouble, Joel realized how in love he was with his wife. He felt the presence of peace and joy in this holy place.

Angel Harper

We lost that demon finally. I guess there was no bitterness around. Joel is not his bitter father. Michael and his angels are working overtime right now with all this havoc in Jerusalem. I am glad to see Joel resting for a bit. This running about the city is wearing them out. I wonder what the plan is next? There are plenty of demons moving about the city, but that ship in the sky is the big guns, the fallen angels. Fallen angels are different from demons—they have human-like bodies and demons don't. My body doesn't look like a human body; remember I'm a sphere. Unlike that bitter demon, Marq, I don't have to run around looking for a place to inhabit. Remember when Jesus made the legion of demons leave that one guy and the demons asked Jesus to let them go into the pigs?

They have to have flesh. Marq was just looking for one of the four of them in this group to be bitter, so he could have legal access to them. It only takes one word with an attitude that sounds bitter and SMACKO, he is in there with full rights, so don't be bitter, people.

Speaking of fallen angels, we don't need trouble right now. They cause havoc whenever they go—even back before Noah and the flood. That was an ugly scene. They intermingled with the women, and those tiny women gave birth to giants. Thank goodness, Noah and his family escaped that mess. Then later, fallen angels showed up and polluted the gene pool again with the poor women of the village of Gath. You would not believe how tall they were. Goliath was six cubits and one span, so imagine how tall his father was. Thank goodness for King David who slayed that giant and put them all in their place. The fallen angels just keep coming back to start a fight. I talked to David about his fight with Goliath. He is quite humble about it, but if he had not killed Goliath, it could have been a major turn for the Israelites in the wrong direction. I am so glad the Almighty was on David's side.

Those fallen angels ruin everything. Through time they have shown up and are mistaken as extraterrestrials because of their fancy stolen ship. They are just fallen angels. No big deal. Well, they are big, but the Almighty always finds a way to thwart their schemes.

Demon Marq

I couldn't follow the box any longer, as Joel is way too jubilant after his newfound belief. It made me ill. The joy of the Almighty is their greatest strength. I decided I had to hang behind with Naomi. She is full of joy too, but I just needed a break from that disgusting ball of joy, Joel. How am I supposed to work under these conditions? Naomi is spending plenty of time on the phone working on deciphering that scroll. I have no idea what it says, but it must be substantial for the fallen angels to show up out in the open in that ship. What are they thinking? Surely people will know who they are and what they are up to, unless these humans still have not learned their lesson?

I have noticed most humans don't even pay attention to history. They either have the attitude of unbelief or just don't care enough to pay attention, which is perfect for us because we get to keep taking advantage of their lack of knowledge and understanding.

It does get tiring knowing so much they don't know; it's almost an unfair fight. Sure, there are a few humans who pick up on truth, but it's rare. Naomi here has more knowledge than most I have noticed. She has certainly done her research. I will have to be cautious as I heard them talking about her being able to see angels, which means she could easily pick up on my presence. I am planning on making myself scarce for a bit until I can catch her being bitter.

52

NEPHILIM

They woke to Rabbi Jacob shaking their shoulders. "Wake up Joel, Hannah," he said.

They sat up, rubbing their eyes as they tried to remember exactly where they were and what was going on.

"You two have been sleeping for a few hours. I'm hoping Naomi may have figured out some of the other information from the scroll. I have completely deciphered the first scroll. It is indeed the list Annas spoke about in his letter regarding other items for the Third Temple. We need to get this information to my group, so they can start trying to locate it. I'm not sure what is going on with the huge black thing outside, but I think we need to hear from Naomi. What do you two think about me going out there for a bit to see if I can get phone service and see if she has a report for us? I just didn't want to leave you here while you were sleeping, in case someone made their way back here," Rabbi Jacob said.

"Sure, sounds like a plan," Joel said, still rubbing his eyes.

The rabbi handed them bottled water from the trunk. "Here you go. We expected this place to be one of protection and provision a while ago. I'm glad we stocked up."

Rabbi Jacob took off toward the official parts of the underground. Joel and Hannah stayed there, still groggy, and decided to take turns sleeping a bit more. Hannah insisted she was okay and told Joel to go ahead and rest for a bit. Joel was exhausted, so he took her up on her offer.

As Joel slept, he had a dream. In the dream, he was standing on a tall cliff overlooking an arid, lifeless valley. Out of nowhere, it started to rain, and the water rose at an alarming rate. It was like the Grand Canyon filling up with water as if it were a small bathtub. As the water rose up, people started flowing out of caves in the water; the carved-out caves appeared to be in the sides of the rocks. The water came higher and higher. As the water rose, the people rose too, floating along the surface of the water, coming closer to Joel. When they got right up to where he was standing on the cliff, the people landed on their feet on the cliff. Several came from different directions, and they all landed upright in front of Joel in a circle. When he looked at them, they were all huge. Some were 12, 15, even 18 feet tall. The dream flipped then, to a new scene.

In the second scene, all the giants were at Stonehenge

in England, and each of the giants had lifted the rocks individually and built Stonehenge. There was a giant standing at every stone in the circle. Joel realized in the dream that they had been the ones who built Stonehenge. Joel looked up, and the ship—the same one now hovering over Jerusalem—was over Stonehenge and it landed right on top of the rocks as though Stonehenge was their landing strip. When Joel looked up, the ship had the same symbols underneath just like Bubbe's necklace. Then he woke up.

"Hannah," Joel said. "Wake up." She had fallen asleep also.

"I should have stayed awake with you," Joel said as Hannah opened her eyes and looked at him wide-eyed.

"Oh, Joel, I'm sorry. I thought I could stay awake, but I couldn't keep my eyes open," she said.

"I know the feeling; it's okay, we're okay. I was so tired! I can't believe I let you take the first shift. I should have gone first anyway," Joel said.

"No, sorry, I should have woken you up when I was catching myself nodding off," she said.

"It's fine. Hannah, I had a dream." Joel proceeded to tell her about the dream. She was astonished.

"Dreaming about Bubbe's symbol and the ship? That has got to be from God," she said.

Joel agreed, "But what do you think it means?"

"Maybe the key to all of this is with Stonehenge. If that ship was using Stonehenge for a landing strip, and those people were giants, that information is part of the solution. The only thing I know about Stonehenge is the rocks are huge, and they are in a circle. It would make sense giants helped put it together, but why?"

"How long have we been sleeping?" Joel asked. "We need internet access."

Hannah looked at her watch. "About two hours."

"We need the good rabbi to get back here with an update soon, or I think we should venture out to get phone access, and do some research on Stonehenge," Joel said.

Hannah agreed. They started making their way out of the tunnel and ran smack into Rabbi Jacob.

"Hey, you two. I have some news for you from Naomi. She has found a similar alphabet to the symbol on your box and the other scroll online," he said.

"Awesome, what did it say about it?" Hannah asked.

"She was trying to contact the local library who had mentioned something in their archives to see if they have other details to help decipher the writing on the scroll," Rabbi Jacob said as he handed them a paper sack. "Here, I brought you some baklava and bagels."

"Great, thank you so much," Hannah said.

Joel was kind of hungry but didn't want to mention it to Hannah because he knew she had to be hungry also.

Joel took the bag, and the three of them headed back to their spot.

"Where were you two going?" the Rabbi asked.

"Joel had a dream about Stonehenge," Hannah replied, "and we decided we needed to go do some research."

"What were you planning on doing about that ship outside?" Rabbi Jacob asked.

"I don't know. So it is still there?" Joel asked.

"Yes, and we still have no idea what it is. Naomi is still looking for answers on the other scroll. The only thing we know is whoever is in that black monstrosity is looking for you two," said the rabbi.

"I know, but we got tired of sitting here. We need some answers," Joel said.

"Well, tell me about your dream and Stonehenge, and I maybe I can help," Rabbi Jacob said.

They sat and blessed God for the food, and Joel shared his dream with Rabbi Jacob.

"Wow, I have no idea what that means, but it has a flood and giants in it, so it could have something to do with the Nephilim or the Fallen Angels," the rabbi said.

"What are the Nephilim?" Joel asked.

"There is a short mention of them by Moses, about how the fallen angels took human women and made a super-race called the Nephilim. The Nephilim—also called giants or Titans—were on the earth before the flood, and then after as well. Noah was not from their bloodline, which is one of the reasons God chose Noah and his family. The flood was supposed to wipe them out and it did wipe out the first batch, but of course, fallen angels are supernatural beings, so they escaped the flood. They took advantage of women again after the flood, and we know this because Goliath of Gath was a giant, probably another attempt by the fallen angels to ruin God's plan," Rabbi Jacob said.

"That is fascinating." Hannah said. "So, wait, the Nephilim were part human and part fallen angel, so the ship could be fallen angels or Nephilim or both?"

"It would explain some of the mysteries here if that were the case, not that I have ever seen a fallen angel and not sure I would want to, but the ship could be fallen angels," Rabbi Jacob said.

"Yes, the angel alphabet and Stonehenge in the dream," Hannah said.

"Then we have more answers to mysteries than I ever imagined. Think about it-the box made by Jesus and Joseph, the writings of Annas as he came to believe Jesus was who he said he was. Then you have artifacts of the crucifixion, a list of priceless Temple treasures, and the key of David, which has something to do with Jesus and the fallen angels. "Something so important that they made themselves visible. But why?" Joel asked.

"Because the information you have will bring truth and clarity to many," a voice said from down the tunnel.

Rabbi Jacob, Hannah, and Joel were frightened by the sound and scuttled to find a flashlight to see who was speaking. They shined it all over the room, and nobody was there.

"It's Him," Joel whispered. "It must be Him again."

"Who?" Jacob asked.

"Yeshua," Joel answered.

Rabbi Jacob took the flashlight down the tunnel, looking for whoever it was. The voice had shaken the rabbi.

"How will it do that?" Joel yelled to whoever it was back in the tunnel.

There was no answer. Joel followed Rabbi Jacob with the flashlight farther down the tunnel but saw or heard nothing. The rabbi made his way back to them, looking confused.

"You two heard that, right?" Joel asked.

"Yes, I heard it," Hannah said.

"So did I," Rabbi Jacob said. He was tense, and unsure about agreeing with the two of them.

"Thank God," Joel said. "I don't want to be the only crazy—" He stopped mid-sentence and looked at Hannah. "I'm glad you heard that too."

"So where did He go?" Hannah asked.

"I don't know," Joel said.

"Maybe Stonehenge is where the Ark of the Covenant is hidden," Rabbi Jacob said. His body was shaking now, the voice and the realization he had a list of items for the Third Temple had to be impacting him. "We need the rest of the information from the other scroll," Jacob said. "Let me go and see how Naomi is doing again. Meanwhile, this is the safest place for the two of you," he said with his eyebrows in high gear. "I'll be back in no more than two hours with an update. By now they may have locked onto your mobile phones to try to find you, so if I were you, I would turn those things off."

Hannah and Joel had not thought of that before now. With today's technology it was only by heaven's protection they had not been caught.

Angel Harper

Yeshua just made himself heard by the humans. I love it when He does that, and Joel even knew his voice. Well, John the revelator recorded that Jesus said, "My sheep know my voice." So sweet, so amazing, so humble, I could go on and on. Yeshua will protect them wherever they go from these nasty fallen angels. Who cares about the ship when you have Yeshua right by your side? I just love Him.

Joel and Hannah need to sleep. They have a huge task ahead of them. The Almighty intends to do a sweep soon, and Joel and Hannah are part of the plan. Sweep in a good way; we are all gearing up to be on assignment across the whole earth once Joel and Hannah take those steps of faith with the courage to reveal to the world the secrets in the box. I have heard, if they step into their calling, it will reap a harvest like heaven has never seen. The people of the world will renew at alarming rates.

Demon Marq

Naomi has no bitterness either and has now moved to the library. Annoying. However, I just realized I had some information to report back to the chief. I was so focused on looking for bitterness I forgot to report back about Rabbi Jacob, Joel, and Hannah heading for the underground tunnels. I'm not sure how that happened. With this high-profile assignment, it could be any number of things put in my way. For example, I was distracted by a group of teenagers in the library, whispering to each other and using tons of curse words. Curse words open doors for specific demons. They don't call them curse words for nothing. Since humans are made in the image of the Creator, they create like He creates, using words.

I should have been paying closer attention to the

conversation when Rabbi Jacob, Joel, and Naomi were talking. I am often just watching for negative emotions to rise so I could see bitterness, plus with all the traffic from cursing, I was demon watching also. You would be surprised how unusual each of us looks. The chief is going to kill me as it just dawned on me the demon traffic is so high because they were looking for Joel and Hannah. I dropped the ball. I hope I don't get punished.

It looks as if Naomi is not afraid of the fallen angels as she is just walking around with that ship out there— where does she get the courage? She has not read what those things can do to humans. I see as Naomi is walking she has the bubble angels around her; now I understand why she is not scared. There are not many like her on the earth with the gift of discerning spirits. She's like a fortified castle with those throne angels surrounding her. I have got to get to the chief—I am just wasting time here.

53

FALLEN ANGELS

The sounds of a group of people talking echoed down the private tunnel alcove.

Joel stood in front of Hannah as a light flashed from somewhere down the tunnel. Joel put a finger to his mouth, motioning to Hannah not to say a word.

A demanding man's voice speaking in Hebrew was heard from the distance as the overhead light made it very clear someone was there.

"Who's there?" Joel yelled.

The group closed the distance faster than expected, shining the flashlight right in their startled faces. It happened so fast, there was no time for them to think.

"Who are you?" said a voice from the direction of the flashlight.

"Hello, we are here with Rabbi Jacob," Joel said.

374 KELLY FITZGERALD FOWLER

"Rabbi who?" the young man asked in broken English.

That was not the question Joel was hoping for, since he had not remembered Jacob's last name at that moment. They shined the lights around a bit more and saw the chests and sleeping bundles.

"What are you doing, camping out?" the man asked with suspicion.

"We are here with one of the rabbis in charge of this area in the tunnel. I guess you could call it camping, but we have every right to be here," Hannah said.

"Nobody has rights right now. Have you seen that space ship outside? Whoever they are, it's likely going to take over the world. It's everyone for themselves. We are confiscating your tunnel," he said.

The rest of the group agreed with him. There were three other young men with him around the age of 25. They did not have weapons they could see, but the group outnumbered them.

"We can share," Joel said. "There's plenty of space down here. As I said, we have permission, so if you want to stay with us until the good rabbi comes back, we can talk to him for you."

Joel looked past him at the others; they didn't seem as sure of themselves. One of them whispered into his friend's ear—Joel thought perhaps either trying to get him to calm down or agree to wait for Jacob instead of taking the hard line with them.

The young man cleared his throat, "Hmmm...ok, that seems like a fair deal," he said as his countenance changed.

"We're all in this together," Hannah said.

"Yes, sure we are, it's true. When people are scared, they say and do strange things. I'm usually very calm. We are just a bit nervous with this huge thing hovering over our city," the young man said.

"Oh, we understand," Joel said.

The other three stayed back in the shadows so Hannah and Joel couldn't see them well. It suddenly dawned on Joel they could probably tell they were Americans from their accent. His next question confirmed his thoughts.

"Where are you from?" the young man asked.

"We are from the United States," Hannah said

"Oh, were you here on vacation?" he asked.

"Yes, enjoying all the sights," Joel said

One of the other three decided to leave abruptly and headed down the hall. It was evident then that they recognized Joel and Hannah from the pictures sent to every mobile phone in Israel. They would have to get out of there fast, with the box intact. Joel grabbed his backpack off the ground.

"On the other hand, we can take off for a while and come back later when Rabbi Jacob is here. He should be back soon." Joel grabbed Hannah's hand and started to leave. The young man blocked Joel.

"Oh, no, it's fine. We can all wait here," the young man said through clenched teeth.

"No, I think we will just go ahead and leave. You're welcome to hang here for now," Joel said as they tried to make their way around him.

Joel could tell they knew they had found the two people the world was looking for, but had no idea how to handle it. By the time the young man opened his mouth to suggest the fugitives stay, Joel and Hannah had dodged the three men and taken off running down the tunnel as fast as they could. The group of young men turned to chase them.

As Joel and Hannah ran, their hearts pounding in their chests, they noticed something peculiar—they couldn't hear any footsteps chasing after them. It occurred to them the angel protecting the box must have stopped them somehow. Thankful, they headed out the hidden alcove, rounding the corner and emerging into the regular tunnel they had come in.

One of the guys had a head start and would have reached someone outside the tunnel by now, so they moved as fast as humanly possible for people carrying a chunk of ancient acacia wood and the most precious cargo imaginable.

They came upon a couple of women praying and blew past them. They finally reached the entrance and spilled out into the street at the Via Dolorosa. They headed up the ancient, narrow road that marked where Jesus had carried his cross. Naomi had walked them down the same street earlier on their tour.

They both looked up and could see the object still in the sky, but it was no longer black—it had changed to an iridescent color. The pattern they'd seen was gone, and it glowed a transparent white with a blue sheen. It looked completely different than what they had seen earlier.

As they climbed the hill through the empty narrow street, without realizing it, they had stepped upon an iridescent ramp that started to elevate. Joel looked at Hannah, and they both looked down and couldn't see anything under their feet except the large stones through the translucent ramp. Before their minds could grasp what was happening, they saw they were getting farther and farther away from the ground as the ramp closed into the vessel.

Joel held Hannah's hand tight while visions from alien encounter movies ran through his mind. He realized they were too high up from the ground to escape. It was as if the invisible wall in the tunnel that held the men back was now far behind them—the thing in the sky had swallowed them up.

"What is going on?" Hannah shrieked.

"I don't know! I don't even know if this is the same ship?" Joel said as he held her tight.

They rose higher and higher and realized hundreds if not thousands of iridescent circular spheres surrounded them. They suddenly felt peace around them as one of the spheres began to talk.

"Joel and Hannah," a voice said in what sounded like a young man's voice set against a peaceful background noise of a harp.

"Don't be afraid. I am Harper, one of the many angels the Almighty sent to assist you," he said.

As Harper spoke, his light grew brighter, as if to show them which sphere was talking to them. Hannah looked around and saw multitudes of these little spheres surrounding them in a vast sea of light.

Joel relaxed as he recognized the voice from his visit to heaven. He attempted to say something, but all that came out was "Okay."

Hannah also relaxed and smiled at Joel, "Do you smell that?" she asked.

There was a thick, sweet smell in the air, like pancakes or waffles. Hannah smiled and inhaled deeply.

"Oh, that's me. I can be a bit over the top in using my favorite scents to help people stay calm. That is manna you are smelling," Harper said.

They looked down through the ship to the ground,

which was still hovering over the city. They could see from a distance the Via Dolorosa below getting smaller and the city with all the tan stones moving farther away.

Hannah reeled in her unbelief and said, "Harper, pleased to meet you."

"Nice to meet you, too," Harper said. "I'm glad the fresh manna is helping you. It gives a whole new meaning to 'daily bread.' Remember, the joy of the Almighty will strengthen you. He shares his strength with all of us through his joy. So, whatever happens, remember the Lord has given you his strength to endure."

"What do you mean, 'whatever happens'? I don't like the sound of that!" Joel said.

"Well, you are currently inside an ancient vessel built by angels but stolen by fallen angels. We have been told by the Almighty to make ourselves seen by you, so you will know you're not alone. A multitude of higher-ranking angels stand guard as well; this is just a sampling of the angelic host protecting you. If you could truly see all of them, it would blind you, and you need your eyesight," Harper said.

"You told us not to be afraid, but..." Hannah said.

Harper interrupted her, "Never fear, sweet Hannah! If anything, they should be scared of *you* - just look around at your backup. You have the Almighty, who has gone ahead of you like a bulwark and prepared the path for you. Fallen angels are bullies—you are a son and daughter of the Most High Almighty! You inherited his Kingdom when you said yes to Jesus. You have nothing to fear, so fear not," he said as the atmosphere changed. Harper disappeared, as did the rest of the host of angels, at least as far as they could see.

The color of the vessel changed back, and they realized they were actually on the dreaded black ship. Joel and Hannah had been scooped up without knowing what had happened. It felt like a setup. The smiles left their faces as they realized they were probably about to face one of the most difficult situations of their lives.

Joel and Hannah looked around, trying to quickly assess their situation. The aircraft was full of what appeared to be powerful men. There was at least ten surrounding them, each unique in appearance. They were all ten feet tall, muscular, with different skin tones, and tattoos on their wrists and bodies. Some had dark hair with blue eyes, some dark hair and dark eyes. Others had blond or red hair with blue or violet eyes.

As Joel looked around, he noticed they were on the main floor of a rotunda, and as he looked up he saw more fallen angels layered on several balconies above them, all looking down.

The inside of the vessel was cylindrical. Joel would not have been able to tell that from the ground since they could only see underneath the ship. His Hollywood-influenced mind had thought the ship was a saucer.

The vessel was futuristic inside and out—a high-tech machine made by supernatural minds, a hive for fallen angels.

"Now we know why we needed strength," Hannah said as she held onto Joel's arm and tried to stay calm.

Joel held her close and felt the power from what Harper called daily bread. Joel stood in the Almighty's strength and decided to get to the bottom of this.

"Why are you here? What do you want with us?" Joel asked in a loud, powerful voice that echoed through the chamber of the cylindrical vessel.

One of the blond angels with violet eyes stepped forward. "Harper told you who we are," he said, sure of himself.

"Okay, fallen angels? So, what do you want with us?" Joel asked.

"You have something that belongs to us," he said.

"What would that be?" Joel asked with confidence.

"The box you carry in your backpack," he said with a loud, stern voice as if ready for this fight. "I know what Harper told you. Don't be so sure of yourself, Adam."

"I'm not sure of myself, but I am confident in what Harper said. The Almighty will be my strength, which means you don't have any power whatsoever. Plus, you must have the wrong person because my name is Joel, not Adam," Joel replied.

Hannah's grip on Joel's arm loosened after he said this. Joel's courage was giving her strength to stand tall and hold her own as well. She stood strong and unafraid like she would if she were working security at the U.N.

"Do you know who I am?" the fallen angel asked.

"No, I have no idea who you are, but I know this box is mine. You will not win this battle with the Almighty on my side," Joel said as his mind flashed back to being a little kid and learning the story of David and Goliath. The thought gave him peace to continue to stand firm.

"I am Zagan. I was the head of Lucifer's light brigade in the heaven of heavens, which may mean nothing to you, but I know how the Almighty works. A deal is a deal."

"What deal are you talking about?" Joel asked.

"I also happen to know the Nazi who secured your great grandfather Caleb in Bologna. Caleb negotiated the release of your great-grandmother Chasia and your Bubbe Rachel by trading the box and its contents. What your great-grandfather didn't do is tell us the whereabouts of the Key. Unfortunately, he died before we could get that information from him. We have been on this wild goose chase for decades. So, you see, you would not exist if not for his negotiation. As I said, a deal is a deal."

The fallen angel came over to Joel and pulled his

backpack out of his hand in one lightning-fast second. Joel fought back, but a couple of the other fallen angels surrounded them and were holding his arms as the blond angel opened the backpack and pulled out the box.

Joel noticed something black drifting toward the fallen angel; he heard Harper whisper in his ear, "That's Marq the demon, a familiar spirit of bitterness who haunted your father." As the demon approached the fallen angel, Joel recognized the feeling of his presence.

"Ah yes, thank you, Marq. I am glad we are all a big happy family again," he said in an insincere tone.

"Marq just reminded me the reason we didn't take the box from your father. Our spy Leona from the SAD organization told us we still didn't have the key. Bubbe Rachel must have had plenty of protection to keep the key hidden from us all those years. We waited forever for your father to produce the key, but it never surfaced. Our little SAD group worked hard to keep an eye on all of you, and now it's paying off," the bully angel said.

"That doesn't belong to you if the negotiation was for the box only," Hannah said with boldness.

The fallen angel motioned to another to hold her as he approached and touched her dark hair. He looked up into the cylinder and yelled to the crowd, "Would any of you like this one for your offspring?"

Hannah started to kick at him, but she was no match

for the angel holding her. Joel struggled to get in front of her, but other fallen angels held him securely. A few in the crowd cheered, while others jeered a few words in an unknown language. Joel couldn't make out what they were saying, but the huge angel looked at Hannah and nodded in agreement.

"You are right; it's not worth it," he said as he walked over to Joel, plucking Bubbe's key out from his pocket. He shot a fake smile at Joel then commanded to the angels holding him, "Dump them out!"

The fallen angels holding Joel back released him, and what looked like the same ramp they had entered on, opened from the bottom of the vessel, and swept them down to the street just as fast as they had been taken up. The massive ship lifted straight up to the sky and was out of sight in an instant.

Joel had lost the box and Bubbe's necklace. His family's inheritance went with them. His father and Bubbe had protected it his whole life, and now it was gone.

Demon Marq

Wow, I barely saved myself by reporting back in time on the whereabouts of Jacob, Joel and Naomi. Chief, my superior, was delighted to have the information, and then booted me out as fast as I arrived. I even told him my father was the head of Lucifer's light brigade in the heavens of heavens. You'd think that would carry some weight.

It's a good thing I was able to sneak in behind Joel and Hannah onto the vessel, so I could tell my father where Joel was hiding the key.

Since I spent most of my time back in the day watching the box in Assisi, I should have recognized the symbol. Harper must have been allowed to conceal the pattern on Rachel's necklace all this time because all I saw when I looked at it was a fish. I had not noticed Rachel's necklace was the key until I saw Joel use it to open the box in Israel. I should get a huge reward for telling my father about the key being in Joel's pocket, but I got nothing. He didn't care.

Zagan is not the head angel. He thinks he's in charge; they all believe they're in charge. Most fallen angels have no appreciation for demons, even though they are related. The fallen angels believe they're special just because they "look" like men. Fallen angels are not superior just because they have flesh. Permanent tissue is a major problem anyway. I don't like having to seek out something to cling to, but at least I can ride words, symbols, and objects.

Fallen angels cause so much more trouble than my type. Look, they caused the flood by messing with the women on the earth. That was a hard time, but somehow the fallen angels managed to thrive. Then they went ahead and started the race of giants again. They could care less about those of us who were bound to roam the earth endlessly.

Then the man, David, slew a famous giant and it caused war after war. David was chosen but they tried to wipe out his seed and failed because the promised Messiah showed up anyway.

I think they skipped from plan A, B and C straight to X, Y or Z because they are at it again, discussing bringing back more giants. It's clear they're looking for female candidates even now; did you hear what they said about Hannah? Since man appears to be a bit wiser and more sophisticated these days, they have had to slowly introduce the idea of a half "spiritual" and half man story into society once again. It's outrageous, all the plans they try to make we can't be a part of. But I'm not bitter.

On the other hand, I'm supposed to get back to Naomi at the library as soon as possible. Speaking of Naomi, there she is, headed out. She looks as if she is on a mission moving very fast... Oh no, what did I miss?

54

OFF THE RECORD

Joel and Hannah gathered themselves up from the street and the core-shaking experience they'd just had. Joel was distraught over losing the box, so Hannah decided they should head back toward the tunnel. She figured Rabbi Jacob might be looking for them at some point, and with the ship and the box gone now, they realized they were no longer in danger.

As they walked back down the Via Dolorosa, people started coming out of their homes and shops. A few of them must have seen the ship dump them out on the ground and stayed clear of them but continued to capture them on video on their phones. It happened so fast—anything could end up on the Internet. Joel and Hannah would have some explaining to do. *Jerusalem had been held hostage by a ship of fallen angels or Nazis or whatever they were*, Joel thought.

"People would never believe such madness. They'll

388 KELLY FITZGERALD FOWLER

think the videos are fake," Joel murmured.

"Do you think since the ship and your box are gone now, there would be no reward?" Hannah asked Joel.

"I have no idea, but I bet they're going to want some answers," Joel said.

As they got closer to the tunnel entrance they had come out of earlier, a group of reporters passed them. Joel and Hannah ducked into an alley nearby to avoid them, but they could hear witnesses steering a reporter toward them.

"Those people are closing in," Hannah whispered. "Should we run or what do you think? What do you want to do?

"I think it's time to tell them something," Joel speculated.

"Like what? I have seen how ruthless reporters can be," Hannah said. "We need to decide what information you would want to tell them."

"I know, I am trying to decide the right thing to do. I would like to tell the whole world they took my inheritance," Joel said, looking down the alley to see a snooping reporter. He put his finger to Hannah's mouth and held her back behind a garbage can so the reporter couldn't see them. He wasn't quite ready to tell everything. The reporter took off in the other direction.

"Wow, close call," Hannah said.

They sat there for a while in a fog over what had happened. The whole area was in an uproar as sirens moved around the city. The hustle and bustle of the city returned as people realized the ship had left the area.

If the Lord was Joel's strength, he needed that strength right now, as his entire family's lives had been in danger forever.

"Well, at least Naomi has a picture of one of the scrolls," Hannah whispered.

"That's true; I forgot about that! I can't believe they didn't open the box before they dumped us out. Everything happened so fast," he said looking at Hannah, who agreed.

"Let's get back to the tunnel and find Jacob and Naomi. Hopefully, Naomi has figured out a way to decipher the information on the scroll," she said.

She was right. *All is not lost*, Joel thought as he looked around to make sure the alley was clear. They popped out from behind the trashcan to walk away. Suddenly, a young twenty-something girl jumped in front of them.

"So, they were right! You did come down the alley," she said.

She was tall and thin with a huge pile of auburn hair piled up in a bun.

"They said you two looked like the pictures they had seen on TV," she said.

"We don't know what you're talking about," Hannah said.

"I know who you are," she said as she glanced at her little notepad in hesitation. "Hannah, is it, um... and Joel? There's a reward out there for you two."

"Oh, and you think you can drag the two of us in?" Hannah asked.

"No, but I could get someone to help me out if I started yelling right now," she said. "Or you could help me out in my job by giving me some details about what happened when that huge canister in the sky scooped you up?"

"Listen, uh, what's your name?" Joel asked.

She put her hand out to shake it and said, "Aubrey. Aubrey MacKenzie."

Joel shook Aubrey's hand. Even though Hannah was a bit hesitant, she shook hands too.

"Look, Aubrey." Joel hesitated and cleared his throat. "We do have a pretty huge story here, and I think we will need to get it reported at some point, but right now is just not the time." He nodded at Hannah and continued, "We were just discussing the need to contact a reporter and share what's happened to us since we arrived in Israel a couple of days ago."

Hannah was nodding her head in agreement.

"Yeah, like all the video they have of you two at the Knesset and other various places around town," Aubrey said.

"You sound American," Hannah said

"I'm from South Carolina," she replied.

"Look, why don't you go ahead and give us your mobile number and we will call you when we are ready to break the story. There is a piece of it missing we have to resolve. Once it's resolved, we're going to need a reporter. I promise you, we will be calling you first thing, once we get to the bottom of it," Hannah said. "I give you my word, as an American, you will be the first person we call."

Aubrey looked at both of them. After a slight hesitation, she started digging in her purse to pull out her phone. "You give me your numbers, and I will verify them right now by calling them and then I will have your number as well. That is the only way I will be quiet."

Joel and Hannah looked at each other and decided it was fair enough. Hannah called Aubrey's phone and hung up, and Joel did the same.

"I have so many questions—could you just give me something about what it was like in that colossal ship?" She was grasping for anything. She knew she was risking letting the story of her life walk away.

"Let's just say, off the record—it was supernatural, and we promise you get the scoop as soon as we get to the bottom of the whole story," Joel said.

"Where are you headed?" she asked

"To the Wailing Wall," Hannah said.

"That's the worst place to go. There are cameras all over the place. People will identify you and find you," Aubrey said. "Let me help you hide somewhere."

"We are keeping a low profile but have to meet up with a couple of people before we do anything. We will call you once we get back with our contacts, I promise," Joel said and started to move as he grabbed Hannah's hand.

"Okay, but call me if you get in a tight spot. I will be waiting to hear from you," she said as they rounded the corner.

Hannah and Joel ran back to the tunnel and were careful to see if she was following them, which she did not appear to be. As they entered the tunnel, sure enough, Naomi was waiting for them.

"Hey, you two, I was getting worried. I went back to the hidden dugout area where Jacob said he left you and heard a group of boys back there talking about video games or something. I didn't want to draw attention to myself unless I heard the two of you, which never happened, so I just came back to this part of the tunnel hoping to either get phone service or see you or Jacob," Naomi said as she was giving them both hugs. "Where have you two been?"

Joel told her the whole sordid story about what happened with the ship and Harper, how they lost the box and the key. As he finished the story his head was hanging low and he was almost in tears.

"I'm confused about why Harper or Yeshua allowed them to take it," Joel said. "At least you have a picture of the scroll."

"Yes, I do. Maybe you don't need the box any longer because I think I have figured out what the writing on the scroll says," Naomi said. "I can't wait to tell you what I found, but we should wait to make sure we're in a safe place before we talk. I also think we need to get back with Jacob and make a plan based on what I figured out."

"What is it?" Hannah asked.

"I can't say here. I honestly don't think it's a safe place. People can sneak up on you in here, and our voices carry. We need total privacy," she implored. "Plus, it's going to involve some planning, so let's track down Jacob and try to relocate."

55

THE PRAYER TOWER

Naomi stepped outside and contacted Jacob on her mobile. She explained about the troublemakers in the tunnel and what had happened to Joel and Hannah with the airship. Naomi indicated the couple needed some prayer covering, so she suggested they all meet up with Rabbi Jacob at the Prayer Tower. She gave Jacob the address, and they grabbed a cab to the location.

The Prayer Tower was on the top floor of one of the tallest high-rise buildings in Jerusalem. The church that founded it was in the basement of the same building. On the way, Naomi explained to Hannah and Joel how the people who go up to pray and worship in the tower feel called to worship with the Holy Spirit for hours and pray for the nations of the world.

"They feel a call on their lives to reveal the light of Yeshua to Jerusalem and the nations. It will be a safe place to discuss our next move, plus Rabbi Jacob is nearby,"

Naomi said.

When they arrived, Jacob was waiting there for them. They all greeted each other, relieved. The rabbi was glad to see them after hearing about the fiasco in the tunnels and the mess Joel and Hannah had experienced with the airship.

Naomi led them into the tower and talked to the woman who was on staff for the evening. She motioned to them, and they followed her up the elevator, then to a room on the top floor of the building.

As they entered the room Joel noticed he felt very lightheaded. Something weighty felt like it had lifted off him the moment he entered.

Two people, a man and woman, were worshiping in the room—the man was on a keyboard and the woman a guitar. They were singing a beautiful song, and they all stood there watching the two worshippers sing. Naomi sang along for a short amount of time. Joel was unaware of time passing as the piece was so beautiful and the woman's voice was angelic.

When they concluded their session, new worship leaders came in, and Naomi led her friends out to another room to talk. The view of Jerusalem from the room on the top floor was stunning.

"Wow, this is such a fantastic place," Joel said to Naomi.

"Yes, I know," Naomi said. "It feels different here because there is an unseen world around us, and here in this space there is total peace, because of the long dedication to prayer and worship. I believe there's an open portal to heaven in this place."

"I have never experienced this type of thing before," Rabbi Jacob said.

"Neither have I," said Hannah. "I had no idea there was a place like this."

"I wanted a secure location where I knew we would be able to speak, hidden from the dark side of the spiritual realm. The details I have here are enough to cause quite a ruckus. There's no way demons can penetrate the Glory of God that covers this particular location," Naomi assured them.

"So, the Glory makes it so the spiritual world cannot have access?" Hannah asked.

"Let's just say, based on what has happened to you two today, with them scooping you up and taking the box, you are being heavily watched by undesirables. Here, they won't be able to hear our conversation, and what I found from the scroll is huge," Naomi said.

Angel Harper

Oh, I love the Prayer Tower. There are so many worshiping the Almighty in this space. I think meeting Joel and Hannah went well. Naomi is so smart to come here. The demon Marq won't be able to get in here. When there is worship, the Almighty is so pleased He thwarts many of those little devils from their assignments. It would astound the humans if they only knew the power of their worship.

I know the Almighty has big plans for this sweet group of four. He has big plans for everyone! I'm so excited to see how it falls into place, and that bitter demon Marq will not be able to report back from this location. I'm not sure why he even tries. Nobody in this group has bitterness, so, they will be free to speak and make a plan.

Demon Marq

They have gone into that place over there covered with too much shiny or glory as they call it. Not for me; I will have to wait for them to come out. Worship causes brilliant glory. I can hardly get near places where worship is happening. If I had skin, it would be crawling! I will just have to bide my time here and wait for them to come out. As I look at this space, I can see there are tons of other demons on assignment for them right now. I wonder where they all were earlier? If something is going to get done, I have to do it myself. Most of these demons should have been following them all day, especially when that monstrosity was hovering over the city looking for answers. I am glad I got to report to my father Joel had the key in his pocket.

56

THE ARK

"So, here's what I found," Naomi started.

"First, let me explain some things to you about the days of Noah. Jesus said at one point, 'As it was in the days of Noah, so shall it be in the last days.' If we go back to the days of Noah, we know there were wars, all kinds of sexual immorality, and most importantly for this discussion, giants or Nephilim in the land. Many have suspected something like this was going on for a while, meaning the fallen angels trying once again to procure women to have babies with them to create yet another new race of giants. Hitler was involved in trying to usher this in during World War II. He was more than likely involved with fallen angels without realizing it. Think about it—Hitler was a short, unattractive man. Joel and Hannah described the fallen angels as huge 'model-looking' males. Why would Hitler agree to create a superior race that looked nothing like him? It's just a theory, but it makes sense the fallen angels had something to do with it, especially since Hitler was involved in ethnic cleansing, which is the work of Lucifer. Anyway, that is a side note," she said as she continued.

Joel interjected, "Plus, I think Hitler was looking for the box and key either for the fallen angel Zagan or Lucifer. My great-great grandfather, Caleb, negotiated for his wife and daughter to be left alone by telling them the box was in Assisi, knowing it would be impossible for them to find a key because the key was still with Jesus at the time according to the Annas scroll. I can't wait to tell Bubbe her dad negotiated with fallen angels over the box and her journal to save her life."

"Oh yeah," Naomi said, "Also, in our current day propaganda, you have movies that perpetuate some intermix between a strong supernatural male and a woman, which creates a hybrid, so to speak. So, I believe they are trying to indoctrinate our youth into thinking this is cool or okay. They could very well be in power already or in place to convince influential people to allow a new race of giants yet again—the same group of fallen angels who polluted the gene pool in the days of Noah, which resulted in Nephilim."

Joel pointed to Hannah and exclaimed, "That's what they were saying about using you for offspring!"

"Yeah, not right! The whole lot of them were sizing up my tiny hips," Hanna said.

"So, yes, they were checking you out as a possible

mother of a new race of giants," Naomi said.

Hannah cringed. "Oh my, thank the Lord I am a petite woman!"

"Yeah, well, you are not their perfect pick because they could see you were going to be problematic with the angelic protection you two had inside the ship," Naomi reminded them.

"Is it possible the prime minister and the government are working with the fallen angels unknowingly?" Hannah asked.

"It's possible, for sure, along with the SAD group Leona reported to. But you don't need to focus on those people anymore; you are holding all the cards. They don't think you have the ability to decipher the scroll or that you have a copy of it, so they think they have you duped," Naomi said.

"Okay, so what did you find out about the Ark of the Covenant?" Rabbi Jacob asked.

"Wait," Joel said, "You can decipher the scroll?"

"Just a minute, you two. The first scroll Rabbi Jacob verified is a list of hidden items for rebuilding the Third Temple, like you said," Naomi said smiling and pointing at Jacob.

"Yes, I know. I'm excited. Our committee is going to be thrilled. Did it say where to find the items?" Rabbi Jacob asked.

404 KELLY FITZGERALD FOWLER

"Okay, so I decided go to the library since I found something online regarding the angel alphabet in their archives," Naomi informed them. "While I was in the library I had a divine appointment. I overheard a couple of students in the ancient manuscript area of the library talking about their research paper on the fire that destroyed the library in Alexandria. Some archeologist uncovered a curious manuscript from the dig site - an unknown alphabet that survived the fire. I started asking them about their research, and they said they had found a document with the manuscript that described a very young genius scholar who had scribed it and brought it to the library with his father. When I started digging, one ancient scholar suggested Yeshua himself was the author of the scroll. I asked them to show me the picture of the scroll, and sure enough, it was our alphabet. I dug further and found an Egyptian translation of the alphabet and Egyptian symbol translation book and translated it into English."

She paused.

"Okay, so what does it say?" Joel asked.

"I'm getting there. Let me catch my breath; my heart is pounding," she said as she laid her hand on her heart.

Joel's heart was pounding fast as well.

"So, I have figured out a few things. With all this time passing through your family preserving the box, with the witness of Annas, the evidence of the nails and the spear, which I believe are from the crucifixion, as well as the list of Temple Treasures, each of those things were gathered up by Annas and stored in the box in the hope it would be enough evidence to prove to the world the truth of who Jesus was, right?" Naomi asked.

"Yes, I think that would have been his intention," Joel said, "but now they are all gone."

Naomi ignored Joel's somber mood. "If the box was made public, those items would require verification and scientific study. Many would try to discredit them, right?" she asked.

"Absolutely, they would try," Rabbi Jacob said in agreement.

"I'm glad you said that, Rabbi, because I noticed your issue with the evidence in the box was related to Noah's Ark, correct?" she asked.

"That's right, but what are you getting at?" Rabbi Jacob asked.

"Then, the evidence in the second scroll is the greatest witness of truth!" Naomi said. "Simply put, many believe Noah's Ark to be a fairy tale, but this is the evidence that will bring in the largest harvest of believers the world has ever seen. It makes perfect sense the fallen angels were after the box and the scroll. They know when it goes public, they have fewer humans to choose from for their 'race of giants,' because many will believe, which will result in angelic protection like Hannah had on the ship. But also their attempt to revive 'the days of Noah' will be shattered yet again. Joel, you found a supernatural key forged by Jesus in heaven and delivered to your Bubbe, a box made by Jesus and Joseph on earth. There is physical evidence of the crucifixion preserved by Annas, who has provided the firsthand witness of the cover-up created around the missing and supposedly 'dead' body of Jesus. But we all know He is risen, might I add," Naomi stated.

"I found it, but don't forget I lost it!" Joel said.

"Nope, listen." Naomi said and continued. "Your family has uncovered the whereabouts of the Ark of the Covenant, which in itself would be enough to make Stephen Spielberg faint—aside from the actual Holy Grail, which was probably just a wooden carved cup," Naomi said.

"So where is it?" Rabbi Jacob asked in earnest.

"Patience," Naomi said, holding up a finger and smiling at the rabbi. "The picture I took of the scroll is all the evidence anyone would ever need to believe Jesus was who He said He was. God has gone above and beyond all you could ask or imagine and sealed the deal. All of this has been accomplished for such a time as this and is being revealed here today."

She paused again. The next words from her mouth were nothing short of incredible. "Joel, we are going to need a team of people and a reporter."

"I know a team of people," Rabbi Jacob said.

"We know a reporter," Hannah exclaimed.

"What else did it say, Naomi?" Rabbi Jacob asked with anticipation.

"Rabbi Jacob, get ready to believe—it gives clear directions on where to find the Ark of the Covenant, which it says is hidden just inside Noah's Ark!"

57

THE INTERVIEW

~Six Months Later~

Joel, Hannah, Rabbi Jacob, and Naomi were seated on a supple leather couch in the studio, their eyes fixed on the screen as the in-depth investigative report was about to begin, featuring a voiceover by the now world-renowned reporter, Aubrey MacKenzie:

"The quest for truth. Last fall his team of four uncovered the most all-encompassing and compelling evidence for truth on the planet. Today we are going to take you on a journey, the same incredible journey this team went through—tracking down every piece of evidence and putting the puzzle pieces together that any rational person would need to confirm the validity of Jesus being who He said He was. Today, we will examine each ancient artifact found, and then talk about how at one time they were stolen, and how those stolen artifacts were finally recovered.

We'll also meet the team of people who worked day and night on the quest to uncover the real Ark of the Covenant and Noah's Ark."

"Let me start with you, Joel," Aubrey said. "Gilbert Grosvenor, the first editor of National Geographic, once said:

'The discovery of Noah's Ark would be the greatest archaeological find of human history, the greatest event since the resurrection of Christ, and would alter all the currents of scientific thought.'

"Joel, what would you say to Gilbert after locating not only Noah's Ark but also the Ark of the Covenant?" Aubrey MacKenzie leaned in with the microphone, posing the most exciting question in the greatest interview of her life, and possibly in history. When it aired, every person on the planet who had access to a screen would be watching.

"I would say, Gilbert, you were right!" Joel said.

58

THE COURTROOM CONCLUSION

~Outside of Time~

The fallen angel Lucifer continued his filibuster before the throne of the Almighty. The original light from his body was now dull following his fall, which he refused to acknowledge. His voice was like nails on a chalkboard to those who were listening. He filed through his thoughts and delivered in detail his accusations on each being who stood before the throne. Thousands upon thousands were witnesses as he plowed through the evidence—each of their transgressions—starting with Cain and now working his way through those Nephilim who were on the earth before the flood of Noah's time. Jesus sat on His throne next to Joel and listened to every accusation.

"Next up, Marqrio, or Marq, for short," Lucifer quipped. "I am familiar with your father Zagan. He was part of my light brigade. I accuse you of major havoc, and

I am sure you will be very proud of yourself, as you have played a helpful role in disgracing a notable family. While you had access to your flesh, you were prideful and bitter, of course, since that is what your name means. May I add I am proud of the work you did to further my cause," Lucifer said, nodding his head toward Marq in approval.

Lucifer pulled out Bubbe's necklace and started swinging it around his bony little finger.

"I contend you are mine forever for your actions and enter this information into the record."

"Time to stop this!" Jesus said with a compassionate look on his face, as Lucifer started to move on to the next half-breed spirit in line.

"What do you mean? I'm not done," Lucifer hissed, grinning as he continued to swing the key.

"Let's save us all some trouble," Jesus said. "What were you planning to do with that key?"

"Bring out the box!" Lucifer yelled.

Zagan, Marq's fallen angel father, carried the now familiar acacia box to the front of the throne room. Lucifer took the key necklace and placed it in the embossed emblem on the box. Nothing happened.

Joel wasn't sure what was going on. Was he dreaming again or back in heaven with Harper? He watched intently as the box failed to open as he had witnessed it do on earth. Nothing moved.

Lucifer flew into a rage, looked at Zagan and yelled, "What is the meaning of this?"

Zagan's face contorted in fear and he said nothing. Marq looked at him, his father who had rejected him from day one. This was the first time he ever saw his father cower. Zagan looked scared and weak and scurried away, knowing Lucifer would blame him.

"That is the key to the House of David!" Jesus said. "Only those who serve me can use the key for access to me, their king. This belongs to my servant Joel," He said as He took the key and box and handed them to Joel.

"We retrieved the box fair and square," the adversary said.

"You are a liar. Your negotiation with Caleb was for the box, not the key. Caleb never possessed the key. I gave it to King David who passed it down through the line of Kings of Israel. Once Herod got it, Annas decided to steal it, so I secured it and passed it to Luigi to give to my friend Rachel who recently passed it to Joel. Plus, Zagan bringing the hijacked Angel Ark into Jerusalem and stealing the key from Joel was illegal. You have been caught and have no legal grounds for ownership," Jesus said.

"Besides, the box does you no good if you can't open it," Jesus said. "Once Joel opened it, no one else can shut it and when he shuts it, no one else can open it. It's my key to give and I gave it to Joel. He and the others who are my friends have my authority on earth to render your power useless using the same authority of the key of David—I give each of them that authority when they say yes to me."

Lucifer tried to open his mouth in protest. "Wait—no, this can't be true!" he screeched as he turned around to sneer at Zagan, who had disappeared to the back of the courtroom.

Jesus continued, "Listen to me, those of you in line waiting. I have defeated this lying, fallen angel Lucifer and his reign of death over your eternity. There is another option for you if you are willing to consider it. You have all been participating in activities you are ashamed of through manipulation. I present you with a way out. If you would like to continue believing his lies, then pay no attention to me. But, if you express remorse for your wrongdoing and do it no more, you can become part of the Kingdom of Heaven rather than remaining in a world of torture and constant accusations. If you want to stay with me, then step out of line, and I shall count you redeemed."

The Angel Harper gasped.

"Why does Marq look familiar?" Joel leaned over to ask Harper.

"He is that familiar spirit who was on the ship and has been assigned to your family for generations. His abilities are focused on attaching to bitterness, which would explain why your father changed into a different person once he inherited the box. Marq has been harassing your family for generations by firing deep roots of bitter darts into your minds, hoping to tear down relationships. Jesus just offered redemption to a whole line of half-bred humans. You know, the Nephilim who were on the earth before the days of Noah. It's astonishing!"

One by one, many stepped out of the line with their heads bowed, trying to avoid Lucifer's glare. About one third of those in line took Jesus's offer.

The rest of them moved up in the line behind Marq, who was facing Lucifer.

Lucifer was seething at this plunder by King Jesus. He grabbed Marq, who was still in place at the front of the line, and turned him around, pointing him to the door, and motioning him to lead out those who stayed under his influence. Marq complied and marched toward the exit with all the others who were following him, under the watchful eye of Lucifer.

As Marq walked by Harper and Joel, he paused and looked at Joel, then at Jesus still at the front of the courtroom, then back at Lucifer. Lucifer watched—his eyes suddenly growing defiant and huge—and took a sharp intake of seething breath when he saw Marq stop.

Marq stopped in front of Joel and with his head hung low said to him, "Your father loved you."

Lucifer screamed at Marq, "Leave now, Marq, demon of bitterness!"

Marq looked at Jesus and Joel and said, "Forgive me!"

Jesus said to Marq, "Your heavenly Father loves you. You are forgiven."

"*I* am his father!" Lucifer hissed, spit flying from his mouth. "He has spent his existence telling lies!"

"One cell from his mother gives him rights as a human. He has free will," Jesus replied in a still small voice.

Marq's father Zagan shook his head in loathing at Marq as he mustered up the courage to advise Lucifer, "Master, we have lost again. Let's go before others defect."

Lucifer was livid. Unleashing a stream of obscenities under his breath, he snatched his list and flew out of the courtroom in a volcanic rage before any of the others could change their minds.

Thank you for reading *Over My Dead Body: A Supernatural Novel.* Gaining exposure as an author relies on word-of-mouth, so if you have the time and inclination, please consider leaving a short review wherever you can and/or telling your friends about the book.

Discussion Questions

1. What part of the story did you relate to the most?

2. If this was not a novel and you discovered the box yourself, what would you do with the box?

3. Which character did you relate to the most? Joel, Hannah, Naomi, Rabbi Jacob, Harper or Marq?

4. Have you considered the difference between fallen angels and demons?

5. Have you ever had an encounter with an angel or demon?

6. A root of bitterness causes grudges, anger and an inability to forgive. Have you ever found yourself with a root of bitterness like Joel's father, Ely? Learn more at Hebrews 12:15 and Deuteronomy 29:18.

7. What did you think of Joel and Hannah's relationship?

8. The theme surrounding the Key of David is one of authority. Do you understand authority? For example, when a police officer pulls you over, he or she has authority to do so, and you comply because you understand authority. You can dig deeper at Isaiah 22:22, Luke 9:12 and Luke 1:3.

9. What do you think Rabbi Jacobs's conclusion was about The Messiah after finding what he had been looking for his whole life?

10. Have you ever considered what it is like to be in the courtroom of heaven?

11. John 14:2 talks of the many rooms in heaven. Name a room you hope to find in heaven?

*Do you have questions you'd like to ask me about the novel? I would love to hear from you! Feel free to email me at kellyfitzgeraldfowler@gmail.com or call me at (843) 800-2025.

*If you would like to stay in touch please join my newsletter at www.kellyfitzgeraldfowler.com and I will send you my novelette called, The Bologna Journal, which gives you the background of Luigi and some more tidbits about what happened to Caleb or find me on my author page on FB, Twitter @kellyffowler, Instagram @kellyffowler, Goodreads & Amazon Author Central.

Acknowledgments

I have to say writing this book over the course of ten years would make for a daunting acknowledgment page. I almost skipped this process but then my gratitude to those who have encouraged me through the years welled up, and my fingers started typing on their own. My first thank you would be to the Holy Spirit whom without His heavenly nudge this book would not exist. The beginning of this story marinated in my head for several months before I realized it could become a novel. I also thank God and Jesus for love and sacrifice as well as being an ever-present truth in my life. To this day I am not sure how anyone can breathe without a personal relationship with the creator of the universe.

To my love, my captain, my husband Judge. Thank you for every bit of energy you have put into loving me. Attempting to write my feelings about how loved and blessed I am to have you are futile, so I will stick with my original promise to adore you forever!

To Aubrey, thank you for enduring all my crazy scenarios and your invaluable feedback on the early manuscript, even though it is not your genre. You have and will always be the wind beneath my wings. I love you and your sweet family.

To MacKenzie, thank you for listening to me ramble on about this story and for your help and patience for ten years. You will never know the joy I had when you said you loved the book. I have learned so much about storytelling from you. You are still the sweetest thing on earth. I love you, sweet girl.

To Abraham and Clementine, you both inspire me! Gigi and Jesus love you!

I, of course, have to thank my earliest inspiration, my Grandma, Marguerite Fitzgerald. She was a schoolteacher who I am sure has been cheering on my journey from the cloud of witnesses. I know she loved and prayed for me so many times throughout her life and for that I am grateful.

To my amazing mother, Linda, who is an avid reader and cheered me on from the first moment I told her I started a book and read several versions of my story. Thank you for your love and support.

To my daddy-o, Jerry, thank you for your glee in listening to all my crazy ideas of what I think it must be like in heaven. Your childlike wonder on the topic as well as your curiosity about Nephilim helped me want to know more too.

To my sweet sisters Jet, Peg and Rose, thank you all for always being a huge part of my circle of support and love for any pursuits in my life. Thanks for just loving me no matter what crazy notion I come up with. Jet, we sure do miss you here on earth!

Others I would like to mention who have contributed to cheering me on. Listed in no particular order below: The Hansens, The Botero Family, The Nelsons, Josh, Taylor, Heather, Shannon, The Weichsels, Gil and Jennifer Truesdale, Teresa Ward, Donna Gleeson, Betts Keating, Susan Sloate, Neil and Carolina McMullen, George Wagner, Janet Schwind, Janet Lockett, Chris and J. M. Khyat, Dana Frazeur, Sandy Cox, Eva Hamm, Stuart Kimball, Suzanne Parada, Brooke O'Friel, Cyril Jedor, Jennifer Tubbiolio, Jill and Rick Chesser, Denise Gellerman, Linda Howard, Joleen Crook, Linda Blankenship and the entire Masters Touch Ministry team, Bryan Ransom, Ben Davis, Danny Steyne and the entire MOW family, my Dreamer group, my Yah Yah's, my "Write it Down" critique group, The Book Lovers Supper Club, my Hokey Pokey family, Bethel Church Kingdom Culture group who I had the honor of traipsing through the Holy Land with in 2013 & my Seacoast Church family, Keven Vachon and the Kings Inn church family in Maine, Terry Ward Tucker, James L. Rubart, Bliss, every person on my OMDB Launch Team.

Made in the USA
San Bernardino, CA
14 January 2019